MW00526566

A BUCKET FULL OF LIES

BOOK ONE

by

Robert K. Swisher Jr.

Text copyright © 2013 Robert K. Swisher Jr.

OPEN TALON PRESS

OTHER PUBLISHED NOVELS
BY ROBERT K. SWISHER JR.

Historical Fiction: Trade and E-book
Published by Sunstone Press
The Land
Fatal Destiny

Contemporary Western Fiction: Trade and E-book
PUBLISHED BY SUNSTONE PRESS
How Far the Mountain
The Last Narrow Gauge Train Robbery
The Last Day in Paradise
Love Lies Bleeding
The Man From the Mountain

Literary: Out of Print
Published by Samisdat Press - Canada
American Love Story

Young Adult: Trade Only
Published by Echo Press California
The Weaver
Published by Sunstone Press
Only Magic

Humor: E-book only
Conversations With the Golf God

Mystery Series: E-book only:
Bob Roosevelt Mystery Series – 4 novels

Contemporary Fiction: E-book only
Hope
How Bridge McCoy Learned to Say I Love you
A Circle Around Forever

Satire: Trade and E-book Published by Open Talon Press
Vent
Grammar Nazis Are Not Always Rite, Right, Write
Vent Revisited
The Lonely Cowboy
Short stories and poetry in literary journals, articles in outdoor
magazines. Reviews by Publishers Weekly, Best Sellers, Library
Journal, and many others.

PUBLISHED BY
OPEN TALON PRESS

EDITORS: Sheila Awalt

COVER DESIGNER: Samantha Fury...Mike Nguyen
PRINT FORMAT: Samantha Fury

Part of this book is a work of fiction. For the fiction segments names, characters, places and incidents are either products of the author's imagination or are used fictitiously. Any resemblance to actual events, locales, or persons either living or dead, is entirely coincidental. Part of this work might be construed as non-fiction. If any of this book reminds you of yourself and you get offended by certain comments or remarks (corporations included since you are by law considered people) no harm, malice, libel, racism, discrimination, in any of the previous terms multitudes of forms and definitions, and any term that would come to mind by any other person, was intentionally intended either by me, my wife, my dog, my cat, my goldfish, my hanging plants, or any relative - this includes all and any life forms in the known and unknown universe that might share some of my DNA, and unknowingly, by either cosmic intervention, or a form of communication as yet unknown to mankind had anything to do with the writing of this book.

If you wish to use portions of this book for anything but reviews you must contact OPEN TALON PRESS or the author. Sorry, what can I say? We all know lawyers run the world. And to be honest we all know our politicians are controlled by big business interests who are also controlled by lawyers.

Library of Congress - In Publication Date
Swisher, Robert K, 1947 –
A BUCKET FULL OF LIVES: A novel / by Robert K. Swisher Jr.
Summary: mystery, humor, satire

LCN: 2020908372
ISBN: 978-0-9979096-4-7

DEDICATION

FOR THE TATTOOED LADY

ON THE CONRNER OF 4TH STREET...YOU'RE RIGHT HONEY

AIN'T NOTHIN GOOD ABOUT HUMIDITY

EXCEPT CORN.

Table of Contents

A BUCKET FULL OF LIES
BOOK ONE

CHAPTER ONE
WHERE IN SPACE IS DES MOINES?

"You had better boot scoot out of here, Roosevelt," my Guardian Angel warned me trying to look like he really cared. "If you don't, you are going to get trapped right in the middle of a murder, a multiple kidnapping, a gun and heroin smuggling ring, and to top it off everyone you meet will only lie to you. And if that is not enough, you are going to get hurt, maybe even killed."

"Please, I'm in Iowa, nobody knows me here," I said. "Besides, I'm in a quandary."

"What's new about that?" my Guardian Angel stated bluntly. "You're 62 years old and you have never found yourself or the love of your life - being in a quandary is all you know."

"Your job is to help me not ridicule me," I said defensively, although he was telling the truth. Since I was twenty I have tried to discover who I really am and searched for the love of my life, neither of which has ever happened.

"Does the truth hurt?" my Guardian Angel taunted like a Catholic who had pulled a fast one on a Buddhist.

I am the only person who can hear my Guardian Angel and when I talk to him it is only through my mind, which is a good thing, if not, people would think I talk to myself all the time. And, thank God, I am the only person who can see him. He is not a pleasing sight. My Guardian Angel is a 14th century monk with a shaved head. He is 5'2" tall and in his early 60's and more than a little over weight – in fact he is as round as a basketball. His eyes are tiny brown slits that show he is not to be trusted. His eyebrows are so bushy birds could nest in them. He has a splotchy uneven black beard and his complexion is close to watery flour paste. He wears sandals with no socks and a knee length, stained, brown wool robe, which exposes mats of black curly hair on his bowed legs. To top it off he does not bathe saying vapors cause disease – people from the 14th century were not known for their intelligence. For many years he would not tell me his name saying it was none of my mortal business, but then in a weak moment, which we all seem to go through, he informed me his name was Wright, which is completely out of character, so I nicknamed him Pea Brain. A name he does not really like, but what the hell, I am his boss, and how many people in life like their boss? But in an effort to be nice, I only call him Pea Brain when he peeves me off. I have also discovered he used to take money to forgive sins and slept with as many women as he could informing them he was a blessing from God. In a lame excuse he told me the Bishop made him do it.

My Guardian Angel was assigned to me, for a reason, or reasons I do not know, when I was in Vietnam. He has been with me ever since. Although I owe him a lot, as he has saved my life numerous times, he is snide, lecherous and sarcastic. He told me that by going against the grain of what most people think a Guardian Angel should be makes him feel like an individual. He also hates the fact I am moral.

I am in Des Moines, Iowa, at Greasy Ed's cafe, sitting at the counter. Greasy Ed's is on the corner of 14th Street and Walnut and serves nothing but chili - I suppose it cuts out the need for a menu. I had taken the exit off I-80 to eat before continuing on to Colorado for some trout fishing.

I was now picking at a bowl of tongue curling Cajun chili, and between sips of my second lukewarm draw beer, I was trying to figure out if the meat in the chili was cat or dog.

"This is Iowa," my Guardian Angel said holding his nose. "It might be possum."

"You're a great help," I told him.

"Or Raccoon," he said.

Greasy Ed, or who I figured was Greasy Ed - who else could be 6'4", weigh 290 pounds, wear a greasy apron and work in a dive called Greasy Ed's, but - Greasy Ed – a few things in life are obvious. Greasy Ed was reading the sports page at a corner table in front of a fan that sounded like the prop wash from a B-52. The fan didn't do much except plaster the warm, June, muggy air to my face like a second skin. It was three in the afternoon and I was the only one in the joint. Greasy Ed grunted at me, "you want more beer, use your feet and get it yourself, I ain't your mother, and if the chili is too hot, don't eat it."

My Guardian Angel threw him the finger.

Like I said, he is not a normal Guardian Angel.

I was drinking another beer while my Guardian Angel was studying the numerous pin ups of nude women on the walls that normally decorate the bathrooms of garages that make a living cheating little old ladies when I heard the door open, and then to my shock, my name sliced through the hot muggy air. "My God, of all the people, Bob Roosevelt, what are you doing here?"

"Heed my warning, Roosevelt," my Guardian Angel said with a truly worried look on his face.

"Bob Roosevelt," echoed through the cafe once again.

A sinking feeling shot through my heart. I turned apprehensively to look at whoever knew me. Seeing Sam Wrench jolted me back to the 1960's.

"You're a sight for sore eyes," Sam said, lumbering toward me like a polar bear with bad feet.

"Murder and kidnapping, heroin and gun smuggling, bodily pain all over your body," my Guardian Angel recited while shaking his finger at me.

I hadn't seen Sam in over 45 years. "You haven't changed a bit," I lied, standing up - my Guardian Angel's words sending distress signals up and down my spine.

Sam embraced me and pounded on my back like he was beating the dirt out of a rug.

In truth, Sam hadn't changed that much. In the 60's Sam looked like a long haired guard for a pro football team - only now the muscle has turned soft - his hair is short, though still coal black, and he doesn't have a beard. Although Sam is a big man, back then he was one of the gentlest men I had ever known.

"I'll get my own beer," Sam bellowed over to Greasy Ed.

Greasy Ed gave Sam a dirty look, which I guess meant, yes. Looking at Sam, I could picture him in the past with long black hair, an earring in one ear and a peace sign hanging around his bull-like neck. He was one of the few hippies in New Mexico the cowboys didn't try to knock the snot out of. They tried to knock me around a few times but found out it was a mistake.

Sam poured me another beer and came back around the counter with two for himself. Without a comment we went to a table. Sam drained one beer without stopping, wiped the froth from his lip, and smiled distantly, like remembering a fond memory. "I sure miss the 60's," he said.

"I bet the 60's don't miss you guys," my Guardian Angel smirked.

I had to smile, thinking back to New Mexico. "Those were the days," I said to Sam, trying to ignore the fact I really can't remember, except in fragments, what had really gone on during my hippie days in a commune in New Mexico.

"Don't blame your memory loss on substance abuse," my Guardian Angel said. "One has to have intelligence to lose his memory."

"It's too bad we all grew up and had to accept reality," Sam said.

"The drugs made us lose credibility," I said.

"They were a bad thing," Sam agreed. "I haven't messed with any since."

"Me either and I wish I never did," I said.

Sam laughed and I laughed - the type of laugh used to cover up things that no longer should be mentioned or should be forgotten.

Sam took another gulp of beer. "We were all dreamers," he said, his mood suddenly going dark.

"You were all stupid," my Guardian Angel said like he had a college degree in human nature.

"Pea Brain, we weren't that stupid, we were naive," I half snarled to my Guardian Angel.

"There are no excuses," he replied sounding like my mother and gave me a hurt look from being called Pea Brain.

Sam took another swallow of his beer and was quiet for a few moments. "I've kept up with you through the years, you're sort of a famous private eye," he said.

"'Sort of' are the right words," I said. "After the commune I went in search of myself. I spent years doing every job you can imagine and then I went to Santa Fe and tried writing for a few years."

"It's hard to be a writer when you can't spell or write complete sentences," my Guardian Angel butted in sarcastically. His feelings don't stay hurt for long.

"I wandered down to Florida," I continued. "In Florida, I ran into an old army buddy who had started a private detective agency and after I got my license he gave me a job. I'd reached a point in my life that I had to do something - either crime or a decent job - and I took the job," I joked.

"You should have taken up crime," my Guardian Angel said. "You might have made some money."

"Have you found yourself yet?" Sam asked seriously.

"No, but I keep trying," I said.

"Idealists are a lost lot," Sam said.

11

"To look for yourself you have to keep your eyes open. Roosevelt has the tendency to close his," my Guardian Angel said.

Sam got two more beers. Greasy Ed was still reading the newspaper - I figured he could only read about three words a minute. "The TV coverage on the kidnapping case you solved in Florida was exciting," Sam said after he sat back down.

I smiled. The case had been the highlight of an otherwise boring career. A rich family's daughter had been kidnapped and, more by luck than sleuth, I had caught the kidnappers. The family was so wealthy the case had made the papers and I even got fifteen minutes on a cable TV crime show and two reruns. For my efforts I received a $10,000 tip. Since the family was making about $10,000 a minute, I felt like I got gypped, but, since I had never had more than $5,000 to my name, I felt like Bill Gates until I found out how easy it was to waste 10,000 big ones. I'd sworn if I ever made any money again I would be content with hamburgers and beer.

"So, what have you been doing since hippie heaven?" I asked Sam. I didn't want to get into my decline in the private eye sector of the world.

"I came back to Iowa after New Mexico, got married and have three kids. I inherited my dad's furniture store when he died and I took on a partner," Sam said. "The wife cooks me dinner, cleans the house and does the laundry, and once or twice a year goes out and has an affair with some stranger she meets, about the same old middle-class America story - lost in the pursuit of stuff. Everything we didn't want as hippies," he chuckled sadly.

By the tone in Sam's voice, I sensed there was a lot more to the story than that, but, I didn't pursue the matter.

"I bet you never got married," Sam said.

"No. I keep hoping, but every time the bell rings in my heart something always happens."

"Fortunately for the women they discover the real you before it is too late," my Guardian Angel said.

"You're lucky," Sam said.

I guess lucky to Sam was sleeping alone, eating pizza and other fast foods for a steady diet and studying the world of loneliness.

I felt like telling him I would trade with him in a minute, but I didn't want to ruin his illusion of what single life is like. I did know that if I wasn't single I wouldn't be in a dive like Greasy Ed's, having eaten chili that should have been used as axle grease and drinking beer that was closer to mouth wash than beer.

Sam drank his other beer. "Let me buy a round," I said, and started to get up.

"That would be a first," my Guardian Angel said.

Sam put his hand on my shoulder and pushed me back like I was a cloud. I am not the biggest man in the world, but at 5'11" and 180 pounds, I am also not the smallest. "No, No," he said, like one 'no' wasn't good enough to get his point across.

Sam lumbered over and brought back two more beers. Greasy Ed went into the kitchen as though expecting a big rush for dinner. I figured a big rush was two people trying to cash stolen welfare checks.

"It's funny I should run into you," Sam said in a tone that made my skin tingle.

"Murder, kidnapping, gun smuggling, heroin, pain all over your body," my Guardian Angel warned again, adding, "let's go to Colorado, Roosevelt."

I didn't want to continue the conversation but Sam went on.

"I'm in big trouble," he said, looking nervously around the empty cafe, as if the pin ups on the walls were undercover agents with no cover. "I'm in so much trouble I don't know what to do."

He sounded desperate. So desperate there was a pleading quality to his voice.

"Dive, dive, time to leave Dodge," my Guardian Angel warned. Even though my Guardian Angels is snide, lecherous, and sarcastic, he is God driven to protect me.

Looking at Sam's worried face I wanted to say, "What kind of trouble can an old hippie living in Des Moines, Iowa who now runs his dad's furniture store be in?" But I couldn't make myself say it. I know I should take my Guardian Angel's advice. I have my own demons to dodge, not some long lost friends who I used to dream about utopia with. I am trying to find myself and wanting a new life, but, when people are in trouble, I feel obligated to help.

"A person only finds themself by helping others," my Guardian Angel said piously.

"You just told me to get out of here," I said.

"It is my job to protect you. It is your job to find yourself," he said shrugging his shoulders and holding his hands out like what was he supposed to do.

13

"I've messed my life all up," Sam said.

I tried to look away from his pleading eyes. I tried to ignore his pudgy, football player's face and receding hairline with the coal black hair that I can see is dyed. Looking at his hands I saw the raw fingertips with the nails bitten down to the quick. I remembered a buddy of mine dying in my arms in the rot-infested jungle, his blood vivid red on the immense ocean of green foliage, saying, "Everything happens for a reason Roosevelt."

I hoped beyond hope that meeting Sam Wrench at Greasy Ed's didn't happen for a reason, but was one of those happenings in life that had no reason at all and would lead nowhere.

I sipped on my warm beer and looked at the pinups on the walls. I felt their sadness creep over me like old age and said to Sam. "Sam, maybe I can help you."

I'm an old softy after too many warm beers.

"No, you're an idiot," my Guardian Angel said, shaking his head sadly.

Sam's face seemed to lose some of its tension. He smiled the way he used to smile when we were sitting in our Tepee back in '69 and telling each other why the world was all screwed up and how easy it would be if the world would only do as we said.

"I know you can help me," Sam said.

"If I'm going to help you, you're going to have to tell me everything that's going on, even the stuff you're embarrassed about," I said, trying not to sound like a preacher.

"I can't tell you here," Sam said, looking around nervously once again. "But we can go to my house and I'll introduce you to my wife and kids. We can sit on the porch and I'll tell you everything."

Going to Sam's house wasn't something I really wanted to do. Wives and kids are two things that confuse me. Most wives, because I am single, treat me like I am going to take their husbands to some far off land where lonely, single men live, and read men's magazines all day.

"I'll flip you for the tab," I said. Luckily I won. I am short on the green stuff right now.

As Sam paid the tab Greasy Ed didn't say a word but I couldn't help but feel Greasy Ed and Sam were more than casual acquaintances. I did notice that as Sam walked away from the cash register, Greasy Ed glared at his back as though he would like to rip off Sam's face. But, for Greasy Ed, his look could have been friendly.

14

Standing in front of Greasy Ed's the hot, humid air, mixed with the gagging car exhaust turned the air a pale, soggy green. "I'm glad I don't have to breathe," my Guardian Angel said faking like he was coughing.

"Boy, there's a car," I said to Sam, looking at a brand new white Lincoln with bright red leather seats that was parked behind my black Volkswagen.

"It's mine," Sam said casually.

"Look at that old Volkswagen," Sam said. "That boy must be living in the past. I bet it has flowers painted on the headliner."

"Daises," I said, "two white ones and a red one."

"How do you know?" Sam asked, puzzled.

"That's Matilda, my 1966 bug," I replied proudly.

Matilda has been a good and trusted friend for many, many, years - for all her sputtering and slow speed, she has never failed to start.

"I couldn't even get into her," Sam said.

I didn't say anything, although I knew Matilda wouldn't want his big rear in her anyway. "You can follow me home," Sam said. He started to walk toward his Lincoln but stopped suddenly and looked at me quizzically. "You have everything you own in that car?"

"Doesn't take much," I replied, not wanting to tell him about my hasty retreat from Florida. When the husband happens to be the Chief of Detectives for homicide and the woman, who had told me she was single and I thought I was in love with, turns out to be his wife, one does not take time to worry about worldly possessions. Having nothing and breathing hot, humid, gas fumed air is much better than having a 357 shoved down my throat by a detective who, on his best days, would make Hitler look like an altar boy.

"Roosevelt," Sam said. "You should have stayed a hippie."

"I still am at heart. It's the convictions that have faded," I said.

"You still have the convictions," my Guardian Angel said. "Don't shortchange yourself."

The only thing I was thinking about as we drove off, was - why would a guy with a new Lincoln drive down to the seedy part of town to drink hot beers at Greasy Ed's? Greasy Ed's wasn't the kind of place to go and try to get rid of one's problems if you have money.

Twenty minutes later we pulled up to a large, walled, two story brick home. The house was covered with ivy and surrounded by majestic cottonwood and maple trees. The sidewalk cost more than I have ever made and the yard was the size of a small farm. The driveway

15

circled around to the rear of the house and there was a parking lot big enough for half of the Kmart Sunday shoppers. Through the trees I could see a tennis court and what I gathered was a covered swimming pool.

Sam was standing by his car door and smiling proudly as I pulled in behind him. He hadn't bothered to open the triple garage. I couldn't see the neighbors' house for the trees but I could hear the sound of a running river and the neighing of horses. I shut of the engine and got out. "You looking for a gardener?" I asked, flabbergasted.

"No he isn't, but he had better be looking for an undertaker," my Guardian Angel yelled in a way I knew he was not kidding. I darted toward Sam, hoping to knock him to the ground, but before I reached him a shot belched from the trees. The bullet entered the right side of Sam's head. For a brief moment there was a look of bewilderment in his eyes and then acceptance, as if getting killed was a relief. As Sam's body slid down the side of the new Lincoln, leaving a trail of blood on the shiny white paint, I knew I should have listened to my Guardian Angel.

"I told you, I told you," my Guardian Angel screeched.

There was another shot. The bullet sang a death song as it buzzed over my head. I sprawled on top of Sam, which was about as smart as trying to stop a runaway train with my hand, since Sam was as dead as dead can be.

After a few moments and no more shots, I quickly checked Sam's pants pockets and took a key from his front right pocket. In his shirt pocket was a folded up piece of paper. I stuffed both the key and the piece of paper into my Levi's pocket.

The next thing I knew, a very attractive lady was standing over Sam and screaming, "Oh Sam!! Oh Sam!! Why? Why?"

I grabbed her hand and yanked her to the ground. I didn't know who she was or how she got here so fast, but in the instant it took to yank her down I noticed the fine female form molded into one of the briefest string bikinis I had ever seen. People will tell you being close to death can heighten your senses. That may or may not be true, but the lady was gorgeous and the bikini she was wearing wasn't made to leave many tan lines. The lady started bawling. There was nothing I could do to help the woman. I am a stranger to women. I am not a stranger to death. I learned one thing in the war, there is no guarantee about this life thing - the reaper takes you when he wants.

After a few minutes and no more shots, I stood, helped the crying lady up and shook her lightly. "Go call the police," I said softly.

She looked at me with pale blue eyes, her soft brown hair was tumbling around her face and her tears had made dark rivers of mascara down her cheeks. She ran to the house. I thought it odd she didn't have on sun tan lotion and was wearing makeup. But, I suppose, most bathing suits aren't really intended to get wet.

"That is one fine woman," my Guardian Angel said, licking his lips.

Because my Guardian Angel is dead, death doesn't bother him too much.

"Your death, since you won't listen to me, won't bother me either," he said but I knew he really didn't mean it.

I looked at Sam's body for a few moments and felt sad. I didn't feel any need to go look for the shooter – that would be the police's job.

My Guardian Angel prayed, "Take this mere mortal, God, even though he was a friend of Roosevelt's, I feel he was a good man."

I had moved away from Sam's body when the lady came back, she was wearing a light yellow summer dress that I could see the outline of her bikini through. She had wiped off her face and oddly, had brushed her hair - people have many strange ways of coping with grief. She wasn't crying.

"I'm an old friend of Sam's," I told her.

"He's dead, isn't he?" she asked in a far off manner, looking at Sam's body like it was a mirage.

I nodded.

She looked at me oddly, examined every inch of my old Levi's, my faded blue western shirt and scuffed brown cowboy boots. She looked at Matilda and then back at me and seemed to be infatuated with my shoulder length gray hair, and short, almost pure white, close-cropped beard. She peered deeply into my pine tree green eyes. "You have to be Bob Roosevelt the private detective, Sam's old friend," she finally said. "Sam and I saw you on TV. I am Lisa, Sam's wife."

I was amazed at how calm she was and started to say, "Yes, I'm Bob Roosevelt," when she fainted and crumpled to the ground at the same instant a police car screeched into the driveway.

Luckily, as four police officers were about to slam my head to the pavement, kick me until I didn't know if my guts were on the inside or outside of my body, Lisa came to. "No, No," she cried, "He's a friend of the family."

The four policemen who had jumped out of the squad car and grabbed me, now looked at me with their, 'I'm talking to the high school gym class eyes,' brushed me off tenderly like I was their favorite child, while wondering if I had enough nerve to sue them.

Within twenty minutes, there were enough police cars around to escort the President and the area was taped off. Police were trampling everywhere while others were taking photographs. Lisa and I, and a detective named Owens, who even a bulldog would think was ugly, were in Lisa's spacious kitchen. Owens looked like a large powerful box with arms and legs. His eyes were bored, talking to criminals all the time can't be too exciting, but his stare and face were menacing. His hair was as long as a Sergeant Major's and he probably shaved three times a day.

"I can guarantee you, you don't mess with this guy," my Guardian Angel said. "He would gut punch his grandmother."

Lisa and I had told Owens everything we knew, including how I happened to be at the house. He had already looked at my driver's license, social security card and library card. He was now holding my Private Investigator's card from Florida like it was so foul even a dog wouldn't sniff it. He finally handed me back all my identification - looked me straight in the eyes with a look that could turn milk into cottage cheese and said, "Roosevelt huh, you wouldn't happen to know the wife of the Chief of Detectives for homicide in Ft. Lauderdale would you?"

His words hung in the air like frost descending to kill the last summer flower. I looked at his broad, Neanderthal face, that was covered with scars he didn't get from shaving, "Must be somebody else," I lied, hoping my voice hadn't gone one octave higher and he hadn't noticed Matilda had Florida plates.

"This isn't good," my Guardian Angel said. "Trying to run from one's past never works."

By Owens' reaction, I knew he knew I was lying and as soon as he was out of here, he would call a buddy in Florida and see what they could do about sending my various body parts back to the Chief of Detectives.

He faced Lisa, smiled like he was talking to his grandchild which I knew would pain him terribly, and said, "There's no need to go over any more of this tonight. You get some rest, my men will be here for a while. I'm sorry for your loss and hope that within a few days we'll find your husband's killer."

He dug into his billfold and handed Lisa a card. "You call me in the morning and don't worry - everything will be cleaned up outside."

She smiled gratefully at him.

He glared at me and I had a feeling he was fighting terribly hard not to reach out and rip out my Adams apple. "Roosevelt," he ordered. "You don't go anywhere, I'm not done with you."

"He's staying here tonight to protect me," Lisa said to Owens.

Her words shocked me. My Guardian Angel did a little soft-shoe eyeing Lisa.

Owens didn't smile at me as he stood.

Lisa walked Owens to the door.

When Lisa sat back down, she looked as fresh as a Glade commercial and instead of being sad there was a funny little grin on her lips. Like I said before, some people have strange ways of dealing with grief.

"You are going to think grief if you don't get your lost and bewildered self out of this state," my Guardian Angel said. "But, wait until morning, you might get lucky tonight. Lisa looks like she needs company and you know I like to watch."

My Guardian Angel is sick - most of the time all he ever thinks about is sex.

"Everybody to their own bag," he said smiling like Charlie Chaplin.

"Where are the children?" I asked Lisa, feeling embarrassed by my Guardian Angel.

"Gone for the night," she told me.

"Don't you think you should contact them and tell them what's happened?"

"I want them to have one more good night," she said sadly.

"I understand," I said, but not really understanding.

Besides Sam telling me the kids were home I felt they should be contacted.

"Would you like a gin and tonic?" Lisa asked.

I nodded. Somehow murder, a pretty lady, gone children, and a gin and tonic seem to go together.

"There's more than enough room for an old friend of Sam's to stay here tonight. You will stay, won't you, for me and for Sam?" her pretty little eyes begged.

"If I told you to stay I would only be thinking of myself. You should go," my Guardian Angel said.

"Don't stay, don't stay," my common sense said.

"If it will make you feel safe I'll stay," I said.

19

Why listen to common sense when I never have before?

Lisa smiled in relief.

Most of the time a smile is the best thing a person can receive in the world.

"You're going to think smile," my Guardian Angel said while looking at Lisa's ample breasts and glad I had not taken his advice.

CHAPTER TWO
STICK ME WITH A FORK

It was close to 10 p.m. when the last policeman left, informing Lisa they didn't think they would be back, but if they had to they would call. We hadn't seen Detective Owens again.

I was slightly perplexed as not one policeman, except Detective Owens, had asked Lisa or me a single question, or even seemed to care that we existed. Maybe the police in Iowa have so few murders they really don't know what to do when there is one.

"I don't know why but I think Lisa is an undercover cop," My Guardian Angel said. "You should ask her. If she is she can help you with the case. You and I both know you are going to try and find Sam's murderer."

"There is no way Lisa is an undercover cop," I stated in a tone that let my Guardian Angel know there is no way I am mistaken.

"Have it your way," he pouted like a spoiled little kid.

By 11, Lisa Wrench, of the late Sam Wrench, had forced me to drink four gin and tonics and eat a most delicious cold roast beef sandwich. I noticed for the first time how beautiful and how young she was. She could be a swimwear model and couldn't be a day over 28. She wasn't much over 5'4', 110 pounds if that. She had distant blue eyes, full lips and dimples when she smiled. Her auburn hair hung to her shoulders and had a natural wave. She had an innocent bearing, but I felt she has a touch of Lolita in her.

"I like the Lolita part," my Guardian Angel said. "And her legs are exceptionally nice"

Lisa sat on the other side of the table from me. The table was large enough King Arthur could have recruited a dozen more knights to fill it - only if they wouldn't fall in love with Guinevere. "Well, Roosevelt," Lisa said, her voice somewhere between a college cheerleader and a late night 900 number call. "It seems that you stepped into Sam's life at the wrong time."

"Everything with Roosevelt is the wrong time," my Guardian Angel said dryly.

"Our reunion was rather short," I agreed with Lisa.

Suddenly all the calm and composure Lisa had maintained while the police were here shot away like a Corvette on a deserted highway in Nevada. Her lower lip started to tremble, her shoulders started to shake, she wrapped her arms around herself so tightly her fingertips turned white and she started to cry. "Oh, Roosevelt," she sobbed. "I loved him so."

I fumbled in my back pocket for my handkerchief, which as usual wasn't there. I darted to the sink and grabbed the dishtowel and brought it to her. She buried her pretty little head in the small red and yellow print fabric and sobbed like a little girl whose Barbie Doll's arms had just fallen off.

I stood there in my manly manner and stuck my hands in my pockets. When it comes to women crying I'm about as useless as an unloaded pistol.

With one deep resounding sob Lisa stood and put her head on my chest. "Hold me please, Roosevelt, I feel so alone."

"I like this," my Guardian Angel said with a twinkle in his eye.

"Pea Brain, you are disgusting," I said to him.

He smiled.

My hands went around Lisa like a puppet being controlled by the string master. She smelled like lilacs and her tears dampened my shirt. I patted her back, trying to ignore the small knot of her string bikini under the light fabric of the summer dress.

"Carry me to my bed," she sobbed. "I feel so weak."

"I really like this," my Guardian Angel said, rubbing his hands together.

I tried to protest, but Lisa's arms went around my neck and clung to me like a chimpanzee holding a banana. I picked her up as gingerly as one picks up a six-foot rattlesnake. She directed me through the large house, up the mahogany stairs, to a bedroom the size of a bank lobby. The carpet was white shag and the walls were covered with photographs of children. The four-poster bed had a soft white mesh hanging around it. I parted the veil and lay her down. Soft light filtered through the veil and made her look like sleeping beauty. She held her arms out to me. "I need you," she said with trembling lips.

I looked at her, feeling like her father, and slowly turned, turning out the light as I left. I knew there was no need to say goodnight, in her grief, she would not have heard me.

"You're no fun," my Guardian Angel whined. "She wanted you."

"She doesn't know what she is saying. She has suppressed her feelings for the time being," I replied.

22

"So?" he replied more than a little bummed out.

Back in the kitchen I made myself another gin and tonic and stood by the window and looked into the darkness. I knew the killer was out there somewhere. Probably sitting with his buddies, eating pizza and drinking a full-bodied burgundy, while gloating about what a good shot he was - not bothering to tell them he had missed me. After the gin and tonic I went to Matilda and got my suitcase. Back in the house, I took my 9 m.m. Browning from the suitcase, put in a clip and wandered around the house until I found a sofa.

Lying in the darkness, my trusty pistol on the rug beside me, I closed my eyes. Even with my eyes shut I saw the beautiful wife of my now dead old hippie buddy. Driving the vision of her body out of my mind I swore, even if Lisa didn't want me to, if it was the last thing I would ever do, I would find the killer, and then get out of Des Moines.

"Heed all my warnings, Roosevelt," my Guardian Angel said, but with a tone in his voice he knew his words fell on deaf ears.

In the morning, I felt like an over done steak somebody had stuck a fork in too many times. My mouth was coated with cheap beer, gin, and Greasy Ed's chili. I needed a shower, a shave, and a gallon of coffee. I could hear Lisa talking on the phone in the kitchen and could smell bacon. I had a flashback of sitting in a room with a group of people who were organizing a march against nuclear power plants. The march went well, the nightsticks on our heads and backs didn't.

"What does that have to do with Lisa talking on the phone or the smell of bacon?" my Guardian Angel asked looking at me like I was going off the deep end.

"Flashbacks have no rhyme or reason," I said.

"Maybe you are a flashback and don't know it," my Guardian Angel said.

Lisa came into the room with a cup of coffee on a silver tray. "Here, my knight in shining armor," she smiled - dressed in short pants, a tank top and wearing no shoes she looked like she had just returned from a vacation in Mexico.

I took the coffee and smiled.

"Lisa is not a connoisseur of grief," my Guardian Angel said.

"Breakfast in fifteen minutes, the downstairs bathroom is down the hall and to the right. I've already set out towels for you," Lisa said and went back to the kitchen.

I felt like a king after breakfast. Clean, with clean Levi's on and a clean shirt, I wanted to get in Matilda and whistle my way to the next nowhere stop, but I know I can't. I have to get serious. "Do you want me to try and find the person who killed Sam?" I asked Lisa.

"Oh, Roosevelt, I'd hoped you would ask," she said. "There are certain things I can't tell the police but I know I can trust you."

"Sad to say Mr. Moral here is trustworthy," my Guardian Angel said.

"You'll have to tell me everything you know," I said to Lisa.

"Ask her if she is an undercover cop," my Guardian Angel said. If nothing else he is persistent.

Lisa gravely nodded her head. "I will when I get back from the police station. Detective Owens called me this morning and he has a few questions. Make yourself at home and when I get back I'll answer all the questions you want and we can decide on how much I'll pay you."

"This will be a second. A job that pays," my Guardian Angel said like he was good buddies with the man who owns the bank in Panama.

Lisa left the room.

When she came back she looked like a sales lady at J.C. Penney's that sells men perfume for their mistresses.

After she left I ambled around the large home, looking - not really investigating. It was spacious, beautifully decorated, and tasteful. There were five bedrooms upstairs - the master bedroom, a den, three for the children, two girls and a boy, but by their photographs, too old for Lisa to be their mother.

"Smart one, Lisa is at least 25 years younger than Sam was," my Guardian Angel said. "She couldn't be the mother."

Why is it in life the obvious is always the hardest to see?

The children's rooms were spotless - beds made, clothes all hung up, pictures on the walls all even. The den walls were covered with photographs of football teams and many hunting pictures of Sam posing with dead deer - there was the same rifle in all of the pictures. I examined the pictures closely, taking in every detail of the rifle. I had no doubt it was a 243. There was also a bedroom downstairs, off the laundry room.

I went outside, the two-story red brick house was on, what I estimated, two acres of land, with a fenced in tennis court and a large swimming pool with a Jacuzzi. It seemed odd, but the tennis court gate was locked. A glass building enclosed the pool. The pool was decorated to look like a Club Med with potted tropical plants and black wrought iron tables and chairs. There was a large well-stocked wet bar in the corner and bathrooms with several stalls and a shower.

The trees on the property were large and close together, it was impossible to see more than 50 feet in any direction. I looked at all the trees for a tree house but couldn't find one. Whoever had fired the shots had to have been on the property but, if they had left any tracks they were now obliterated by the meanderings of the police. I walked around the outside of the house. In the weed free flower beds were all sorts of flowers, red ones, blue ones, yellow ones, the only ones I know are roses. But, looking at the flowerbeds and having seen Lisa's hands, I know she must have a gardener. About the only calluses on Lisa's hands are from opening the top of a nail polish bottle.

"She might wear gloves," my Guardian Angel said.

The back and sides to the property were fenced with an 8-foot tall chain link fence without a gate. I found no sign of anybody coming over the fence or going back over the fence. By the back fence there was a river that was over a hundred yards wide. The water was brown and listless.

"That's the Raccoon River," my Guardian Angel said.

"How do you know that?"

"Elementary my dear dummy. I saw the sign when we drove over here yesterday."

Walking to the front of the house I heard horses like I had the day before - they must belong to the neighbors. A wall made of round river rock surrounded the front yard of the house. Where the chain link and the rock wall met a mouse couldn't squeeze through. The rock wall was at least twelve feet tall and stained with light and dark green moss giving the wall a look of age and respectability. The driveway has a wooden gate that Eric the Red could have built to keep the Cossacks out. The house looked like a home for a judge, or senator, or at the least, a retired boss for the mob.

"They are all the same, aren't they?" my Guardian Angel stated with a disgusted look on his face.

I opened the garage. Inside were a two-year-old light blue Mercedes and a new silver Mazda. I thought it strange Lisa would have taken the Lincoln to see Detective Owens. There were also three plastic garbage cans with the snap on lids that were labeled - CANS ONLY - PAPER ONLY - PLASTIC. It was nice to see there are a few things the

25

hippies did get people to think about. It would be nice if more people would think about radiation, ozone, the dying oceans, alternative fuels - "Enough is enough, Roosevelt," my Guardian Angel cut in. "Most people have to work too hard from day to day to look too far into the future."

"The future is all we have," I said.

I stood where Sam had been killed. I was pleased the police had cleaned up everything and not left any sign of a murder or an investigation. If this was Florida, the body might still be in the driveway.

By the way the bullet had entered Sam's skull, the bullet had to have been lead tipped and there would be no fragments - except those floating around in what had been Sam's brain. The shot had to have come from the area of the swimming pool or tennis court and by the loudness of the shot it had to have been a large caliber rifle. Walking toward the kitchen I wondered if Detective Owens, out of the kindness of his heart, would give me any information they had discovered. I decided that was as possible as the United States giving Texas back to Mexico.

Close to the door, leading into the kitchen, I stopped by a brick barbecue pit that was big enough to cook hot dogs for the entire Chinese Army. For some reason it seemed out of place.

In the kitchen, I suddenly remembered the key and paper I had taken out of Sam's pockets and half ran to my dirty clothes and dug them out. The key looked like a key a cheap hotel room would have - the kind with air fresheners in the wall sockets, cigarette burns on the nightstands and rented out by the hour. There was no name on the key, only a worn room number, number 23. I carefully unfolded the piece of paper and read in what looked like a woman's writing - "C'est La Vie Mother Goose." It was written on what appears to be a torn off section of normal 20 pound bond typing paper. I put both the paper and key in my back pocket. I had no idea what they meant but they had to mean something.

"I bet they don't mean anything," my Guardian Angel said.

"If we bet and I won you couldn't pay me," I said.

"Existence is much simpler when you don't need money," he said.

I took my trusty note pad and pen out of my suitcase and began jotting down everything that might be a clue and things that might not be clues but could turn out to be. Although I quit drugs years ago, after several years of trying to find myself with mind-altering drugs and only

26

getting further and further from the truth, I have to write down everything as it comes to me. If not, I forget it in about three seconds and normally only remember it three years later when the knowledge is as useful as finding the phone number to an old girlfriend who is now married. I also do not own a laptop or a cell phone. I like the old paper and pencil over a laptop – a pencil never needs batteries and when it comes to cell phones I hate the fact that by law any conversation on a cell phone is considered open airways and can be monitored and recorded without needing permission for a wire tap. The long arm of the law can be very, very, very, long even for the innocent. And, there are so many laws on the books now who knows when we are breaking one? My Guardian Angel thinks I am paranoid. Sad to say he is right.

I was so engrossed in my work that I didn't hear Lisa return until she was standing over me like a schoolteacher watching one of her students who thought he was getting away with cheating on an exam.

"You're cute when you're thinking," she said to me, but she looked nervous.

"If you think he's cute a baboon must look handsome to you," my Guardian Angel said. "And he doesn't think. He is more like an amoeba."

"I'm going to change," Lisa said.

When she came back, she was once again wearing short pants and a halter-top, widows wearing black must have gone out of style. She picked up my suitcase and showed me to the guest bedroom, which was off the laundry room. I now have my own bed, a bathroom, and a large picture window that over looks the side of the property. I even have my own door, which meant, if I wanted, I could go out and take a late night swim or Jacuzzi - even during bad times life can be good.

Standing by the picture window I could barely see the outline of the roof of the neighbor's house. "Do they have horses?" I asked Lisa.

"They have everything," Lisa said in a tone that chilled the air and then abruptly left the room.

I hung up my clothes in the closet and taking my note pad and pen went to find Lisa. Lisa was in the kitchen drinking iced tea. "I suppose it's time to get down to work," she said, as if a minute ago I had been a friend and now I was the man who had come to unclog the sink.

I sat on the opposite side of the table. "I should tell you a few things about myself," I told her, having found it was nice to have a little personal touch before all the dirty work begins.

"I know all about you, Roosevelt," Lisa said. "Sam always talked about you when he got drunk, which lately has been all the time. It seemed you and that commune back in New Mexico left a lasting impression on his mind. I know you're a Vietnam Veteran, one of those brave enough to have volunteered. I know you have so many karate belts you can't count them and you were shot twice in Vietnam, and Sam said you could shoot the eye out of an ant at 100 yards. I know that people looked up to you at the commune. I know you gave peace a try and that you were in the S.D.S. at The University of Texas and you marched for every cause there was except anti war rallies."

"War is not good, but until there are no enemies, our country must be prepared," my Guardian Angel said sounding like an Army recruiter.

"My history isn't much, is it?" I said to Lisa.

"Oh, I don't know. It has its rough romantic edges. I will say you're a good looking guy and have to do more than lift beer bottles to stay in shape."

"I only ran into Sam by accident," I confessed. "I was headed for Colorado."

"Dream boy thinks the faster he runs he will find himself and that the love of his life is always around the corner," my Guardian Angel said like I was dumber than a jelly fish.

"Detective Owens told me you had to leave Florida because of certain improprieties with a powerful man's wife," Lisa said, eyeing me suspiciously.

"She didn't tell me she was married," I said truthfully, trying not to sound bitter. "I thought I loved her but I was only a game."

Lisa looked at me like I was lying.

I opened my notebook. Lisa had enough of my personal history.

"What did you tell Detective Owens?" I asked.

"I told him I didn't know who would want to kill my husband. That we have received no threats or anything that would lead to such a crime."

"Why was your husband killed, Lisa?" I asked gently.

Lisa got up and brought back a glass and a bottle of white wine. She didn't offer me any, which was fine by me. After pouring a glass and taking a large swallow she began, "It all started three years ago after his divorce and our marriage. We lived in an apartment at first. We were happy, the kids seemed to be adjusting well and then Sam started to be gone a lot. I don't think it was another woman."

I raised my eyebrows but said nothing.

"Look at me, Roosevelt," Lisa said mockingly. "Men who have me don't need another woman."

"That's no lie," my Guardian Angel said really looking at her.

There was nothing I could say. True is true.

"Soon, Sam started buying me clothes, then a nice car, then one day he drove me over to this house. He had a big, red ribbon on the front door with my name on it. The house is in my name, he gave it to me. He enrolled the kids in private school and sent them on summer trips. We took exotic vacations. Sam's store did not make enough money to pay for any of this, but I didn't ask any questions, although it worried me. As the months passed he grew more and more distant. He started to drink, would yell at me, stay away for days and when he did come home, he wouldn't tell me where he'd been. Then he started getting phone calls late at night when he was home and would leave immediately."

I remembered Sam mentioning his wife having affairs. "Who do you think killed him?" I asked again.

Lisa gulped the wine, slammed the glass down on the table, and exploded. "His ex-wife is who. Sam kept a $500,000 dollar life insurance policy for her and for me. She would do anything to get her hands on that kind of money. She's so unfit the judge gave Sam custody of the kids."

"Shouldn't the kids be home by now?" I asked casually. Working on a case I have to stay level headed and not get emotionally involved. Emotions have the tendency to cloud reasoning.

"Don't get hung up on it, Roosevelt," my Guardian Angel said. "Reasoning isn't one of your strong points."

All the color drained from Lisa's face like dirt going down the bathtub drain. Her bottom lip began to tremble. "Where are the kids, Lisa?" I asked again.

"I don't know," she stammered fearfully. "When I got home today this was in the mailbox."

She reached into her pocket and slid me a folded sheet of typing paper. "Don't read it, give it back, time for the nowhere man to head to nowhere," my Guardian Angel begged.

I carefully unfolded the paper and read the typed message. I HAVE YOUR CHILDREN. DO NOT TELL THE POLICE OR YOUR KIDS WILL END UP LIKE SAM. I WILL BE IN TOUCH.

I felt as though somebody had hit me in the stomach with a ball bat.

"Murder and kidnapping, only two more to go before bodily harm," my Guardian Angel whispered in my ear.

"I have money," Lisa went on, composing herself. "I'll pay you whatever you want to get the kids back, but I don't want the police involved and I don't want to tell Sheila."

"Is Sheila the ex-wife?"

Lisa nodded her head.

"We can talk about money later," I told Lisa gently. "And I've never been one to love the police. I'm afraid of the law anymore."

"What are you going to do?" Lisa pleaded. "You have to do something."

"I'm going to sit here and you're going to tell me everything you and Sam ever did and try and remember everybody you ever saw him with, now, and before you were married. I imagine you two were having an affair before his divorce."

"Who wouldn't, married to that witch," Lisa snapped, baring her claws.

"I like it when they are angry," my Guardian Angel said.

"And you will tell me everything as calmly and rationally as you possibly can," I went on. "I'm really pretty good at this job when I get my head into it."

"You and Pinocchio are best buddies," my Guardian Angel smirked.

Lisa got another glass and poured me a glass of wine. I like wine about as much as I like quiche, but now wasn't the time to be rude. I looked again at the typed message - it puzzled me. "You really didn't know that lady in Florida was married did you?" Lisa asked me.

"No, I didn't," I said.

"I'm glad," she said, believing me this time.

"You're in for a lot of trouble, more than I thought at first," my Guardian Angel told me.

"I know," I answered, wondering if somewhere in the trouble to come I would discover who I am or what my purpose in life is.

"Maybe about ten seconds before you are killed, which, by then, will not do you any good," my Guardian Angel said.

30

CHAPTER THREE
FRIED EGGS OVER EASY

By the time Lisa went to bed, she had told me all there was to know about her and Sam's personal life. "You didn't ask her if she was an undercover cop," my Guardian Angel said.

"She is not an undercover cop," I replied like he should never bring the subject up again.

Lisa had met Sam at a bar. What started as casual conversation soon turned into a torrid affair. He divorced his wife and married her. They had been married for three years, but not all of them had been happy. She told me if he was doing anything illegal, she didn't know what it was, and had no idea why anybody would want to kidnap the kids. She admitted she had several affairs, but added, "They were nothing serious, just good sex."

"She must read Cosmopolitan," my Guardian Angel commented. He has read every Cosmo in print, or I should say, looked at all the pictures.

I was in bed, going over my clues, and hoping something would jump off the page and hit me with the truth so hard it would knock me out. I was also wondering why I think Lisa had not told me a single word of truth.

"You like it when they lie to you," my Guardian Angel said.

"I don't think that's funny," I told him.

"With the divorce rate like it is in this country I suppose it isn't," he said. "Sorry."

I have little hope of solving the murder. My deepest hope is that the children are safe and Lisa will be contacted soon, and by some miracle I can get the kids back. I told Lisa what to do when she is contacted. If it was by phone, she should remain calm and listen carefully so she would not forget anything she was told to do. If she was contacted by letter or note she should not do anything until I read the note. In my opinion, it would be better to go to the police and tell them what had happened, but, Lisa was against my advice and, it is her family. In most cases, the police are set up to handle kidnappings much better than anyone else. Most kidnappers don't release the people they have kidnapped. Once the money is handed over, all people get for their trouble are bodies.

"Kidnappers are cold-blooded people and when they are caught, they should be turned over to the family of the victims and the members of the family should skin them alive. Not quickly either, but six or seven inches a day, beginning with their eye lids so they can't shut their eyes and block out the nightmare of what is happening to them," my Guardian Angel said grimly.

"That is not nice for a Guardian Angel to say," I said, slightly taken back.

"I am not that nice," my Guardian Angel replied truthfully.

I turned off the reading lamp and stared into the darkness. Sam and I used to sit out at night and gaze at the stars that blanketed New Mexico. Back then life was a big dream that went on and on forever. Whatever Sam's worldly dreams had been had killed him. Still, I couldn't picture big gentle Sam, old hippie, a man I never witnessed angry at anybody, getting himself tied in with anything that would get him killed or endanger his family. The old capitalist system can spin a mean web. I hadn't really dwelled on what Sam had been doing to make so much money. That would come in time. What I really wanted to know was why Lisa didn't want to contact the police about the kids?

"She can fool you easier," my Guardian Angel said.

"What do you mean by that?"

"I don't trust her, Roosevelt. I think she merely wants you around so she can keep tabs on you. Undercover cops are like that."

"I don't think so," I said, ignoring the undercover cop bit.

"I'm only trying to help. If you don't want my advice I'm not going to lose any sleep over it."

"You don't have to sleep."

"That's one bummer about being an angel," he said with a frown.

As I shut my eyes, I know what I had to do in the morning. I had to start at the beginning. To dig a hole, you have to start with one shovel full of dirt. Hopefully, I don't dig a hole I can't climb out of.

"Roosevelt, you're always in a hole," my Guardian Angel said.

"You haven't been nice to me lately," I told him.

"I think my biorhythms are off," he said holding his wrist like he had a pulse.

In the morning Lisa was in the kitchen. The strain had finally gotten to her. Her eyes looked like dark river soaked sandbags and I could tell she had been crying. She had the phone sitting beside her in hopes whoever had the children would call. She smiled faintly at me but didn't say good morning. Standing by her I gently patted her on the shoulder. "It will all work out," I said as confidently as possible.

She looked at me like hope is a lead balloon.

After a quick cup of coffee I went to my room and locked my pistol in my suitcase. I had visions of a distraught Lisa blowing her pretty brains out.

Back in the kitchen, Lisa hadn't moved. "I'll be back before dark. If you get a call don't do anything stupid," I told her.

I didn't see any reason to tell her what my plans were for the day.

She nodded at me like a little lost puppy that only wanted to curl up in my lap and have its ears scratched.

"You could rub her tummy," my Guardian Angel said.

Matilda was her usual reliable self, starting with one turn of the key. I decided to take a tour of the neighborhood. The road curved gracefully. Each house, mansion in my mind, was set back from the road and barely visible either over the high walls or behind the large trees. I thought how strange it was that nobody in the neighborhood had come over to give Lisa condolences or at least called. But, I suppose, people in the situation that these people were in don't want to get their images tarnished in any manner.

My first stop was at a convenience store called Quick Stop. Iowa is one of the few states that still have pay phones. Luckily the phone book in the phone booth hadn't been ripped off by some jerk looking for an all night bait shop. There were only two addresses under Wrench, one was where I was staying.

Des Moines is not a large city as cities go, but, contrary to popular belief, it is modern, and has a feeling of tranquility to it. It does not make me paranoid like New York or Miami or downtown Amarillo.

The neighborhood I drove to is north of the V.A. hospital. The houses are solid middle class, ranging from white to blue in color, with one-car garages. The yards are all neatly trimmed, with blooming flowers along driveway edges and next to the houses large Oaks and Cottonwoods hang gracefully over the roof tops. The narrow street had cars parked on both sides. Every house had a Neighborhood Watch sign in the window. It was the type of neighborhood where everybody knows everybody and the kids are either in dance classes or little league.

Finding the house I was looking for I parked in the driveway behind a 2003 blue Ford Taurus with a dent in the driver's door that looked like it came from a wayward baseball. Next door, two small children were splashing in a wading pool decorated with yellow Donald Ducks. A man across the street, mowing his yard on a riding mower, waved. Most people in the Midwest are prouder of their lawn mowers than their kids - of course, lawn mowers don't steal cars or get kicked out of school.

I rang the doorbell and as if on cue two dogs inside the house started barking. There was no doubt they are the kind of dogs that look like drowned rats and would sneak up and bite me on the heel.

The door swung open. This is Iowa, people in Iowa still answer their doors and don't have to take six chains off the inside to let someone in. An attractive, middle aged woman, with short black hair streaked with white, cut almost military style, with large brown eyes, and a pleasing receptive face looked at me and said, "Yes?"

"Mrs. Wrench," I said. "I was a friend of Sam's."

Her calm, composed expression, changed instantly. "I'd like to talk to you, if I could?" I said, trying to sound as imposing as a grocery store cashier.

"What about?" she asked, eyeing me suspiciously.

The two miniature poodles by her feet barked viciously at me, but were about as vicious as a mosquito trying to bother an elephant.

"I want to find out who killed your ex-husband."

She grimaced, as if finding the killer of her ex-husband was the last thing she wanted to do. "Oh, I suppose," she said, after a moment. "It couldn't be any worse than talking to that detective. That guy would make a bulldog look good. But you'll have to wait until I put the dogs in the bedroom. They don't like strangers."

"I take it Owens was here or Des Moines is into ugly detectives," my Guardian Angel said.

Looking up and down the street it was nice. The man mowing the yard went back and forth dreaming he was at lawn mower Indy.

Mrs. Wrench came back and let me in.

The living room was neat and connected to the dinning room. I could see into the kitchen. There was a large pot if spaghetti sauce cooking on the stove, which I thought was strange. Sheila directed me to a chair and she sat on the sofa with a coffee table between us. On top of the TV was a photograph of each of the children when they were younger. Everything was so clean I doubt if dust was even in the air.

Mrs. Wrench was dressed in a loose fitting skirt dotted with small purple flowers and a sleeveless tan blouse. She was attractive in a

34

dignified way, and looked like a schoolteacher who teaches 8th or 9th grade and wouldn't take any excuses. She seemed like a much better match for Sam than Lisa.

I expected her to offer me coffee and cookies but instead she said, "Sam was a jerk," her tone wasn't bitter or hateful but matter-of-fact and she didn't sound like a schoolteacher.

"I know why you two divorced," I said.

"You've met the tramp," she retorted, sounding hateful. "Well, I hope she enjoys what she has caused."

I could see this conversation was getting me nowhere. I have yet to meet an ex-wife who likes the new wife, especially if the new wife is pretty and much younger.

"That is also true for ex-husbands," my Guardian Angel said.

"I was wondering if you would know anybody who would want to kill Sam," I asked Sheila, ignoring my politically correct Guardian Angel.

"You mean besides me," she half-chuckled and then leaned back on the sofa. In her new posture, she was much prettier than I had first thought. Her legs, now partially crossed and outlined by the soft fabric of the light skirt, are long and graceful.

"I'd like to see her in short pants," my Guardian Angel said.

God must really have it out for me to tax me with such an obnoxious Guardian Angel.

"When I married Sam we were both young. Looking at you, I would think you were one of his old hippie buddies. In fact, I think I saw you on TV once, something to do about a kidnapping."

"That was me," I answered, trying not to sound proud I had done one good deed in my life.

"You must be Bob Roosevelt. I'll be."

I felt like a fool, I had not introduced myself.

"You don't know how many stories Sam used to tell about you two. I think you were the best friend he ever had. It was old Roosevelt this, and old Roosevelt that."

"Those were different times," I said.

"Tell me about it. I left Iowa in 1969 and hitchhiked to San Francisco. Can you imagine? Sticking out my thumb, wearing bell-bottoms and a little halter-top. In Frisco I lived in a house on Haight Ashbury with 14 other kids. We sang, danced in the streets, marched against anything that needed marching against, it was great until the junkies moved in. Dear lord, looking back, it scares me almost to death wondering how I survived."

"Would you do it again?" I asked.

She smiled ruefully. "If I hitchhiked now you'd find my naked and mutilated body in a cornfield in Nebraska."

I smiled, it beat frowning.

"You want some coffee?" she asked, seemingly relaxed.

"Please."

As she walked by me I could see the young girl in her hitchhiking. I could picture her sparkling eyes, carefree smile, and her naive Midwest mind filled with fairy tales and dreams of a better world. Now I can see the reserve in the eyes, and the fear the world has gone a muck and her youth had been wasted on trying to change a world that would never change.

"Don't be a pessimist, Roosevelt," my Guardian Angel said, "there is always hope for the world."

"I am a pessimistic optimist," I replied.

"My name is Sheila," Sheila said, handing me a cup of coffee.

I did not tell her I already knew her name.

I sipped the coffee and wished I would have been driving to San Francisco years ago and been the one to pick up Sheila as she stood by the road.

"I suppose you wanted to see Sam dead," I said.

"He put me through hell, what with his lying, and his other women. Lisa wasn't the first you know. She was only one of a string of young beauties. Young beauties that Sam thought would keep him young. You might not have known it but Sam was morbidly afraid of growing old. But, no, I don't want to see anyone dead."

I thought of Sam's dyed hair.

"Did you kill him, Mrs. Wrench?" I asked, seeing no reason to not get right to the point.

"You can call me Sheila," she said. "And no, I didn't kill him. He got himself killed."

I don't know why, but I didn't believe her.

"I do. She didn't kill Sam," my Guardian Angel said.

"You can call me Roosevelt," I told Sheila, and wondered why her two dogs weren't yapping? Most little dogs when they are taken out of a room scratch and bark at the door.

I happened to notice a bookcase with three trophies on it. Two of the trophies were of horses in the process of jumping. The other one was a trophy with a person holding a rifle in the shooting position. "You ride?" I asked casually.

"I was raised on a farm and we always had horses. But I haven't ridden in years."

"I don't want to offend you," I said carefully. "But why did you lose custody of the children?"

Sheila looked at me like I was a used pooper-scooper. After a few moments she took a deep breath, and replied, "Whoever told you I lost custody of the children is a liar. Sam and I had joint custody. But, what with his new house and his money, I felt he could do a much better job for them and they stayed with him most of the time. The youngest is 14 now. It isn't like they need their diapers changed."

I felt like a bug that had just hit the windshield of a pickup truck that was going 90 miles an hour. "I'm sorry," I stammered. "I was misinformed."

"I think I will start calling you big foot in mouth," my Guardian Angel said.

"Do you know anything Sam might have been involved in that would have gotten him killed, Sheila?" I asked, regaining my composure.

"I know he didn't get involved with drugs. When he came back to Iowa he never touched the stuff. But I know he had to get involved with something. See this house? This was our house, the store barely paid for it. In ten years we never took a vacation, and then suddenly he buys a house, a Lincoln, and sends the kids to private school." Sheila smiled coyly at me. "He didn't win the lottery, Roosevelt."

"Did the detective leave you with any indication that they might have a lead?"

Sheila shook her head.

I could think of nothing else to ask and I felt like a suitor who had finally made his play, had been rebuked, and was now looking for a way to get out of the house. As with Lisa, I felt Sheila was both holding back from me and lying, especially about Sam and drugs. I wanted to, but couldn't, mention the kidnapping. In my mind Lisa is responsible for the children and I have to follow her wishes.

Sheila looked at me from head to toe like I was a prize bull about to be put up for auction. It made me feel like I was only a piece of meat - she didn't want to know me for the real me - only for my body.

"Tell her she has nice eyes and you want to see her naked," my Guardian Angel said. "She is sizing you up. She wants you, Roosevelt."

It was time for me to make my exit. I set the coffee cup on the table and got up. "I'm sorry to have bothered you," I said. "I'm sure we'll find the killer."

"Who are we?" Sheila asked, puzzled.

"Tell her about me," my Guardian Angel pleaded. "You don't know how hard it is to spend so much time in the shadows.

"The police and I," I replied to Sheila.

"Thanks for nothing you ego freak," my Guardian Angel said trying to make me think he feelings were hurt. What feelings?

Sheila stood by me. "A couple of old hippies like us should get together," she said like an old lover as she put her hand on my arm.

Her eyes were like an Indian's eyes, dark, penetrating, with no discernable pupils - eyes that pulled me into their center but revealed nothing. "Maybe when this is all over," I said.

"You don't know when opportunity smacks you right in the middle of your forehead," my Guardian Angel sighed.

As I drove away Sheila waved like I was her long lost brother. I felt strange, like I haven't eaten in two days. Out of impulse, I drove a block and parked the car. Ten minutes later Sheila drove by me and luckily didn't see me.

I drove back to her house, parked in the driveway, and waved at the man across the street who was now edging his yard. On the back porch was a pair of black riding boots with polo spurs and hanging on the clothesline was a pair of lady's riding britches. The two dogs inside the house started barking but then suddenly stopped.

As I drove away, I wondered why I felt Sheila was lying to me when I knew Lisa had lied, but even with the lying, I knew Sheila would be a lot of fun to sit down with on a warm summer night and talk about the 60's.

"If you remember, oh famous private detective, I told you when you first got to Iowa everyone would lie to you," my Guardian Angel said like he had never been wrong in his life or death.

Stopping at a pay phone I called Lisa. Lisa answered sounding like a young lawyer's secretary who had lost her manicure set. "I take it you've heard nothing," I said.

She hesitated and then said, "No."

"Don't worry, I'll be back soon."

"I hope so," she answered, no longer sounding like the secretary, but like somebody who had no friends in the world.

Looking at my four-dollar quartz watch it was already 12:30. 12:30 seemed to be a good time to visit Greasy Ed's. I didn't think it would be hard to find a seat.

Nothing had changed at Greasy Ed's, including Greasy Ed. He hadn't changed clothes, and it was obvious he hadn't changed his apron.

"You back again?" he said as I sat down at the counter - like having a repeat customer was as rare as a lobbyist who really cares about the country. Once again, I was the only person in the place.

"Your chili gave me so much heartburn last time I thought I'd try it again," I said, noticing another pin up had been added to the wall. This one was of a naked girl riding a copper frying pan.

My Guardian Angel walked around the room looking at the pinups mumbling something about great art and superb lighting.

Greasy Ed went to the kitchen and came back with a bowl of chili and four crackers. "Beer," he said, setting the bowl of chili down like it weighed two hundred pounds.

"Waters fine," I replied, "and a few questions."

"I'll give you some water, but I don't answer questions," he said like answering a question would be like taking a bath.

"Did you know Sam was killed?" I asked as I took a bite of chili - like murder and chili went together. I noticed a slight flinch in Greasy Ed's jaw at the question before he said, "Who's Sam?"

I wanted to reach over the counter and grab him by his nose for playing with me but I controlled myself. I have always found great enjoyment in beating the p-dunk out of big guys who think they are tough. An enjoyment I try to keep under control, but, at times, it flares up like the volcano on the Big Island. I know he knew who Sam was as well as he knows the names of every pin up girl in the place. "Sam was the guy I was with the last time I was here," I said, holding my temper.

"I never seen that guy before," Greasy Ed half smirked.

"Greasy Ed," I said calmly. "I'm going to ask you a few questions. You are going to answer the questions to the best of your slow-witted mind. If you don't answer the questions, I'm going to jump over this counter and make you wish you were the dog meat in this lousy chili.

Now, how did you know Sam?"

Greasy Ed looked at me like I was some cockroach he was about to kill and toss in the chili. He leaned on the counter and, with his nose about once inch from mine, said, "Mr. Nosey, I'm going to cram that bowl of chili down your skinny long haired throat if you don't change your attitude."

"My throat doesn't have long hair my head does," I said, and slammed my forehead into the bridge of his nose. He went down like a cow at a slaughterhouse. As he lay behind the counter, bleeding, I jumped over the counter and kicked him twice in the ribs. I then grabbed him by his greasy apron string and dragged him into the kitchen. As he lay wheezing, I quickly looked around the kitchen. There was nothing spectacular about the kitchen, except the phone on the wall that for some reason caught my attention.

Greasy Ed was trying to get up and had managed to get on his hands and knees. Blood was pouring out of his nose like a broken water line leading to a washing machine and he was growling like a dog. "Greasy Ed," I said. "You are one big dumb son-of-a-Cheerio." I stepped back and kicked him in the stomach. The wind went out of him so loudly it sounded like a tire blowout. As he fell to the floor, I know there is at least a small stadium full of people who would have loved to have seen Greasy Ed go down.

"When I come back, you will talk," I told the unconscious form.

"Temper, temper," my Guardian Angel chastised, but added, "he needed a good whipping even if you did sucker punch him."

"It wasn't a sucker punch, it was a head butt," I said, still angry.

"Don't get huffy with me," he said sticking his jaw out. "Remember, I am impossible to hit."

To my surprise, two older black men were sitting outside on a bench. They had to be in their late 70's and looked like they had never seen a lucky day in their lives. "You men like a bowl of Chili?" I asked, like I was the new waiter. "Come on in and sit at a table."

Both men nodded their heads apprehensively but went in. I went to the kitchen, stepping over Greasy Ed, and filled four bowls and gave

40

them each two bowls. I then drew them two beers apiece. "On the house," I said.

The two men grinned at me like I was Santa Claus.

Driving away I knew it would take more than four bowls of chili before Greasy Ed woke up.

I remembered when I first got out of Vietnam and had become, in appearance sake at least, a hippie. I had long, light brown hair, a beard, and wore a bell earring my girlfriend had given me. I used to walk around The University of Texas wearing Levi's, sandals, a T-shirt, and a fringed leather jacket with my two purple hearts pinned to it. One day I was walking by a frat house that football players belonged to - THE FRATERNITY OF MY GIRLFRIEND DOES MY HOMEWORK AND I HAVE NO NECK. Two big guys, who thought they were Greek Gods, were sitting in front of the house grunting. When they saw me, they laughed like I was the funniest thing they had ever seen in their life, which, looking back, I was. The frat boys were famous for beating hippies half to death and cutting their hair. Twenty minutes later when the ambulance was taking them to the hospital to set their broken arms they weren't laughing. War has a way of reminding one that peace is all well and good but all people have to embrace the idea before you throw your club away. Pity the world.

Two blocks from Greasy Ed's, Lisa, driving the white Lincoln, went by me going the opposite direction. I wanted to slam on the breaks and do a quick U-turn but there was too much traffic.

I turned around at the next light, but I had lost her. Although at times I am stupid, I am not always that stupid. I drove by Greasy Ed's and saw the white Lincoln parked in front. I know Lisa wasn't inside posing for one of the calendars and I really doubt if she was there to eat the chili.

"This is interesting," my Guardian Angel said rubbing his chin like he could think.

I felt like an all day sucker that somebody had left out in the sun and was covered with ants. Heading back toward the house I did know, that at the present time, it would be better to not tell Lisa I saw her at Greasy Ed's.

I was about three blocks from Lisa's house when the red lights from a squad car came on behind me. I pulled over.

"I didn't know this relic from the past could speed," my Guardian Angel said.

41

"Don't listen to him Matilda. He's running his head as usual," I consoled my car - her feelings get hurt easily.

The city policeman had seen too many Robo Cop movies. He was wearing sunglasses that were so dark he couldn't have seen the road if he was in Arizona. "You Bob Roosevelt?" he asked politely, much to my surprise.

I was used to Florida police who pull a gun on you if you have a moustache.

"Yes I am, officer," I replied, like a high school kid who is on the honor role.

I have found it's always smart to be polite to the police. My good old papa taught me that a guy with a gun usually has all the power.

"If you would be kind enough to follow me in your car," he said in a manner that I knew I really had no choice.

I followed the squad car half way through Des Moines, but when he stopped, to my relief, it was not at the police headquarters downtown, but at a truck stop off of I-35. I followed the policeman inside, trying to ignore the glances of the truck drivers. Truck drivers like police like farmers like skunks under their houses and broadleaf weeds in their corn and soybean fields.

Sitting in a booth eating chicken fried steak and mashed potatoes smothered in gravy, and of course, no salad, was Detective Owens.

"Here's your rabbit," the policeman told Owens.

"No, chicken," my Guardian Angel said.

Owens's cheeks were so puffed out with steak he looked like a fat chipmunk - an ugly fat chipmunk.

I slid into the booth. Owens looked at me like he thought I would only order the salad bar.

He swallowed the hunk of steak, slurped on his cup of coffee, wiped his mouth with the back of his hand and grunted, "You ever slept with my wife I'd cut your tongue out."

I wanted to say, "Anybody that would be married to you, my dog wouldn't want to sleep with," but prudence is the better part of valor and I sat there quietly.

"So you're staying with the Wrench widow," Owens said, sticking a bite of chicken fried steak in his mouth that was so big a Mississippi catfish would have choked.

"She asked me to," I said. "It wasn't my idea."

"Your private eye license isn't worth squat in Iowa you know?"

42

"I'm only helping her as a friend," I replied, thinking how good the chicken fried steak looked.

"I bet her little sad naked body is about all the friend you need," Owens said, trying to sound mean, but sounding like he had spent all last night wishing he was staying at Lisa's house.

"Have you brought me here to buy me dinner," I said, "or to talk about women?"

For a moment, Owens stopped chewing his steak, his eyes became mere slits and I thought I was going to have to put his nose all over his face like I did Greasy Ed's. Then he smiled, or what I took to be a smile, and I smiled knowing if I put Owens's nose all over his face, I would be scrubbing floors at the jail for more than one birthday. "You got guts. I made a few calls and everybody told me you got guts. To sleep with the Chief of Detective's wife, you got to have guts," Owens said.

I could see no reason to tell him I hadn't known she was married.

"Listen, Roosevelt," Owens went on. "I don't give a rat who you sleep with. Truth be known that sassy little lady you were hijacked by down in Florida used to be my wife. There was a convention three years ago in Ft. Lauderdale and the Mrs. had been riding me hard to take her somewhere, you know, the old, 'you are never home, we never do anything,' so I took her with me. Within two days she's sleeping with the Chief of Detectives and when I came home, she stays."

"I'll be," I stammered, trying not to picture in my mind, Owens, with the body of a bulldog, making love to his ex-wife, who was one good looking lady.

My Guardian Angel was laughing so hard he sounded like a donkey with a head cold.

"It's not at all funny," I told him feeling sick.

"Har, har, har," he laughed harder - tears running down his face.

"My turn will come oh laughing one," I warned him.

"Har, har, har."

My Guardian Angel should have a small amount of respect.

"It's a small world," Owens said, swallowing the last bite of his steak.

He then reached across the table and swatted me playfully on the shoulder, like two good old boys from Laredo, who, on different days, without knowing it, visited the same Mexican pawnshop.

"You want something to eat?" he asked.

"I'm not hungry right now," I answered, my appetite having flown out the window faster than a pro wrestler takes a dive.

Owens burped and looked at me. "Listen up Roosevelt, first off, you don't carry a gun in Iowa. And, I think you should know we've been following Sam for months. We think he was a key player in a gun smuggling ring."

I felt like a twenty-pound bowling ball that couldn't knock over the ten pin.

"And we also think he was involved with smuggling heroin."

I now felt like a twenty-pound bowling ball had landed on my foot.

"Do you have anything that could help me?" I asked which I knew was a stupid question as soon as I asked it.

"Nope," Owens said. "I thought you should know what you were getting yourself mixed up in and hoped it might make you decide to get in your flower child bug and get out of my state."

"I've tried to tell him," my Guardian Angel said. "But, will he ever listen? Not old know it all."

I could see myself in Matilda with the windows rolled down, the 93 degree hot air as thick as mud blowing around my face as I drove through Nebraska on my way to Colorado. I haven't been trout fishing in years. I used to love trout fishing. I would go up in the mountains where the Aspens started and camp out and catch trout. I'd catch a skillet full and fry them in butter with an onion and sit there listening to the breeze and feel as happy as Bob Dylan after he dumped Joan Baez.

"We think they were taking the guns to revolutionaries in Mexico," Owens said.

I really didn't know what to say. "Have you gotten any concrete evidence?" I finally asked.

"No, we got a report from the Texas police that they had picked up a Mexican national who gave them the information. As to anything else, we've never been able to find anything. In fact, we had written it off until your old hippie buddy ate the big one."

"How do you know he was an old hippie?" I asked.

Owens laughed and it sounded like he was choking on a meatball. "There isn't a hippie alive in this wonderful free country of ours that the Feds don't have a file on."

"Big Brother don't need no stinking permission," my Guardian Angel said.

"Did you find anything at the murder scene?" I asked Owens.

Owens made a dour face. "We didn't find a thing, no shell casing, no footprints, it's like the murderer swung through the trees like Tarzan. We do know the bullet was a 243 with a lead tip.

"Can you trace it?"

"Maybe, if we find the murder weapon."

"That's really not likely," I commented, but remembering Sam's hunting photographs.

He grunted.

"Do you think either Lisa or his ex-wife knows anything about what he was up to?" I asked.

Owens looked at me like I was as stupid as a fence post. "A wife always knows everything. Men come home and talk about their business, even if it's killing people. But remember there are laws. A wife can't be forced to testify against her husband."

"Even if he is dead?" I asked.

"I don't know about that," Owens said. "Good question."

Owens slid out of the booth. "One last thing," he said. "You pick up on anything you'd better trip your old hippie tail down to see me and fill me in."

I nodded in agreement, like withholding evidence was the last thing I would ever do.

"I didn't know you had a tail," my Guardian Angel said.

Back in Matilda, and headed back to my gun and heroin smuggling, dead old hippie buddy's house, where his lying ex-wife waited - looking as delicious as a keg of beer to a Georgia chain gang - I had the sobering thought that I don't own a fishing pole anymore, and the place I used to go trout fishing and listen to the breeze in Colorado was now probably paved and has $200,000 log cabins everywhere. I also felt that Owens had been far too nice to me - he was up to something - something, that if I knew what it was, I wouldn't like.

It was one of those days, when the eggs I tried to cook over easy, turned out as hard as a rock, and I didn't have the money to feed them to the dog and try again. When this happens,

I put the over hard eggs between a couple of slices of white bread and smother them with ketchup - it's not half bad. Remember though, I didn't say it was good. Like my mother used to say. "If I cook it, you eat it, I don't want to hear any of this it doesn't taste good stuff, man only eats because he has to, if you're worried about taste you are spoiled."

My mother lived through part of the depression in the Midwest. No Wendy's or Big Mac's in the belly can leave a lasting impression.

"You think depression," my Guardian Angel said. "I lived through the dark ages."

"Maybe that is why you are such a sick-o," I said.

CHAPTER FOUR
RUB MY TUMMY

When I got to Lisa's, the Lincoln was parked exactly where it had been when I left - she had taken pains to cover the fact she had gone to Greasy Ed's. Looking at the tennis court I wondered once again why the gate was locked.

"The tennis court has nothing to do with this case," my Guardian Angel said.

"How do you know?"

"Heavenly intuition," he said, like he and God are best buddies.

"You let me be the detective and you be the Guardian Angel," I said, "I don't like people getting into my business."

"I'm not people and you might be sorry."

"I'll take my chances."

Lisa was sitting at the kitchen table. She didn't look as bad as she had in the morning. I didn't tell her that I had seen her parked in front of Greasy Ed's. She didn't tell me that Greasy Ed had told her some middle aged guy with long gray hair and a beard, not more than half his size, had been in and had his way with him, like a bunch of guards in a Mexican prison that had picked up a college boy from Austin and they really didn't care if he was innocent or that his dad owned the biggest tortilla factory in Houston.

"I take it nobody has called?" I stated, more than asked Lisa.

Lisa shook her pretty little, Sheila lost custody of the kids, lying head.

"Did you find out anything during your travels?" she asked, sounding as concerned as a parole board member interviewing Charlie Manson.

"I found out I don't know anything," I said truthfully.

"Keep trying, Roosevelt, you might get lucky, since you don't want any advice," my Guardian Angel said, "and won't ask her if she is an undercover cop."

I gave him a shut-up look.

"I might as well make us something for dinner," Lisa said.

While Lisa busied herself in the kitchen I took a shower. It felt strange taking a shower while a murdered friend of mine's wife was cooking. Life goes on. It's sad.

47

"Being overly practical can be a bummer," my Guardian Angel said.

Lisa had thrown together a salad that had about everything in it but lettuce - salad isn't exactly my idea of dinner but I kept my mouth shut. For a period of my life I tried being a vegetarian, but my greasy hamburger addiction was too strong. I kicked drugs and tobacco but fat has my number.

I kept trying to figure out why I thought Lisa was lying to me about her and Sam's history.

"Don't forget Sheila," my Guardian Angel said.

He has never been one to stay out of my business for long.

After the salad, Lisa brought out a bottle of red wine. I can say one thing for Lisa, her grieving process has many twists and turns. Pouring my wine, I don't know if it was by accident or intentional, but she brushed tantalizingly against my shoulder. One part of my mind said, 'Accident', one part of my mind said, 'Intentional'.

Either way it made me uncomfortable.

Lisa smiled and went to her side of the table.

"Your morals make me sick," my Guardian Angel said.

"It can be a bummer," I said.

As we drank the wine, Lisa and I said nothing. I took my empty glass to the sink. When I turned, I ran chest to chest into Lisa. She didn't smile but I could read her mind like a book. A book filled with dirty pictures and few words.

"I like those kinds of books," my Guardian Angel drooled.

"Lisa, I have to get up early in the morning," I said.

"I admire your dedication," she said, and gave me a you don't know what you are missing look. "Have good dreams."

I went to my room.

"I can see Lisa taking off her clothes," my Guardian Angel said.

"Keep it to yourself," I told him.

I took out my notebook and began to write down all the happenings of the day that I thought might have a bearing on the case. When I was done, I turned off the light, but it took far too long for me to fall asleep. Temptation is not an easy vice to fight.

Lisa wasn't up when I got out of bed. The sun hadn't risen above the trees and the sky was a pale golden yellow. The dew was so thick on the ground it was like I had gotten the first tee time on Sunday morning. I was looking out the window at two robins shadow boxing over a worm when I heard the horses from next door. Dressing quickly,

I left the house, went down the driveway, and up the street to the neighbor's house. I had no idea why I was going.

"Warning, warning, white boy might be better off going back to bed," my Guardian Angel informed me, sounding like Custer's guide the day Custer lost his hair.

If Sam's house was large, the neighbor's house was obese, it had enough stained glass to buy all the homeless in Des Moines lunch for two years and enough red brick in the walls to build Texas another prison. Behind the house, about thirty yards away, was what I gathered to be the caretaker's house or guesthouse. It would have made any middle class American proud. Not far from the caretaker's house was a horse barn, made to look like a miniature of the master house. Three horses, expensive thoroughbreds, were prancing around in their individual paddocks. I could see three other empty paddocks. A man leaning on the fence of one of the paddocks saw me, looked apprehensive, but then waved. I waved back and headed toward him. As I did, he tossed hay into the feed bins for the horses.

When I was next to him, I knew he wasn't the owner of the house.

A Mexican man in his late thirties and dressed in work clothes, doesn't own a home like this one unless he is living in Mexico City and bribing the president. The man was slim, hardened from years of work, his hands looked like he could use them to drive nails. He had eyes that are as dark and intense as a heavyweight prizefighter and a nasty looking two-inch scar on his right cheek. He had on a gold bracelet and a gold chain around his neck that struck me as odd. The man smiled at me and looked at the horses. "They are nice, no?" he said in English, which should have been, "They are nice, yes?" but I did not correct him.

"Beautiful," I lied.

I worked on a ranch for several years and I've thrown enough hay bales to have a bad back and shoveled enough horse manure to fill Yankee Stadium.

"Does the owner race them?" I asked the man.

"They are only pets, a few people come and ride them, but besides that, they only eat and poop."

"Are the Browne's in?" I inquired.

"No, they are in Mexico for a week or so."

"Too bad," I said. "I'm staying next door and merely wanted to meet the neighbors."

49

"I will tell them you stopped by," the man said, not asking for my name.

There really wasn't anything to say, and after a long moment of silence, I mumbled goodbye and drifted back toward the road wondering why the Mexican man had not asked me anything about the murder or how Lisa was doing?

There was a tennis court close to the chain link fence that separates Sam's house from the Browne's house. I got close enough to the tennis court to see that the gate was also locked. People build fences around swimming pools so they can lock the gates to keep kids from drowning, but I didn't know people built tennis courts so they could lock the gates. I have never heard of a kid drowning on a tennis court.

"I told you, get off the locked tennis court obsession," my Guardian Angel said.

By the time I got back to the house, Lisa was in the kitchen. She had on short pants that were so short normal short pants would be considered long. Her halter-top looked like a reject from a bikini factory it was so small. "I take it nobody called?" I asked, trying to ignore her seven miles of cleavage.

My Guardian Angel was drooling. "I'll be," he said. "She has an outie belly button."

Lisa didn't answer my question but demanded more than asked, "Where have you been?"

"Women do not like being rejected," my Guardian Angel said.

"I went to see the neighbors," I replied, feeling like a hen pecked husband.

"You have never been married. How do you know what a hen pecked husband feels like?" my Guardian Angel asked.

"It's in every man's gene pool," I told him.

"You went to the Browne's," Lisa said, like Browne's is a cuss word.

"Only the caretaker is there. They went to Mexico for a few weeks."

She seemed to relax and placed a plate of peaches on the table covered with yogurt and wheat germ. "Eat," she ordered.

I wondered where the ham, fried eggs, butter, toast and coffee were.

As Lisa was about to start eating the phone rang. I could see genuine fear in her eyes. "Wrench's," she answered.

50

I knew the phone call was from the kidnappers. I stood up, glad to get away from the peaches, and stood by her.

"Yes, yes, yes, I understand," and she hung up.

"What did they say?" I asked, trying not to convey any fear in my voice.

"It was a woman I think, a woman with something over the phone to disguise her voice. All she said was the kids are fine and to quote her exact words – 'I will be in touch as soon as I feel everything is safe.'"

"No demands?" I asked, confused.

"Nothing," Lisa answered.

I could tell she felt better having at least heard something.

Eating my peaches I wished I could hold my nose. Eating peaches for breakfast is like, when I was a kid, having to drink my milk after it got warm.

As the last peach slid down my throat, I wondered what kind of kidnappers these were that were waiting until everything was safe. Being a kidnapper isn't safe. If it's safe it's about as safe as being a belly gunner on a B-52 during World War II.

"Do you know anything about the Browne's?" I asked Lisa.

"I know he's a tramp and all that he wants to do is get me in bed."

"I can't imagine anybody not wanting to get Lisa in bed," my Guardian Angel said, adding, "Except you, oh idiot one."

"What does Mr. Browne do?" I asked Lisa.

"He made his first fortune by bringing cable TV into Iowa. After that, he started an import company out of Mexico. I guess he's doing well with it and it gives him and his wife time to travel."

"Who are he and she?" I asked.

"Bill and Connie."

Looking at my empty peach plate I wished I had a greasy hunk of sausage. "Do you know where Sam's ex-wife works?"

Lisa didn't even bat an eye at the mention of the ex-wife. "She has a store close to Merle Hay Mall. I don't know the name of the street, but it's next to a Chinese restaurant."

"What's the name of the store?"

"Mother Goose," Lisa replied.

The peaches in my stomach felt like Salmon wanting to swim back upstream as I remembered the paper I'd found in Sam's pocket - Ces't La Vie Mother Goose. My plans for the day had changed.

I left the house so fast Lisa didn't have a chance to say, "What do you think of my tan lines?"

Matilda, as usual, kicked right off, but before I headed for Merle Hay Mall, I stopped at a Wendy's and got two hash brown potatoes and a large coffee.

"Don't you ever wonder about Lisa's reaction to the murder and kidnapping?" my Guardian Angel asked. "Lisa seems awfully calm."

"Maybe she is practical and accepts life," I replied.

"An American woman, come on now," my Guardian Angel said.

"Be careful about gender generalizations, this day and age they can get you in a lot of trouble," I said.

After wolfing down the hash browns and drinking the coffee I felt human again and promised myself a greasy hamburger for lunch.

It wasn't hard to find the store. The sign in front pictured a large gray goose with a white bonnet on its head. Streaming from the bonnet was a trail of white daises. The goose was holding a wicker basket that has blue and yellow butterflies flying out of it. In a half circle over the goose is painted - MOTHER GOOSE. The store sells dolls and stuffed animals and smelled like lavender.

Sheila was arranging a display of teddy bears that range in size from two inches to three feet and were every shade of black and brown imaginable. They all have little glass eyes and button noses - even I thought they were cute.

"Does little Roosevelt want a teddy bear?" my Guardian Angel taunted.

"If I could, there are times I would punch you," I told him.

"Being a spirit does have a few advantages," he smiled.

Sheila didn't see me as I watched her work on her display. I noticed how graceful her hands were, and how attractive she was wearing an old type, loose fitting hippie skirt, and a light fluffy blouse. She had on sandals but, unlike the old days, her feet were clean. She was even wearing multi-colored beaded bracelets on her wrist and ankle. She would be perfect working in an organic supermarket in Oregon.

When she turned, and saw me, she wasn't surprised at all, but smiled a grin at me so large you would have thought I was bringing her a truckload full of stuffed animals.

"Roosevelt," she said. "You don't strike me as the kind who would want a stuffed toy.

"Do you have any blow up plastic women?" my Guardian Angel asked.

"This is a nice place, Sheila," I said. "It suits you."

"I like it. You'd be surprised how many ladies come in here and buy my babies. I get more older people than kids."

"It's a fantasy island."

"We all need our fantasies," she smiled and winked at me. "I'll show you around."

I had never seen so many stuffed animals in my life. When she was done, she was beaming like a little girl at a carnival with cotton candy all over her face and two more tickets to the roller coaster. I hated to ruin her day but I had to. Trying to solve a murder and a kidnapping can get in the way of a nice day. "When Sam was shot I was there," I said slyly. "I managed to grab a few things out of his pockets. One of them was a note. The note said, "C'est La Vie Mother Goose."

Sheila didn't give me the response that I expected. Instead of being shocked, or trying not to show guilt, she looked at me like whatever I had said had been said in Latin, and since not many people speak Latin anymore, she didn't have the foggiest idea of what I was talking about.

"Don't you get it," I finally said, looking into her eyes, trying to find a trace of anything sinister.

"I suppose you think because you found a note with 'Mother Goose' on it, that I'm the one who shot Sam."

"Well, something like that," I replied. "I was hoping you would be so overcome you would fall on the floor sobbing and confess to his murder."

"Roosevelt," she said. "Get grounded."

"He keeps trying but it never seems to work," my Guardian Angel said. "Grounded to him is being stuck in the mud."

"Why don't you come over for dinner tonight," Sheila asked out of the blue.

"What time?"

"Around 8 and you bring the wine."

"It will be cheap wine," my Guardian Angel said.

I don't know why I accepted the invitation so quickly. I didn't even ask what we were having.

Driving away from the Mother Goose I was disappointed. I felt sure Sheila would have a reaction when I mentioned the note. I wondered if she was on Prozac.

"You could brighten up my life if you seduce Sheila tonight," my Guardian Angel said.

"I'm not going to sleep with Sheila," I said.

"Boring," my Guardian Angel said.

I drove to Army Post Road. Army Post Road is on the southern edge of Des Moines - second-rate car dealerships mingle with run down gas stations and adult video stores. There were cardboard signs nailed on all the telephone polls advertising garage sales. On the corner of Army Post and 9th was Sam's furniture store. One of those stores with the perpetual 'going out of business' sign out front, 'everything slashed 50%,' the sale had been going on for 27 years and would end any day now. The balloons out front of the store had probably been there for at least 5 years. In the parking lot were half a dozen rusted out Chevy's, Fords, and a few dented pickups. Several fathers were standing out front smoking and watching the kids run in and out of the traffic. I know there is no way this store could make enough money to buy a house with a pool and a locked tennis court. The store couldn't buy all of Lisa's halter-tops and short pants.

It was close to noon and I decided now was as good a time as any to eat a greasy hamburger and besides, I needed time to think. "There isn't enough time left in the world for you to start thinking," my Guardian Angel said.

Sitting in the plastic fantasy world of a modern hamburger joint, eating my double Whopper with onion rings and a large Coke, I know I haven't discovered a thing. About the only thing I know is that either Lisa or Sheila could have been the murderer, but - if either of them was, then who was the kidnapper? Sam's involvement with gun running and heroin was so far above me, it might as well be a satellite. But, there was no doubt Sam had to be doing something illegal to afford his little corner of the capitalist dream.

With the hamburger sitting in my stomach like a charcoal briquette and the onion rings guaranteed to give me heartburn, I watched the stream of short panted and short sleeved throngs of humanity that poured in and out of the restaurant and wondered how I have developed such a weird taste in food. I remembered Sheila had told me to bring a bottle of wine. Telling me to pick out a bottle of wine is like telling me to explain an opera. The only wine I know about costs four dollars a gallon.

Before I drove off I checked Matilda's oil, which was its usual half-quart low, and then drove toward Greasy Ed's. I have no doubt he will be in a question-answering mood today.

The two older black men I had given the chili and beer to were once again sitting on the bench in front of the restaurant. "You working here now?" one of the men asked me.

"No, just stopped by for a chat."

He looked disappointed but also worried. "Me and Harold ain't seen nobody inside, but the door isn't locked," he said.

"Don't go in," my Guardian Angel warned.

I went inside. The fan was not on and Greasy Ed wasn't in the front.

"Hey Greasy Ed, you old crafty dodger, come on out," I called like the Big Bad Wolf to Little Red Riding Hood.

The two black men looked at me through the window. I guess they were hoping I would give them more chili and beer - they probably figured I am a liberal trying to atone for the way white people had treated the black race throughout the years. They didn't know that having been a hippie and a Vietnam Vet, I had experienced every prejudice imaginable from every race in the country including Jane Fonda - movie stars should be a separate race.

I looked over the counter to where I had split open Greasy Ed's nose the day before. The blood had been cleaned up. I went to the kitchen.

In the kitchen, I could smell chili burning. A large, army sized metal pot of chili was on a gas stove. There was about two inches of paste left in the pan that smelled like burning dog hair.

Turning off the burner I checked the back door, it was open and I could see a yellow 1985 Cadillac. It had to be Greasy Ed's. An old Cadillac was about the only car he could fit in. I went back into the dinning room. The two black men were still looking in the window. They reminded me of alley cats behind a Kentucky Fried Chicken. I went outside. "What time did you guys come down here?" I asked.

"About ten," the man who had spoken to me earlier said. "Me and Harold always come for coffee and to see what horses Ed has picked out for the day."

Harold looked at me like he wanted to trust me but couldn't.

"I never seen Ed not here," the man who wasn't Harold continued.

I went back into the restaurant. I don't think Greasy Ed made a fast exit from town as all his pin-ups were still on the walls. As ugly as he was, about the only thing he could date is an 8" by 11" glossy.

Going back to the kitchen I noticed a walk in freezer. It had only taken me three trips to the kitchen to see it.

"That's why you are a lousy detective," my Guardian Angel said.

I started to open the freezer door.

"Please, Roosevelt, don't open the door," my Guardian Angel pleaded.

I pictured a naked Greasy Ed hanging from a meat hook. When I opened the door, Greasy Ed wasn't hanging from a meat hook. He was lying on the floor, frozen like an Eskimo who had forgotten to take his woollies with him. His eyes were wide open in bewilderment, staring at the frozen sausage hanging above him, and there was a neat little hole about as big around as my little finger directly in the middle of his forehead. A pool of blood was around his head that looked like cherry Jell-O that had too much water and it would not set up. Greasy Ed wasn't going to be killing anymore of the dogs and cats in the neighborhood and putting them in the chili.

"Roosevelt, I warned you," my Guardian Angel said, shaking his head.

"I know," I relied, "you have never steered me wrong."

My Guardian Angel swelled up with pride like a male prairie chicken with six hens.

I have to call the police. I don't want to, but, my fingerprints are all over the place. I asked for Detective Owens, who, after about ten minutes, picked up his phone. "Yea, what do you want?" he grumbled.

"This is your old wife-swapping partner," I said.

Owens, much to my surprise, laughed.

"You know where Greasy Ed's is?"

He grunted, which I took for a yes.

"Well, you'd better come down here. Greasy Ed found out he couldn't dodge bullets."

Owens didn't even bother to say goodbye. I felt offended.

Mr. No Name and Harold were looking through the glass as I came out of the kitchen. I motioned for them to come in. As they did, I pointed toward the counter and they sat down. "I'm having a party," I said. "Beers on the house."

Harold smiled as I drew two beers for each of them. "What's the party for?" Harold's friend asked - free beer made him trust me.

"It's a wake."

"For who?"

"Greasy Ed is dead in the kitchen."

"Well give us a couple more beers before the cops get here," Harold said.

I liked Harold. He had his priorities right.

Owens showed up with sirens blaring and tires screeching, like Greasy Ed really gave a hoot. Owens and three other officers stormed in with their guns drawn. Harold and Mr. No Name shook their heads sadly as they knew the party was over.

"These two men are ok," I told Owens. "Tell your men not to shoot any innocent people."

They put their guns away and I could tell they were disappointed. They wanted to at least smack somebody a few good ones so they could have something to talk about over coffee.

When I opened the freezer door and showed Greasy Ed to Owens, Owens didn't even flinch. All he said was, "good shot."

"Greasy Ed wishes it was a bad shot," I said.

"This time hippie boy, you and me had better have a long conversation. You've been in town a few days and already two people have died around you."

"Only one," I countered.

I told Owens it was an accident when I met Sam at Greasy Ed's. He informed me he liked the Chili and made it a point to stop by at least once a month. I didn't tell him about punching out Greasy Ed or that I had seen Lisa at about the right time of day she could have shot Greasy Ed - judging by how hard Greasy Ed was frozen. There was no need for Owens to call her in and let the cat out of the bag that I knew she wasn't entirely on the up and up. I spent the next three hours sitting at a table watching the police run all over the place - excited they had something to do besides write out parking tickets and respond to domestic violence calls.

"You look like you have a date tonight," Owens said noticing the way I was twitching around. "She must be an old dope head with no morals."

"I hope so," my Guardian Angel said.

"I'm not that kind of guy," I said.

"Roosevelt, get out of here, but don't leave town," Owens ordered.

"The last time I saw you, you wanted me to leave town," I said.

"I changed my mind."

"I wonder if he is really a woman?" my Guardian Angel asked.

The two black men were standing on the other side of the police barricade. "It was a good party," Harold said to me.

I was glad to see the Des Moines police hadn't picked them up. Nobody would kill somebody, put them in a freezer, and then wait for somebody to happen along and give them free beer. But as I started Matilda, it really wasn't that bad of an alibi - I have heard worse.

By the time I got back to the house, it was 6:30. Lisa was in the shower.

I ran upstairs and went to one of the children's bedrooms. "You could do this when Lisa isn't around," my Guardian Angel said.

"I am a spontaneous kind of guy," I told him.

"Give me a break."

The boy's name was Rick - a wooden nameplate was on his desk. His room was filled with baseball trophies, pictures of baseball players, and there was a Playboy under the bed. On the dresser was a photograph of his two sisters and one of Lisa and Sam. I could see no trace of Sheila in the room. There was nothing out of the ordinary - except the two rifles in his closet. Both were 22 match rifles with expensive Zeis scopes. I figured the trophy for shooting I had seen at Sheila's was his.

The next room belonged to Kathy - another wooden nametag. By a photograph she looked about 14. She resembled her mother, as she has dark hair and a pixie smile with just a trace of larceny. Her walls were almost bare except for one poster of some rock group that looked like they were trying to make love to their guitars. At least this way they couldn't pass on any form of VD. Her room was painted a light blue with a matching bedspread. On her desk was a stack of 'Teen World', a small clock radio, and a computer and printer with a ream of 20-pound bond typing paper next to it.

The other room belonged to Margaret, complete with nameplate. I wondered if Sam and Lisa have a nameplate in their room. Margaret was older, taller than her siblings and prettier than Kathy. From a photograph on her dresser, taken with what I presumed was her boyfriend, she looks 17 going on 28, and I hope she is on the pill. But, beneath the smile, I have a deep feeling she is a lonely and confused little girl. Of all the rooms, hers is the only room with a photograph of her and Sheila. They are standing in front of the Mother Goose, arms on each other's shoulders with content smiles on their faces and holding a teddy bear in their other arm.

Lisa had told me all about the children, as far as she knew, none of the children held any animosity toward her.

I would take more time searching the rooms when Lisa was not around. I also want to search Lisa's room and Sam's den. I went quickly to my room, looked my door, and took a shower. Sometimes I feel uneasy when the door isn't locked and I'm in the shower. It's like sleeping in a room with the door open, I can never turn my back to the door. To this day, I feel like there is a bogeyman living in the hallway, waiting for me to fall asleep so he can come in and heist my underwear.

I put on my best Levi's, my best white, long sleeved western shirt, and splashed on some Old Partner aftershave. Don't ask me why I wear aftershave when I have a beard?

"Because it's cheaper than cologne," my Guardian Angel said.

Lisa was pacing in the kitchen. "Sheila called me today," she declared. "And she wants the children to pack up and leave here within two days. She has filed papers so she will get full custody."

"You are about knee deep in it now," my Guardian Angel said.

"You didn't adopt the kids? Did you?" I asked Lisa.

"I never wanted kids." Lisa said looking at me the way the Jolly Green Giant looks at cheap peas. "What are we going to do if we don't have the kids back when they're supposed to go to Sheila's house?" she whimpered.

I could see it now. "Well Detective Owens, I know I haven't told you everything I know about Greasy Ed's murder, and I know I took evidence from the body of Sam, and, well, I really want you to know I wanted to tell you about the kids being kidnapped but."

I could see myself doing ten years in the Iowa Pen - Iowa, where it's cold six months out of the year and I would have to become a Methodist to try and make parole.

This case was becoming a big bowl of Gumbo, but the worst thing about it was I could turn out to be the seasoning.

I had nothing to say to Lisa that should be said. I wanted to tell her I knew she had lied to me about Sheila losing custody of the kids and I had seen her at Greasy Ed's. Instead, I headed for the door. "Where are you going?" she demanded, like I was her kid and hadn't done the dishes like I was supposed to.

I waved at her like a cocky construction worker, "C'est La Vie Mother Goose," I said.

She didn't even bat one of her pretty little eyelashes in surprise at the remark.

"I'm paying you $100 a day and you're walking out without telling me where you're going?"

"I'm glad that's settled," I replied, since we had never gotten to my fee. "So far you owe me $300."

Lisa looked at me like I am an unclean, two-week-old cat box and stomped out of the kitchen.

I bought two bottles of cheap champagne at a HyVee grocery store. I figured it tasted like the stuff at New Year's Eve parties where they advertise party favors and champagne - the champagne comes in a plastic glass and makes you sick because you've been drinking whiskey sours and beer all night.

As I got nearer to Sheila's house I asked my Guardian Angel, "What do you think about this case?"

"Now, after lambasting me, you want advice?"

"Give me a break, just answer the question."

"I told you from the beginning, you should get out of Iowa."

"It's truly that bad?"

"I don't know how bad, that bad, really is, but, it's going to get as bad as bad can be," he said, "and, you should ask Lisa if she is an undercover cop."

"Would you miss me if I got killed?"

"I'd get over it."

My Guardian Angel is at least truthful.

CHAPTER FIVE
EXCUSE ME

The porch light was on to Sheila's house and the curtains were drawn. I clutched my cheap champagne like it was the Queen's jewels.

Women have stood me up before so after I rang the doorbell, I watched intently for the doorknob to turn - at one lady's house I watched the doorknob for thirty minutes before I got the hint. As the doorknob turned I felt relieved.

I had to step back a few steps as Sheila opened the screen door, as I did so, a blue Mercedes slowly drove by - by the dim illumination from the street lights I could make out a grim faced Lisa.

"Danger, danger, fighters at 7 o'clock," my Guardian Angel said, which was too late.

"Did you come to see me or stand on the porch and look at the street lamp?" Sheila asked, sounding like the Mother Superior at an all girls Catholic school.

In the house, Sheila smiled at me like a Turkish belly dancer smiles at a fat Greek who owns 35 oil tankers and kept stuffing $100 dollar bills in her waistband.

Sheila had on a pair of faded Levi's, a light cotton blouse, and was barefoot. The skin on her arms and face was rosy like she had just taken a steaming hot shower.

I looked around the living room for the two dogs, expecting to be ambushed at any moment. Sheila, reading my mind, laughed. "The dogs are at the neighbors."

I handed Sheila the bottles of champagne.

"My favorite," she said. "The cheap stuff."

"I tried to warn you," my Guardian Angel said.

I followed Sheila into the kitchen. It was a nice kitchen as kitchens go. There was a wooden table with four chairs, a Kitchen Witch by the phone, a note pad that stuck to the wall with phone numbers scribbled on it, and assorted little feminine things scattered around that would need cleaning once a week, or, at a bachelor's house, would soon have nests of spiders in them.

She took two fluted champagne glasses out of the freezer and proceeded to pop the cork off a bottle of champagne like she has had years of practice. She poured the champagne and we sat down at the table. "To life," she toasted.

She seemed to have about as much grief over Sam being dead as Lisa does, which, if they were a toaster, wasn't enough to burn toast.

The champagne wasn't even close to being good, it tasted like the cough syrup my mother used to make me take when I was a kid and sick - the stuff was so sweet it made me gag and promise God, or whoever else would listen, I would never have another cold in my life.

It was so bad Sheila poured us another glass. "Have you had any breaks in the case?" Sheila asked, looking at me over the edge of her glass with her dark, soul stealing eyes.

"I have a few solid leads," I lied, not wanting her to know I really don't know a thing.

"I don't think you'll solve the murder," she said, in a tone a woman has when she knows she's right - the tone women usually use when they talk to men, especially their husbands.

"If he does solve it, it will be by accident," my Guardian Angel said.

For some reason, I felt Sheila didn't want me to solve the murder. I also felt offended, but what could I say? She and my Guardian Angel were probably right.

"I never give up," I responded, a lame statement to prove I was a real man and not one of those guys who has to hug another man to find his inner self.

"I know," she giggled, she had to have less tolerance for champagne than I do, "You practice putting your head down and running into brick walls until you can no longer move."

"See these scars on my forehead," I said grinning, "They're not from being smart."

Both of us laughing she poured us another glass of cough syrup.

"Have you seen your children?" I asked, doing a little fishing.

"Sam sent them to camp for three weeks. Rick is in Colorado at an outward-bound camp. One of those places where they make kids crawl around in the dirt to try and give them more self-esteem."

I choked and blew a spray of champagne across the table.

"How can the kids be kidnapped when they are at camp?" my Guardian Angel asked. "It's a fantasy kidnapping."

Sheila ignored my choking like people ignore you when you pass gas at a family reunion.

"Kathy is in up state New York at a music camp, and Margaret, who was at a swimming camp in Missouri, has run off with her boyfriend. The camp called me the day before Sam was killed and apologized. She was seen driving away in a car."

"Have you heard from any of them?" I asked, knowing she had, and wishing I had Lisa's pretty little neck in my hands, shaking the make-up off of her.

Sheila smiled, a, 'my kid's love me' smile. "Rick calls me about everyday. He wants to come home. He told me eating dirt doesn't give him self-esteem it only gives him diarrhea. Kathy called me once, the day after Sam was killed. She could stay in camp for the rest of her life, she is so happy. Margaret called me from somewhere in Colorado. I told her she had better be on the pill or using some kind of protection or I would break both of their necks. Poor Margaret. She is my lost lamb. I have never been able to reach her like the other children. It is as though she goes through life alone."

I felt like a duck that couldn't fly and all my buddies had just flown south for the winter.

"You look weird," Sheila said, "maybe this cheap champagne is too much for you."

I could envision her getting up and getting a thermometer and making me hold it under my tongue for 3 hours. "No, I'm fine," I replied, sipping the champagne to prove it to her. "I take it you haven't told the kids about their father?"

"I can't see any reason to until they get back home. No need to ruin their vacations. Sam will still be dead when they return."

Old hippies can be very pragmatic.

Sheila poured herself the last drip of champagne, drank it, and got the other bottle. I was still reeling from the information about the kids and didn't know if I could get out of the chair. My feet felt like I had climbed Mt. Everest, barefoot.

"Why would Lisa tell you Sheila wanted the kids back within two days?" my Guardian Angel asked, perplexed.

"I wish I knew," I replied.

"And why would Sam have told you to follow him home and meet the wife and kids? And what is the purpose of a fantasy kidnapping?"

"What are you the question man?" I snapped. I hate being asked questions I can't answer.

"Sorry, oh grumpy one," he retorted, but I knew he wasn't sorry.

The cork popped and bounced off the ceiling. Sheila poured us another glass. I noticed the two top buttons of her blouse were unbuttoned and she wasn't wearing a bra. She put her bare foot on my boot and tantalizingly rubbed my calf.

"Skip dinner," my Guardian Angel said.

"So, Mr. Private Eye," Sheila said, "How would you like to have me for dinner?"

"I thought you were cooking dinner," I said.

"You make the word lame seem erotic," my Guardian Angel said.

Sheila looked at me strangely and started to laugh. "You mean you really want to eat?" she said.

"I don't mix pleasure with business," I said, feeling like Clint Eastwood.

"I have six jars of body paint by my bed," she said, smiling provocatively.

"Give them to Van Gough," I said, but smiled at her.

"Roosevelt, you are breaking my heart," my Guardian Angel said and held his head in his hands like it weighed about seven hundred pounds.

"I didn't cook anything," Sheila said, showing no animosity that I turned down her advance.

"Soup is fine."

"I didn't know Sam had any friends that were gentlemen," she said as she opened a can of soup.

"Stupid is the word for it," my Guardian Angel said.

Sheila heated chicken and noodle soup and poured us another glass of champagne. "I think Lisa killed Sam," Sheila said out of the blue.

"Why?" I asked.

"She would get the $500,000 dollar life insurance policy Sam had for her."

"You also get $500,000," I said slyly.

"You're not as dense as you look," Sheila said, much like a District Attorney who had been caught lying to the jury.

"Most of it will go toward the kids," Sheila went on. "Sam set up a small policy for each of them, but left me a big policy to make sure if anything happened they would have the money to go to college."

"Sam seems to have covered all the bases," I commented.

"Except getting himself killed," Sheila replied sarcastically, but with no trace of sadness in her voice.

"You really don't have any idea of what he was up to? It seems like after all the years you were married you should have been able to read him like a book."

Sheila pursed her lips and seemed to remember something. "I went to the store once to see him after our divorce. I was in the area so I thought I would stop by. There were two Mexican men. They wore suits and had enough gold dripping from them to put a run on the Bank of America. They stopped talking to Sam when they saw me. Sam looked like he was scared half to death and used me as an excuse to get away. When I asked him what was going on, he only laughed and dodged the question."

Sheila got me a bowl of soup but did not get herself one. "You're not hungry?" I asked.

"I only wanted sex," she smiled.

I decided it was time to drop a bombshell. "I heard Sam might have been smuggling guns to rebels in Mexico."

For an instant Sheila's face changed, but she quickly caught herself. "That's ridiculous," she said, brushing the comment off like a horse swats a fly on its back. "Sam didn't have enough sense to put gas in his car let alone smuggle guns."

"He had enough sense to make enough money to get himself killed," I replied.

"That's as absurd as saying Sam was mixed up with a bunch of heroin smugglers."

"You said it, I didn't."

"You have to be kidding?" She seemed genuinely shocked.

"Word is, an informant out of Texas told the police Sam was involved with a ring of gun and heroin smugglers."

"Sam would never hurt a thing," Sheila said defensively.

"People change, Sheila. I've seen the most violent men become preachers, and preachers become killers."

"And hippies become private dicks," she added, like a private eye was two steps lower than a snail.

"How about three steps lower than a snail," my Guardian Angel said, adding, "I don't think Lisa killed Sam."

I looked at Sheila closely, at the fine lines edging the corners of her eyes, the way her lips were set, the short cut of her hair, and her dark penetrating eyes. She could be as soft as a teddy bear, yet, underneath the surface I could feel a coldness - a coldness caused by who knows what, but it was a bone chilling cold.

"I want to find Sam's killer, Sheila. I want to find him for the old days. The old days when we all played in the traffic and didn't know the cars and trucks would kill us. When we all carried flowers and laughed, and life was something we got up to every morning and felt we would change - felt that we were the first generation of people who would stop the wars, and the killings and the poverty. We thought the whole table of life was set out for us with the finest silver and the best food and that all humanity would dine with us."

"We failed," Sheila said. "We all failed." Her words fell around us like mini atom bombs.

I went around the table and kissed her on the forehead, much like one kisses his sister. "Maybe we didn't fail," I said. "Maybe we just quit in hopes one day somebody else will pick up the torch."

"The Buddhists have been trying for thousands of years," my Guardian Angel said.

Starting to walk away Sheila reached out and held my arm. "Thanks," she said, with a sad smile.

I smiled at her, knowing my smile wasn't enough, and started to leave. "Are you going to the funeral tomorrow?" she asked. "Sam's getting buried in the morning."

I felt like an idiot. I hadn't even thought of Sam's funeral and Lisa had never mentioned it. "I'll see you there," I replied.

The fact I hate funerals did not enter my mind, but the fact Sheila didn't find it necessary to have the kids come back for their father's funeral burned into my mind like a California brush fire.

On Sheila's porch I looked up at the night sky. There's no city where one can look up and see the stars. Our world has washed them from the sky. I felt old.

Standing by Matilda I once again looked up at the night sky. A faint memory stirred in my mind and by surprise, took form. Sam and I had been cutting wood for the upcoming winter in New Mexico. Northern New Mexico is cold in the winter and the annual trek to get wood was in full swing. It was a beautiful fall day just cool enough I needed to wear a warm shirt. The Black Eyed Susan's were in full bloom, their yellow sun filled faces darting to and fro in the slight breeze. We took a break and Sam shrugged his shoulders and said. "You know, sometimes people have to do radical things for the right things to get done."

66

At the time I didn't think a thing about what he had said, now, years later, I wondered what he meant exactly or if he was trying to tell me something he wanted to expound on?

Sheila turned the porch light off as I got into Matilda. Driving down the street, my mind was partially in New Mexico, partially in the no star night, when my Guardian Angel hollered, "duck, incoming."

I ducked my head and stomped on the gas pedal just as the side window blew out, showering my face with glass. I raced down the center of the street - which in an old Volkswagen is about as fast as a donkey can walk. Another bullet slammed into Matilda, but didn't hit a window.

I ran the stop sign at the end of the street, took the next right as fast as I could and sped toward the interstate. My normally 'cool under fire' heart was racing like a quarter horse that had run two miles. Blood was running down my face from the glass and I was lucky none had gotten into my eyes. I did know one thing for sure, somebody wasn't too happy about me seeing Sheila. "Thanks," I told my Guardian Angel.

"It's my job," he replied casually.

I didn't stop speeding until I got close to Lisa's. Then, pulling over, I watched behind me in case I was being followed. After about ten minutes, I hadn't seen a car and drove on. By now my heart had settled down.

Before going inside Lisa's house, I examined Matilda. The first bullet had shattered her right front side window, but I couldn't see a place where it had exited the car. It hadn't missed my head by much. The second shot hit Matilda over the right rear tire. There was no reason to call the police. Why complicate matters with the police when I really don't know what is going on anyway?

I touched the hood of the Lincoln, it was warm. Lisa had come back home in the Mercedes and then gone somewhere in the Lincoln.

To my surprise, Lisa was sitting at the table in the kitchen, but she wasn't her normal self. A half-empty bottle of Quervo had been keeping her company and it looked like the Quervo had won. "You've been hurt," she slurred, seeing my bloody face, but sounding like it pained her more to talk than the fact I was bleeding.

She tried to stand up, but fell back into her chair as loose as a Raggedy Ann doll made in Taiwan.

I left her sitting there in her make-believe Mexico and went to my room and cleaned up. I only had a few cuts. They had bled far more than they should have. It made me angry that the blood had ruined my white shirt. I should start carrying my pistol even if it is against the law. All the karate in the world can't stop a gunshot or kick somebody 100 yards away.

I went back to the kitchen. Lisa had been drinking the Quervo straight, and was trying to pour herself another shot, but was finding it hard to hit the glass.

"I think you've had enough," I told her, taking the bottle from her hand.

"What happened?" she asked me, which sounded more like, "Whaaaaat, hap.....pe....ened."

I couldn't see any reason to tell her the truth - she might have been the one who took a pot shot at me. "Some kid tossed a rock through my window and the glass cut me," I said.

"She's drunk, she couldn't shoot a cap pistol," my Guardian Angel said.

"She might be faking she is drunk."

"No, oh wise one, Lisa is truly pie-eyed."

I had the urge to pick Lisa up by her pretty little shoulders, shake her until her brains turned into a malt and ask her why she'd lied to me? Why the kids were at camp? Why she had gone to Greasy Ed's and Sheila's? And, to top it off, why she hadn't told me about the funeral?

"That's a lot of whys," my Guardian Angel said. "You sound like a ten year old girl."

I had almost talked myself into shaking Lisa until her brains turned into a malt when I let reason once again take over - a quiet man has a wise mind - but I had also heard, a frog with no legs can't jump, sometimes you eat eggs and sometimes you eat feathers, and, believing my Guardian Angel, if you shake a lady drunk on Quervo they will probably throw up on you.

I would rather get shot at than thrown up on.

"What time is the funeral?" I asked Lisa, not bothering to ask her if the make believe kidnappers had called.

"Eleven," she slurred and then started to cry. Her bottom lip trembled and tears the size of peas splashed down her pretty lying face.

I hadn't done anything, I wasn't the one lying, but still, weak man that I am, looking at a sobbing Lisa, I felt guilty.

It's strange, when a woman cries, men feel guilty. If a man breaks down and shows his feminine side, and cries, a woman will laugh.

Lisa staggered to her feet, held onto the chair for support, and with what must have been nothing but will power, stood straight up. A transformation came over her - the Quervo turned her into a stripper. She smiled a smile that a topless dancer learns to smear on her face just before she goes on stage in front of 39 tire salesmen from Toledo. She began to hum and gyrate her hips as she ran her hands down her sides. She looked at me and moved her tongue around her lips. She unbuttoned her blouse, letting it fall to the floor like a faded rose. My Guardian Angel whistled. She stepped out of her skirt and twirled her underpants around on her finger and tossed them at me, hitting me in the face. Before I could say, "I'm not that kind of guy," her body was against mine with her pelvis grinding against my leg like two Flamingo dancers in a cheap bar in Barcelona.

I pushed her away. "Not us, it wouldn't be right," I said gently. "Fun, but not right."

She looked at me like she couldn't believe her ears and then the last shot of Quervo hit and she crumbled to the floor like she had been shot with a deer rifle.

"Of all the luck," my Guardian Angel muttered.

Lisa has about the best body I have ever seen up close and a few moles in very interesting places. I gathered her clothes and carried her to her bedroom. I laid her on her bed, King Arthur would have been proud of me, at least much prouder than he was of Lancelot.

I gently covered her with the sheet and tiptoed out of the room like a daddy who had read his daughter a fairy tale and she had fallen asleep looking like all that is innocent in the world.

In my own bed, propped up by two pillows, I scribbled away in my notebook. It was beginning to get so filled it resembled research notes for a masters thesis on futility. But futility has always been a close friend of mine.

"You don't have faith in me?" my Guardian Angel said out of nowhere, sounding hurt.

"I suppose I do," I replied.

"That's good, Roosevelt. It's nice to have a friend."

"Yes it is," I agreed.

"But friend or no friend you should ask Lisa if she is an undercover cop?" my Guardian Angel said, giving me an imploring look.

I shut my eyes.

CHAPTER SIX
TENNIS ANYONE

Funeral homes are all well and good I suppose. Funeral directors are like people who work in jails, it takes a different breed of man or woman to want to go to a jail everyday when you don't have to be there.

In our modern world somebody has to be a funeral director - the fact that it takes about 7,500 to 10,000 bucks to put old George in the ground has a lot to do with it.

The room for Sam's funeral had enough flowers for the Rose Bowl Parade, and about the normal amount of people in the bleachers for a double A baseball game, six, not counting me. There was Lisa and Sheila, both sitting in the family section, and several men from the store that Lisa didn't know their names. I would have liked to seen the children there - and the look on Lisa's face.

The taped organ music sounded like it was recorded at the turn of the century by a 98-year-old frustrated music teacher. I was sure Sam would have liked to have Eric Clapton ripping out a few Blue's cords or at the least Donovan tripping on about bananas.

The preacher was so old he looked like he should have been in the box, not Sam, and gave his sermon with as much emotion as his $40 fee would allow. Neither Sheila or Lisa cried during the service or showed any animosity toward each other - maybe it was a dead man respect thing.

When all the good things had been said about Sam that could be said - it's funny how when we die we are all so good - I took my turn passing by the casket. They had done a good job on Sam. I couldn't see where the bullet had gone in, and the white satin that lined the casket had been fluffed up around where a portion of his skull had been blown away. He looked like he would stand up any minute and tell me he had found his center and that life was now good.

Still, looking at dead people has always given me the willies. I'm not afraid of dying but I don't want to be dead. I can see myself in a casket and trying to tell people as they parade by, "Hey wait man, it's some kind of mistake, I'm not supposed to die, I wanted to live forever."

"You're funny, Roosevelt," my Guardian Angel said.

I felt like telling Sam, "Sorry the funeral was such a flop, but afterwards 200 people and I are going to have a keg party out in the

70

country, pretend we are dead heads, and dance until the sun comes up."

At the graveside service, Lisa and Sheila didn't look at each other, both probably wondering what Sam could have seen in the other one.

There were two new faces at the service. Mexican men, well dressed, one was so large he could have been a pro wrestler. They stood in the back looking like if you walked up to them to say hello, or how saddened you were by Sam's death, they would shoot you for getting into their business.

After the service I jotted down the license plate of their new Cadillac as they drove away. Lisa was standing by me, looking like the star witness for the defense, so clean soap would run off of her skin. "Did you know those two Mexican men?" I asked.

She dabbed at a tear. "I have never seen them in my life," she replied.

I had driven Lisa to the funeral in her Mercedes, and as I opened the door for her to get in, Sheila glared at me like from now on I wouldn't even be allowed to clean up the dog poop from her back yard.

"It's too bad the children couldn't have been here," I said as we drove through the cemetery.

"Did you take advantage of me last night?" Lisa asked curtly.

"No, I didn't."

"You are such a nice man," Lisa told me, adding, "How dare you bring up the children."

"It's strange the kidnappers haven't called back," I said.

"They did, while you were gone last night. They told me they would call tonight at 8 and I had better be there and that you had better be there too. The Quervo made me forget to tell you."

"When there is no kidnapping, why would the fantasy kidnappers want you there?" my Guardian Angel asked. "And, how would the fantasy kidnappers know who you are?

"Maybe Sam's killer is going to try and extort money out of Lisa?" I said.

"You didn't answer my questions," he said. "But, perhaps you should get Lisa and Sheila together and get to the bottom of this kidnapping thing."

"I think you should call Detective Owens and tell him about the kids," I said to Lisa.

She didn't reply.

"You should at least tell Sheila, she's their mother."

Lisa started to cry. I felt like taking my Guardian Angels advice and driving her to Sheila's house and demanding to know the truth. Funeral or no funeral, I was losing my patience. I'm not a pretty sight when my patience decides to take a trip to the seedy side of town and go slumming for a while. But, I decided it was better to wait.

When we got to the house Lisa saw my gunshot Matilda but didn't say anything. I thought I heard her mind muttering, "I have to practice on my moving targets."

Matilda looked like she'd come off a used car lot on the Gaza strip. At the moment, I couldn't really think of anyone but Lisa who could have shot at me. I knew for sure it wasn't Greasy Ed or Sam.

"Undercover cops don't kill innocent people," my Guardian Angel said.

"The C.I.A. is good at killing innocent people," I said.

Lisa went to her room and changed clothes. When she came back to the kitchen she informed me she had to go to the lawyers. There was paperwork to sign about the insurance policies and Sam's partner was buying out the other half of the store. Business does not grieve too long over death - in fact - business does not grieve - if you don't believe this ponder the statement - with every misfortune there is a fortune.

"I wonder if Sam's partner killed him?" my Guardian Angel asked nonchalantly.

"I didn't even think about that," I said, feeling stupid.

"Too obvious," my Guardian Angel said.

I watched Lisa drive out of the driveway, waited ten minutes, and made a straight line to her room like a bee headed for a honey tree.

Lisa was neat. The bed was made and all her clothes were hung in the closet in a specific order, with the hangers hooked in the same direction. Her shoes were all in a straight line. The photographs on the walls were of the kids doing all those cute things kids do. There were also photographs of Sam and her on various vacations - one of them standing in front of a castle - one of them in front of the Vatican - and also a set of them in a small town that had to be in Mexico. In all the photographs Sam was smiling, except the ones in Mexico. He seemed somber - it could have been a case of drinking the water.

I went through Lisa's dresser. There were the normal female things that make men uncomfortable unless a woman is wearing them: bras, panties, silk teddies of various colors.

"Nice," my Guardian Angel said.

All of Sam's clothes were in two large boxes by the door. It wouldn't take long before the photographs came down too. I imagine Lisa would sell the house, get her insurance money and run like a cat with a field mouse.

In the nightstand drawer was a 32 caliber Berretta, a small box of Kleenex, and a romance novel.

"The Quervo mom packs a punch," my Guardian Angel said, looking at the pistol.

"A small pistol killed Greasy Ed," I muttered.

Standing in the center of the room, I felt there was something I was missing.

"A brain," my Guardian Angel said.

I looked once again at the set of photographs of Sam and Lisa in Mexico and removed one off the wall and turned it around, nothing. I removed another photograph off the wall, nothing. I removed the last photograph off the wall and taped to the back was a business sized white envelope. I carefully peeled the envelope off and opened it, the glue hadn't been licked. Inside, on a folded up sheet of paper, was an area code and phone number.

"You memorize this for me," I told my Guardian Angel and put the envelope back.

I went to Sam's den. All the curtains were drawn and I could tell Lisa hadn't touched anything. It was as though the room no longer existed. I started by looking behind all the photographs, nothing. I went through his desk, but there was only the same old junk that collects in desks: rubber bands, stapler, paper clips, pencils with no points, and about 50 cheap ball point pens.

I went through his closet, there was nothing unless an old wool shirt is exciting? I wondered where he kept his hunting rifle. I stood in the middle of the room, like I had in Lisa's room, and looked around. I examined all the electric cover plates. Seeing one that had chipped paint around its edges, using a dime, I removed the screws and popped the plate off. Stuffed in amongst the wires was an envelope. I did not bother to return this one, but put it in my shirt pocket and put the plate back on.

I went to Margaret's room. There was something strange about her room that had been bothering me. It suddenly dawned on me. On her desk was a stack of typing paper, an ink jet printer, and a pad for a computer to set on, except there was no computer.

"That's earth shattering," my Guardian Angel said sarcastically.

"Little things can mean a lot," I said.

"That almost sounds like a song," he said.

Going to my room I locked the door, like a kid about to read the Playboy he kept hidden from his mother, and opened the envelope that had been in Sam's room. There was a piece of typing paper with an address in Nogales, Mexico, an address that, if there wasn't something shady about it would have been where most addresses are kept, in an address book.

"What was the phone number I had you memorize?" I asked my Guardian Angel.

I wrote the phone number in my clue book, went to the kitchen and called the operator, and asked her where the area code was for the number. It wasn't surprising when she told me it was in Nogales, Mexico.

Nogales is a border town, just south of Tucson. Like all border towns it's a center for everything illegal that's worth money in the United States. If the government would make ashtrays illegal because some politician said they led to smoking, within one week you could buy ashtrays by the ton in Nogales. Ashtrays that once cost 10 cents would suddenly be worth $10.

With the sound of Mexican music in my ears, the smell of cheap beer and the sight of children begging for food, I went out to Matilda. I carry a small toolbox in the trunk and it didn't take me long to bang out the bullet hole over the right rear tire so it didn't look like a bullet hole. What was unnerving was that it was a 22-bullet hole. I swept the glass out of Matilda.

"Aren't there two 22 rifles upstairs in Rick's room?" my Guardian Angel asked.

"I am afraid so."

"Maybe the reason Lisa was drinking was because she missed you," my Guardian Angel said. "Missed shooting you I mean not heartfelt."

I went to the tennis court and stood by the fence. The net was taut. In the far corner was a small metal shed. I suppose it holds tennis rackets, balls, and maybe even a tennis ball-throwing machine.

I examined the lock on the gate. It was not a cheap lock but one of those they advertise that a bullet cannot open. Trust me, there isn't a lock made that a good set of bolt cutters, purchased at any hardware store in the world, won't open.

At one time in my life I was a fairly good tennis player. This was due to a lady I was dating that I felt I might be in love with, she liked tennis. I figured it was a quicker way to her heart if I took up tennis. It was a good idea but she dumped me for a golfer. At least she dumped me quick enough I didn't have to buy checkered pants and some stupid looking little hat and learn how to say "Good shot" when I really meant, "You lucky dog," although I like golf – it's great to watch on TV when you need a nap.

I kept looking at the lock like my will power alone would open it, much like fake prophets make spoons bend. Knowing my will power couldn't even open a loaf of bread, I headed toward the well-hidden chain link fence separating Sam's property from the neighbor's. I had to go a round about way because of all the trees. When I got to the fence, the neighbor's tennis court was almost in a direct line with Sam's tennis court.

I followed the fence until it met the stone wall and then followed the wall to the 'Eric the Red' gate. I decided to once again visit the neighbors.

The Mexican man I had met was by the corrals unloading hay bales from a pickup truck.

He waved at me like I might be dumb enough to help him toss a few bales. "I didn't get your name last time I was over here," I said to him, playing the stupid gringo.

He jumped down from the back of the truck. "My name is Manuel," he said with a large smile and shook my hand like a shark that was trying to rip my arm off. Once again he didn't ask my name.

"The owners are still gone?" I asked casually.

"They called me and said they would be gone for a few extra days," Manuel said in a clipped fashion.

"Do you play tennis?" I asked him.

"I don't have time to play," he said. "And tennis is for sissies."

"Don't ask him if he likes badminton," my Guardian Angel said.

"Are you related to Lisa?" Manuel asked.

"Just friends," I replied, thinking, tennis is not for sissies.

"It is too bad about Sam. He was a good man."

"It is too bad," I replied, not telling him he and I were old friends.

I wanted to grill Manuel somewhat, but I didn't want to make him feel like he was sitting in an interrogation room, filled with six Border Patrol agents that joined the Border Patrol because they hated Mexicans. "How long have you been in the States?" I asked.

Manuel stiffened, but caught himself. "I've been here three years, my wife and children will be coming up in another six months. The Browne's have been very good to me."

Like most old hippies I'd spent some time in Mexico. Mexico is a nice place if you have money. If you don't have money it's tougher than a high school bully in the Broncs.

"I am from Nogales," Manuel said. I think he sensed I was going to ask him where he was from.

"Nogales must be the hot spot in Mexico," my Guardian Angel said.

"I'd better let you get back to your work," I said to Manuel. "Nice talking to you. I suppose one day I'll meet the Browne's."

Walking away, I could feel Manuel's eyes burning so deeply into my back he could tell what I had for lunch.

"You had better watch out for him," my Guardian Angel told me.

Back at the house and in the kitchen, I made myself a gin and tonic. Sitting at the table, I sipped the drink and tried to block out all thought from my mind, which wasn't a hard thing to do when my mind is half mush anyway. At times in my life, when I'm trying to solve problems, the more I think and the harder I try to figure things out, the more confused I get. If I can relax and get as far away from the problem as possible, my subconscious seems to pull out things I've overlooked or been too stupid to think were important.

All that my subconscious told me was that I wanted another gin and tonic and wonder what is so nice about Nogales, Mexico, except cheap rugs, pottery that breaks before you get it home and silver jewelry that leaves green stains all over people's skin. Another drink in hand I went back to Sam's den.

Sitting behind Sam's desk, I tried to picture myself as Sam. I tried to think what he would think sitting at his desk, knowing he was in big trouble and having nobody he could trust. All I could come up with was a cold, lonely feeling. I suddenly jumped up and half ran down the stairs to my room and got the key that I had taken out of Sam's pocket - good old number 23. I ran to the tennis court and presto, the key opened the lock.

76

"I am not going to tell you again. The tennis courts don't mean anything," my Guardian Angel said.

I was about to go into the tennis court when Lisa drove in. I didn't think she saw me but I locked the gate and walked toward the house like I was merely taking an afternoon stroll. Why I felt guilty about breaking into a tennis court I don't know?

"Guilt is a funny deal," my Guardian Angel said.

As Lisa was getting out of the car, she saw me, and I waved. Surprisingly, she waved back at me with a big smile on her face like I was her husband that had been on a Navy ship for six months and was making port.

As we walked to the door, all she said was, "The insurance went without a hitch, and since the house is in my name it will not go into probate. Sam's partner is borrowing the money to buy out the business. Everything else in Sam's will is split four ways - the three kids and me."

"Sheila is not in the will?" I asked.

"Not one word," she said proudly.

"Who is Sam's partner?" I asked.

"He sold half of the store to the local Catholic Diocese," Lisa said.

"They might be thieves but they don't kill people like they used to when I was alive," my Guardian Angel said.

"They are not into guns and heroin, either," I said.

I could see why Lisa was happy - she was soon going to be a very wealthy lady and, if she played her cards right, she would never again have to worry about buying silk teddies.

"You like a gin and tonic?" I asked her when we were in the kitchen.

"I'd better have one to try and catch up with you," she said, like I was some drunk that had done nothing all day but snoop around the house and drink. "You make it and I'll go change clothes."

I don't know what it is about women, changing clothes seems to be a hobby.

When she came back, to my surprise, she had on short pants that were really short pants, and a blouse that didn't let everything hang out. She took the drink I handed her, looked at the clock on the wall, drank half the drink before sitting down, sighed and then said. "It's 6, we only have two hours to wait."

I had completely forgotten about the fantasy kidnappers calling at 8.

While Lisa and I drank our drinks, Lisa seemed nervous. She looked at me, seemed to remember something and left the room. She came back in a minute and handed me $500 in cash. "This is what I owe you so far," she said.

Think again if you think the I.R.S. is going to hear of this or if I am going to pay Social Security. In my mind, Social Security has about as much chance of surviving as a bleeding gold fish in a tank full of piranha's who haven't eaten in three weeks.

"Social Security will never fold," my Guardian Angel said. "You worry too much."

"I haven't done anything yet," I said to Lisa, looking at the money, but with no intention of giving it back.

"You know more than you're letting on," Lisa said, eyeing me like I was a palmist in San Diego with 25 rich clients that believed my drivel.

I smiled at her like she never did anything but tell the truth.

"May I use the phone," I asked her.

"Of course," she said giving me a strange look.

When the owner of the house is in, it's always polite to ask to use the phone. If I'd slept with Lisa, I wouldn't ask, asking permission to use the phone is one of those little courtesies that go away after a couple has been intimate.

Lisa made us another drink.

Waiting for police switchboards to transfer a call is like waiting for an airline-recorded message to end so you can listen to it again. The only difference is police lines don't play music - they could give a run down on the best crimes that have been going on and how many they have solved, but I think the solved rate is about as bad as The Cleveland Browns football team record.

Finally my call went through.

"Owens, how's life?" I said, acting as happy as an oyster without a pearl in it, and noticing Lisa was intently interested in my phone call.

"This job is about as much fun as being the smallest guy in a prison filled with sex offenders," Owens laughed, thinking he had told a funny.

"Listen, I need help," but before I could go on Owens cut in. "I don't lend money to old freaks," then he laughed so hard he sounded like a turkey with a sinus infection.

I felt like telling him there was no way he could make a living as a comedian but said, "I need a run down on a license plate number."

"You on to something with the last of your three brain cells?"

"If I am, I promise I'll tell you."

There was a long pause. I didn't figure Owens as the kind of guy who went out of the way to do anybody a favor. I bet he even makes his mother mow her own yard.

"Give me the number," he said, like an older kid who was going to borrow my baseball and never give it back - unless I had the money to hire a Mafia muscle guy to break his fingers.

I gave him the number.

"Call me in about 30 minutes."

"You're working late," I said, trying to sound sympathetic.

"No, I'm on my Christmas vacation," Owens grunted and slammed down the phone.

"What are you going to do when the kidnappers call?" Lisa asked me.

"Freak out," my Guardian Angel said.

"I still think you should contact the police," I said.

"I can't say I love Sam's kids, but I don't want to see them dead," Lisa said.

Lisa paced around the kitchen with her arms crossed over her stomach. After thirty minutes I called Owens back. "You fall right in with a good crowd," he said, instead of, "How are you, nice to hear from you."

"I take it the plate doesn't belong to a priest from Our Lady of Good Intentions Church."

"It belongs to Salvador Moralis. He controls the heroin market for here and Kansas City. He cleans his money through two topless bars on the edge of town and an escort service."

"I take it you've never been able to nail him on anything."

"He's as slippery as a sidewalk in Buffalo during the winter," Owens replied, then added, "How did you run into this guy?"

I could sense more than curiosity in his voice, but I could see no reason to lie to him. "He and another man were at Sam's funeral."

The line was quiet for a moment, all I could hear was Owens breathing, like Moralis being at the funeral bothered him. "We haven't been able to find out anything about the murder," he finally said.

I was not surprised - murder is the least solved crime in the nation. Most murders that do get solved are husbands and wives killing each other, or their lovers. Most hired killers are about as paranoid of getting caught as a Colombian who has dusted a few Jamaicans in New York. "Can you give me Moralis's address?" I asked.

I could hear Owens's mind clicking before he answered reluctantly. "Sure, it's public record. He lives in West Des Moines at 257 Prince St."

"Thanks for the help," I said. "If I dig anything up, I'll let you know."

I wondered why Owens would know Moralis's address by heart.

Owens hung up without even asking me how my health was, or telling me if I was smart, I shouldn't snoop around Moralis's house unless I wanted to be fertilizer in some remote cornfield.

"Have they found anything out?" Lisa asked me.

"The cops can't even figure out who killed Hoffa," I answered.

"Maybe they did it," my Guardian Angel said.

At 8 o'clock the phone rang. Lisa let it ring three times and then picked it up. "Lisa Wrench speaking," she answered in a nervous voice. Lisa should be an actress.

I stood next to her as she listened. After about 30 seconds, she handed me the phone. I took the phone like it was a water moccasin that had a thing about old hippies. "Yes," I said.

The voice was muffled, though I could tell, female. "You will be behind the house at the rivers edge at eleven tomorrow night. Don't bring a gun, don't call the cops."

The phone went dead.

My Guardian Angel whistled, "A fantasy kidnapper with a voice."

I hung up the phone. "What did she tell you?" I asked Lisa, who was about to cry.

"She said there is no need to worry as long as you do what you will be told tomorrow night."

Lisa didn't do a strip tease tonight, but went off to her room without even saying goodbye.

I went to my room and locked the door.

I spent a long time jotting in my notebook before I went to bed. About the only new thing I had discovered was that it is really hard to get a tennis game in Des Moines.

Almost asleep I pondered once again why both Lisa and Sheila were lying to me.

"Maybe only one of them is lying," my Guardian Angel said.

"It seems like both Lisa and Sheila want me around but they want me confused," I said.

"I told you that two days ago," my Guardian Angel said.

80

"And they really don't want me to find out who killed Sam."

"You should know better than to try and figure out women," he said.

I decided to keep acting dumb and see what happened. Acting dumb has never been hard for me - acting smart is what's difficult. I know one thing though, in my dumb smart way, Lisa knew that one of the Mexican men at the funeral was Moralis. She had known, as I know for sure, Sam didn't hear the dirt hit his casket.

But why would Moralis, a heroin smuggler, go to Sam's funeral?

"Maybe he wanted to make sure he was really dead," my Guardian Angel said.

CHAPTER SEVEN
TOPLESS WONDER

When I woke up it was still dark. The horses next door were neighing. I had an eerie feeling something was wrong.

"You should get out of bed and do some investigating," my Guardian Angel said, which for a reason beyond me sounded like good advice.

I put on my pants and boots, a dark T-shirt, stuck my pistol in my pants and slipped quietly out of the house.

It was a nice night, cool for summer, with a slight breeze. Creeping through the trees, and by gauging the shadows, I made my way to the chain link fence between Sam's and the Browne's. I worked my way down to the fence to get as close to the corrals as possible.

A match flared, and for an instant, I saw the dim outlines of two men standing next to a delivery truck by the corrals. "I'm getting about sick of this," one of the men said in a hushed voice.

"The money is good," Manuel said, "do you want to go back to working in a factory?"

"At least I wouldn't end up in jail," the man answered.

There was no more talking, but I saw the shadowed forms of several men carrying large boxes from the corrals into the truck. The doors to the back of the truck were shut quietly and the truck, with its lights out, pulled out of the driveway. It was too early for the milkman.

I put in my mind that I was a shadow and inched along the fence trying to find a better viewing point. Two muted voices cut through the darkness. I stopped and held my breath, not wanting any noise to interfere with my hearing. "When will you be back?" Manuel asked.

"When you have the money." The voice that answered Manuel filled me with both fear and disillusionment. Adrenalin poured into my body. It was like sitting on an all night ambush - listening to the eerie sounds of the night and then hearing the unmistakable sound of men - men who wanted to kill me - but I was one step in front of them - I was going to kill them. I was not one step in front of this voice.

"Now you're really in over your head," my Guardian Angel whispered, which was strange as I am the only one who can hear him.

"You're the one who told me to investigate," I said.

"You don't often do what you are told," my Guardian Angel said in defense.

A car door slammed, the engine started, and the car drove away. I heard footsteps going away from me.

Making my way back to the house, I felt like I had been betrayed by my brother. I have to find a way to get into the Browne's house. There is a connection between Sam and the Browne's as sure as Jack Daniels doesn't like beer. Back in my room I reread my notes and added several. I now have 42 clues.

I read them from 1 to 42. I then read them from 42 back to 1. I started in the middle and worked forward. I started in the middle and worked backward. When I could hardly keep my eyes open I read them once again from the beginning. In the little grubby notebook in my hands was the answer to the fake kidnapping murder mess.

"The only thing in your notebook that is worth a darn is the paper," my Guardian Angel said like a cop who is writing out a speeding ticket to his mother.

I didn't feel like arguing, but I know better.

Once, during the night, I woke up to the sound of the voice I had heard in the dark, knowing if I was smart I would pack my bag and be gone with no goodbyes. I was fighting a battle there is no way I should win. It would be like Oklahoma telling the United States they no longer wanted to be part of the nation and wanted to be their own country. By the time the Federal government was done with them Oklahoma would be happy to say they paid more taxes than any other state in the Union.

The next morning when I went into the kitchen Lisa turned and smiled at me, showing off a halter top, that was really only Band-Aids with a string between them.

"Nice Band-Aids," my Guardian Angel whistled.

I poured myself a cup of coffee from the Mr. Coffee, sat at the table, and for a reason beyond me wished I had a morning paper.

"Then you would have to learn how to read," my Guardian Angel said.

Lisa started eating her yogurt. Yogurt excites me like putting ketchup on a steak.

"What earth shattering facts are you going to go out and find today?" Lisa asked.

I didn't know if she was being sarcastic or not.

"I have some things I want to follow up on," I said.

"Forget Sam's murder," Lisa said seriously. "All I want you to do is get the kids back, hand them over to Sheila and then you go your way and I'll go mine."

"Good advice," my Guardian Angel said.

"I would like nothing better than to get out of here," I told Lisa.

I didn't tell her I was not going to forget Sam's murder. I can go through life trying to be as happy as I can, letting things roll off of me that should bother me but then suddenly, like a thunderstorm, I get serious. Once my mind is serious I do not rest until I see the task done.

"Your serious ego trip is not worth dying for," my Guardian Angel said.

I wanted to tell Lisa I knew her kidnap story was a sham, but there was still a shadow of doubt in my mind. Maybe my Guardian Angel was right and it was Sheila who was lying to me and the kids are not in camp and Margaret didn't run away. But, in either case, what was the purpose of lying?

"That is the biggest of the big questions," my Guardian Angel said.

"No kidding, oh smart one," I replied.

"Touchy, touchy," my Guardian Angel chided.

So far in my investigation I had been too trusting and hadn't asked enough questions. I have to get forceful and step on a few toes.

"Do you know Salvador Moralis?" I asked Lisa.

Lisa looked at me like the only Mexican she knew worked in the garden. "I didn't know him, but Sam knew him, and had introduced us. I saw him at the funeral."

Lisa's answer shocked me - why would she tell me the truth now, after telling me at the funeral she had never seen Moralis? The thing about lying is you never know when you're telling the truth, plus you forget the lies you've told. I'm not trying to sound like a saint - I know this from experience.

"Boy, do you ever," my Guardian Angel said.

"Did you know Moralis is a crook?" I asked Lisa.

Lisa looked confused for an instant and then shrugged her shoulders.

"Not good body language," my Guardian Angel said.

Lisa got up from the table. "I'm going swimming, whatever it is you're doing today, just make sure you're back by 11 tonight for your meeting at the river."

"You'd better forget about your river trip tonight," my Guardian Angel said. "There's catfish in that river that would love to nibble on your carcass. They don't care if you're trying to find meaning in life or not."

I went back to my room and went over my notebook once again. "If you were smart, you would get one of those lap top computers to organize your clues," my Guardian Angel said.

"It would ruin my image," I said.

"That's funny, Roosevelt."

I dug out the note Lisa had first given me that was supposedly from the kidnappers. It still struck me as strange. I read my notebook one more time, looked at the phone number for Nogales and the address. I was not going to drive to Nogales and find out where the address was. White boys sticking their noses into other people's business in Mexico have a death wish.

Tired of clues I ambled out to the pool. Lisa was lying on a fold out chair with her top off. She was covered with suntan lotion and she didn't bother to cover herself. If there were 50 women, I could have pretended I was on a beach in France where bare breasts are no more uncommon than seeing a lady's knees, but since I was not, I tried to look at everything but Lisa.

"Want to put more lotion on me," Lisa teased.

"I do," my Guardian Angel said. "Please, please, please."

How he made it to heaven I have no idea.

I looked directly into Lisa's eyes. "Has Sheila called you about the kids?" I asked, acting as calm as Robert Redford about to kiss Barbara Streisand.

Her eyes didn't leave mine and a tantalizing smile creased her lips. "No," she said, like a challenge.

I wanted to go over and take the lotion from her. My feet wanted to move, my hands wanted to rub her body, my mind spun like a fishing reel when an 800 pound marlin on the other end. I turned and walked away, her laughter followed me like it was meant to knock me down and break my legs.

"Roosevelt," my Guardian Angel said. "You are one strange man."

"I have morals," I said.

"Like I said, you are one strange man."

Matilda, good girl that she is, although shot twice, started with one turn of the key. I drove to 9th street where it only took thirty minutes for them to put in a new window.

Matilda purred in appreciation.

I stopped at a pay phone. The only credit card I have ever had in my life is a phone card. If I was lucky, the Phone Company hadn't cancelled my card after I moved out of my apartment in Florida without paying any of my bills.

They hadn't, and after about three minutes the phone in Nogales, Mexico began ringing. I let it ring at least ten times when an answering machine came on, and to my surprise, in English, said. "Since you know this number, leave yours. You know when I will call you back."

There was no way to make the voice as it sounded like a computer programmed voice. The way things are going, besides computers doing all our thinking, they will soon do all our talking - then we can lay around and invent ways to give them arms and legs so they can mow the yard and tell robots what to do.

It was slightly after 12. I called Owens. "Good buddy, what are the names of the topless bars Moralis owns?" I asked.

"The Pussy Cat Retreat One and Two," he said, adding, "I am not your good buddy," letting me know our friendship was a long way from being cemented.

"Is that all you wanted to know?" he growled.

It must have been a bad cop day.

I started to say, yes, but he hung up.

"Let's go to the seedy side of town," I told my Guardian Angel.

"It's about time you did something for me," he said like a wolf that had nude pictures of Little Red Riding Hood.

The parking lot to the Pussy Cat Retreat was full. As topless bars go, it wasn't a fancy place like in the bigger cities where they seem to be proud of what they call, 'gentlemen's clubs'.

The guy working the door was almost as big as Greasy Ed had been. He had on sunglasses, although, it was seven shades of dark inside. There was a round, raised stage in the middle of the room. In the center of the stage was a pole that went to the ceiling - gaudy lights illuminated the stage. Around the stage was a counter where men could sit eyeball to eyeball with naked women - away from the counter was scattered tables. The type that are inexpensive to replace. The Pussy Cat looked like it broke up about two fights an hour.

86

"Nice place," my Guardian Angel said. "We should come here more often. I like the ambiance."

I could tell by his voice he was being serious.

Three naked girls were serving drinks. All young, tired looking, with plastic smiles smeared on their faces. The girls were wearing an elastic piece of ribbon around their stomachs that had money stuck in them. There was no show going on.

Along a wall was a bar and stools. The bartender looked like he eats Harleys for lunch and never washes his hair because his mother had told him if he did it would make him be able to think.

There was a menu scribbled on a chalkboard behind the bar and the smell of greasy hamburgers mingled with the odor of cigarettes, beer, and the cheap perfume the dancers were wearing.

The customers ranged from men in suits, to a few farmers who must have told their wives they had to go to town to get tractor parts. There was also a contingency of bikers. Without a doubt, there were a few guys selling dope and, somewhere in the lower gene pool of humanity, an undercover vice cop.

The juke box was playing a country western song about some guy whose pickup was sleeping with his wife, while his dog had run off with a another man, and now he was so poor he can't afford chewing tobacco. I sat at the bar. The bartender didn't say anything. "Beer and a burger," I ordered.

The three naked bar maids circled around, smiling and letting people put money in their ribbon belts, or for a few bucks more, they would sit on the men's laps.

To my surprise, the hamburger was delicious and the fries were real potatoes, not those frozen mass-market things one buys at fast food joints all over the country. The beer was ice cold and served in a glass mug. I supposed the management figured if somebody was going to hit somebody, they might as well give them something that would do a good job.

As I ate my last fry, a girl walked out of the back dressed in a wedding dress. She had on white high heels and a garland of plastic white daisies in her hair. I doubted she was a virgin.

Several men whistled and as if on cue the juke box stopped and The Doors, Light My Fire, blared over the loudspeakers. The girl stepped up on the stage and within five minutes was naked and hanging on the pole in the center of the stage like it was the sexiest thing she had ever seen. It wasn't my kind of power lunch.

My Guardian Angel was breathing so deeply he sounded like a foghorn.

I went outside - life for many is not good.

"Let's go back in," my Guardian Angel begged.

Coming from the darkness of a tomb into the sunshine it took awhile for my eyes to adjust. I was about to start the engine when I saw a piece of paper stuck underneath the windshield wiper, or I should say what passes for a windshield wiper on a Volkswagen. About the only thing it will keep off the windshield is dew.

I grabbed the note, thinking it was probably a flyer advertising amateur night when all the college coeds could come out and feel seedy. Instead, it was a message typed on 20 pound typing paper in all caps: BE THERE AT ELEVEN OR ELSE.

I felt like the trick on Halloween and wondered what the, "or else," meant.

"If I was you I'd be in Denver by eleven," my Guardian Angel said, which was a stupid remark because in a Volkswagen it would take two days to drive 800 miles.

The Pussy Cat Retreat Two was only a few blocks away. City zoning laws always keep the topless bars in little clusters. Topless bars next to churches don't go over too well - or having little Johnny or Mary walk by one on their way to 5th grade.

The second bar was more upbeat. The parking lot was paved and the bouncer was dressed in slacks and a tie. It cost five bucks to get in the door and the inside was almost as nice as the lobby to a Howard Johnson's.

There were no bikers in this bar, only suits. Since a beer was $4.00 a draw I understood why. The naked girls walking around looked like coeds, and all of them were smiling with gleaming white teeth their fathers had paid about $4,000 for.

"Why is the older American male infatuated with coeds?" my Guardian Angel asked.

"Because they ignore us," I said.

"What will you have, sir?" The bartender asked me.

The bartender looked like somebody's gentle uncle, who, without a doubt, would always watch the kids.

$4.00 beers aren't my cup of tea, but I didn't want him to think I was a wimp by ordering a coke so I ordered a beer.

There were two stages, each had a girl going through whatever throngs of passion one goes through while dancing naked in front of 32 pot-bellied business men.

My beer was almost gone and I didn't have any reason to stay. Going to the topless bars was just one of those useless things I had to do, in case, by a miracle, something to do with the case would happen - the odds being about as good as the government telling me I had given them so much money I wouldn't have to pay taxes anymore.

I was about to get up when my Guardian Angel ordered, "Don't move, look away from the door," just as Sheila walked in.

I turned away like a deer in deer season who knows 22,000 half drunk men with rifles are trying to shoot him because he is a vegetarian.

Sheila, luckily didn't see me, and said, "Hello Frank," to the bartender.

She went to a door and without knocking, opened the door and went in. The door had a sign stating, MANAGER, over it. I felt like the invisible man after he had caught his girlfriend with his best friend.

"She run the place?" I asked Frank.

"I have no idea," Frank replied. "I only work here. I don't ask any questions."

"Smart man," my Guardian Angel said.

I made a hasty retreat.

"Roosevelt, this case is one mixed up mess," my Guardian Angel said.

"Tell me something I don't know," I replied, feeling bewildered.

"It would take too long," my Guardian Angel said, "but, Lisa is an undercover cop and don't you ever forget it."

There were no more love notes on Matilda. I saw Sheila's 98 blue Ford Taurus parked in a reserved parking spot. I know it was her car by the dent in the door. I drove and on a hunch I parked where I thought Sheila might drive by.

After about twenty minutes I was ready to leave but decided to wait awhile longer. I have spent days watching someone's house, taking pictures of people coming in and out. It's nothing that will give you ulcers, but it could give you a heart attack from boredom.

Sheila drove by fifteen minutes later. I pulled in several cars behind her and followed. I wondered what her little critters at her store do while mommy went to see how business was doing at the topless bar. I didn't think they would approve.

Close to downtown, Sheila parked in a private parking lot. I was lucky as there was a parking spot I zipped into. I watched Sheila walk across the street.

There was an old building with the windows painted over in black so nobody can see in. Over the door was a sign stating - THE OUTER LIMITS.

Sheila wasn't inside for more than five minutes when she came back out and drove away.

As she pulled out of the parking lot, I tried to fall in behind her, but was cut off by a long line of traffic.

I stopped at a convenience store and went to the pay phone. THE OUTER LIMITS was listed under Escort Services, out call only, men or women.

I called the number. A lady sounding like the receptionist at an airport Hilton answered. "Outer Limits, how may I help you?"

"Is there a way I can see the lady I wish to be escorted with?" I asked.

"Yes sir, all you have to do is come to our downtown office and we can show you photographs."

I went back to the Outer Limits. The lady who sounded like a Hilton receptionist was really about 55 and looked like she could twist my arms off and would do so if I held my lips wrong. She reminded me of Godzilla with a face-lift.

I looked through a photograph album with plastic pages photographs can be slipped in and out of. On the eighth page was Sheila.

"Surprise, surprise," my Guardian Angel said. "But not a good surprise."

"How much for her?" I asked Godzilla, feeling like a guy at a farm auction trying to buy a horse before it went into the sale barn.

"Our standard fee is $150," Godzilla answered me in a voice that let me know there was no negotiation, but then she added with a knowing wink, "What you work out with the lady is your own business, but if you want one of our escorts, you must pay me, then I'll tell the lady where she is to meet you."

90

There was no doubt Moralis ran the Outer Limits and that it drove the police mad. The way the business was set up he was not doing anything illegal, and it is an almost foolproof way to clean money.

I continued to thumb through the pages of women while wondering how they had lost their dreams.

"Most of them are desperate but they still have dreams," my Guardian Angel said. Even though my Guardian Angel is snide and sarcastic and lecherous he does have a heart.

Godzilla pointed to another book, "We also have men," she said.

"I quit men," I told her. "Trying to turn my life around."

The lady didn't bat an eye - she wouldn't have cared if I wanted a cow. And I knew, for the right amount of money, she would find me a cow I could put a dress on and take to dinner.

I flipped the album back to Sheila. Her name was Patricia Smith and her number was 28. It reminded me of a menu where you order by number because the waitress hasn't learned how to write grilled cheese.

I closed the book, smiled at Godzilla, and started to walk out. She gave me a look like a shoe salesmen after you've tried on 10 pair of shoes and leave without buying any. By the door I stopped. "You wouldn't happen to have any lady Guardian Angels would you?"

"What is that? Some new kind of sex toy?" she asked.

"Thanks for trying," my Guardian Angel said sadly.

Driving back to Lisa's I wondered why Sheila would be an escort unless she liked it. I've heard of many large rings of call girls made up of young housewives. I guess it beats working for minimum wage at Walmart. Although the chances of catching a serious case of VD at Walmart would be a lot slimmer. But still, Sheila had a store and was the manager of a topless bar. It didn't seem like she would need the money unless she was in trouble. I know she would soon be getting $500,000 big ones in insurance money - $500,000 can get rid of a lot of problems or buy one a lot of massage oil.

If I had $500,000 I wouldn't let some lady from Chicago, whose husband didn't understand her, fondle me for a few hundred bucks - no matter how good the dinner had been.

"I would," my Guardian Angel said.

"You wouldn't charge them," I said.

"Some things should be free," he grinned.

I felt like everybody around me was a Venus Fly Trap and I was the only fly for miles.

When I got back to the house the Lincoln was gone.

I went as fast as my cowboy booted feet would carry me to my room and got the key to the lock for the tennis court - good old number 23. Most of the time people buy locks in matched pairs so they don't need to carry keys for every lock on their place. I was in luck as the key also opened the lock on the shed. In the shed was, as I had expected, one of those machines that shoots tennis balls. Around the machine were enough tennis balls in large wire baskets for 100 tennis players. I moved all the baskets, looking for a crack in the floor. I moved the machine. I looked at the bottom edge of the shed to see if it covered a crack. There was nothing. I jumped up and down all around the floor to see if anything sounded hollow. The only thing hollow was my head.

I locked the shed and examined the tennis court. I wanted to find anything that could be a hidden trap door. There was nothing.

Locking the gate I felt like some guy who thought he was a tennis jock that had just been beaten by his girlfriend who had only been playing for two months.

"What are you looking for?" my Guardian Angel asked.

"A tunnel between this property and the Browne's," I answered.

"Why?"

"I wish I could tell you," I said.

I decided to go for a swim. I might need the practice for tonight. I hadn't noticed the expensive tile around the pool before. They are those light red tiles, each about two feet square that Arizona thinks they invented. They also get slick when they are wet.

The chair Lisa had been in still had her towel on it, with the sun tan oil on a stand next to the chair. There was a facedown, opened book on the towel. I picked up the book. I'm always interested in what people read. Lisa was reading a vacation guide to Spain. There was no doubt she could find lots of men in Spain to rub sun tan oil on her.

I took off my clothes and dove into the pool, practiced my backstroke, sidestroke and swam underwater. I had just come up and was getting my hair out of my eyes when I heard a whistle.

Lisa was standing there, dressed like the little mother who had just thrown something on to go to the grocery store and get little Johnny some milk. She had my clothes in her hands. "I'll leave these in the kitchen for you," she said and winked.

"Wait," I protested, but she was gone.

I ran as well as I could, naked, except for my cowboy boots, to the house. Lisa was in the kitchen when I came through the door. She looked at me like I was a marble statue on display at the museum, shrugged her shoulders, and said. "Not bad, not too bad at all for an older guy."

I took my clothes from the table and went to my room with as much dignity as I could.

"Funny, funny," my Guardian Angel laughed so hard he was crying.

After taking a shower, I returned to the kitchen. Lisa was pacing. "I don't think it's a good idea for you to go to the river tonight?" she said, sounding concerned, at least she was not gloating over her child like prank on me.

"How do I get to the river?" I asked.

"You have to walk around the property. When Sam bought the house, he had the fence built with no gate so kids couldn't get to the river. He didn't want to take any chances. The river looks tranquil enough, but there are some strong undertows. At least four or five people drown each year thinking they can swim across it."

"Are there any snakes in it?" I asked. I'm morbidly afraid of snakes.

"There aren't any poisonous snakes in the river," Lisa told me, like a park ranger about to give a ladies club a tour of the park and I was a sissy for being afraid of snakes.

I had three hours before I was supposed to be at the river, but I decided I would go down just before dark. I couldn't think of anything I wanted to talk to Lisa about. I wouldn't get a straight answer anyway.

"You would if you asked her if she was an undercover cop," my Guardian Angel said.

"Get over it," I told him.

I went to my room and changed into an old pair of Levi's, put on a white shirt - it would be easier to see - and a pair of tennis shoes I've had for six years. I locked my pistol, notebook, and all the notes in my suitcase and hid it in the bushes outside. I then lay down.

"It's good to be rested before you get killed," my Guardian Angel said.

After my nap, when I returned to the kitchen, Lisa put her arms around my neck and kissed me gently. "I don't want to see you hurt," she said.

"If I don't come back, give Matilda to some college kid who was too stupid to get a scholarship," I told her.

She gave me a sad little smile, it reminded me of a Mayan priestess who was about to cut my heart out and let my blood run down the sides of the temple so the corn would grow.

The sun was setting when I went out the back door.

"Roosevelt, this is a big mistake," my Guardian Angel told me.

"I know," I replied.

I followed the fence to the river. The river was pretty in its own brown muddy way. The shore was littered with remnants of the city - cereal boxes, cigarette packs, Kleenex and other garbage caught in dead branches that stuck out of the water like skeletal hands. There was a small beach between the arms of the trees. In the middle of the beach was a large rock. I sat on it - there was no recliner in the area.

It didn't take long to get dark, and with the dark came the bugs. I discovered, the hard way, you don't sit outside at night in Iowa unless you put on military strength bug repellant - the kind that will strip paint off of a car.

I closed my mind like I used to do in the war. There was only the dark, the lights from stores across the river, the stars, the rock, and me. There were no bugs, no time, no hurry. What would happen would happen. I put myself into this situation and there were no excuses.

"You're right, Roosevelt," my Guardian Angel said. "Being stupid is not an excuse."

I hate it when my Guardian Angel is right.

CHAPTER EIGHT
CATFISH BAIT

It was soothing sitting by the river in the dark, even though it was bathed by the glow of the city. In my mind I saw Indians, hundreds of years ago, paddling their canoes along the river. They were discussing how raccoons were down from the previous year. The corn was doing well, but fishing had been bad. Running Bear was having trouble with his wife. Sleeping Dog was trying to marry off his daughter to somebody with a new canoe and a few good buffalo robes. And, Man Who Always Sleeps Late, was tired of his neighbor letting his kids play outside all night, plus his mother-in-law had been staying in his tent and was always cranky.

Even the Indians had problems before we showed up, but they didn't have to dodge oil slicks and worry about getting poisoned because they ate the fish they caught. In Iowa, people can't drink the river water because it's filled with so much pesticide and fertilizer residue that if they did, somebody would plant corn in their ears and sell them for $3.00 a bushel.

A mosquito was sucking out a quart of my blood when I heard the engine to a small boat. It was 20 minutes until 11. I saw a fishing boat in the middle of the river with two figures in it. The outline of fishing poles stood out against the glare of the city. Two men's voices carried to me, but I couldn't make out what they were saying. The boat didn't turn, but continued on a steady pace down the middle of the river. They were heading to their favorite catfish hole, not to beat the stupidity out of some private detective from Florida.

By now the mosquito was so full of my blood he flew off like a wino that had finished a gallon of warm Ripple.

Hearing a noise off to my left I tensed up, it was only a mouse scurrying through some dead leaves.

Checking the time, it was straight up 11 o'clock.

For the next thirty minutes, I swatted mosquitoes that by now had made me mad, and watched a few beer cans bob down the river.

By midnight, I was pacing back and forth on my little private beach, head down, like a professor pondering light, time and infinity. Only my infinity was back to murder. I had no doubt Sam had been mixed up in something. I know the kids were not kidnapped. I figured Lisa and Sheila were both lying to me, but I can't figure out why. I know both Lisa and Sheila knew Moralis and I figured Owens was telling me the truth about Moralis selling guns and heroin. I know there is a connection between Sam and the Browne's, but I don't know exactly what it is. The voice in the dark in front of the Browne's was the most disturbing. One thing positive I have an idea on how to set a trap.

"Watch out you don't get caught in your own trap," my Guardian Angel warned me. "Thinking and planning have never been one of your strong points."

"What are my strong points," I asked.

There was a long silence. "I will have to get back with you on that," my Guardian Angel mused with a confused look on his face.

By 1 a.m. I'd had enough. I'd been stood up by make believe kidnappers. I felt like a court jester who couldn't make the king laugh and if I didn't get my act together, I would be back on the streets juggling on the corner and worrying about getting the plague.

Picking my way around the fence like a buck private on guard duty, my attention was somewhere on Mars. As I rounded the corner where the chain link fence hit the stone wall my Guardian Angel shouted, "look out," as the bat hit me on the side of the head. Whoever was at bat didn't strike out. I hit the ground like a frozen tuna coming off a Japanese fishing boat.

Waking up, my head felt like the inside of a diesel engine with a rod knocking and blood was caked on the side of my head, getting up slowly I steadied myself against the fence.

"Your reaction time is getting sloppy," my Guardian Angel informed me.

"Your warning was not exactly timely," I groaned.

"I am getting old," he said, which wasn't much of an excuse.

I staggered along the stone wall and fell more than stepped into the kitchen.

The kitchen looked like 16 kids had a party while their parents were gone for a week. The drawers were pulled out and everything was tossed on the floor, all the cupboards are open. Lisa was sitting in a chair, eyes wide open like she had seen a ghost. Her hands were tied behind her and a piece of packing tape was wrapped around her mouth.

Before I untied her, I stuck my head under the faucet and ran the cold water. After washing off the blood, I tenderly felt the golf ball sized bump on my head.

I untied Lisa and, as gently as possible, ripped the tape off her mouth. She slumped in the chair like a person who has had to sit in the same seat in an airplane for 14 hours.

She started sobbing and covered her face with her hands. My head was pounding and I felt certain I had a concussion. I went from room to room and turned on all the lights. The house had been gone over like a drug swat team bent on destroying everything they touched - drawers were dumped on the floor, lamp shades were taken off lamps, the pictures on the walls had been removed. The kid's rooms were all destroyed. Lisa's room looked like a coed's dorm. They hadn't found my suitcase outside. I didn't bother to put the pistol in my belt - the chickens were all gone - eloped with the fox.

It had been a set up. Whoever had come to the house only wanted me gone. But why didn't they just come in when they knew I would be gone? As I headed back to the kitchen I knew one thing, Lisa was not going to lie her way out of this one - the throbbing bump on the side of my head is a testimony to that.

Lisa made us a gin and tonic. Her face was flushed and her hand trembled as she handed me the drink. "There were two people," she said, her voice shaky and her speech quick. "They had on Halloween masks and surgical gloves. One looked like Porky Pig and the other one like Daffy Duck. It was exactly 11 o'clock when I answered the back door. They didn't do anything to me except stick a pistol in my stomach. After they tied me up they searched the house. I kept hollering at them, trying to find out what they were looking for. They got tired of listening to me and taped my mouth shut."

"Did they ever say anything to you?" I said between throbs in my head. Ball bats can give you Excedrin headache number 184.

"They never said a word."

"Nobody showed up at the river. I must have run into their guard by the wall, he bushwhacked me."

She looked carefully at my head, mumbled something and then left the room and came back with a bottle of something to swab on the cut and two aspirin. "Will it sting?" I asked.

We both laughed. Somehow it seemed funny.

When she finished she made us another drink and we sat at the table like we had lived through a bombing and were glad to be alive.

"Why have you lied to me about the kids being kidnapped?" I asked Lisa, not harshly. I didn't want to talk too loud - my head might explode into thousands of tiny baseballs.

Lisa looked as though a volcano would blow out of the top of her head. "Why would I lie about that?" she snarled, reminding me of a not very happy tiger.

"Not good, Roosevelt," my Guardian Angel said.

"Sheila told me Sam had sent the kids to camp just before he got killed," I said.

But no sooner had the words tumbled from my mouth when I remembered a statement Sam had made to me, "Why don't you come to my house and I'll introduce you to my wife and kids."

Did Sam forget he was sending the kids to camp or was he lying to me also? Did he know the kids had already been grabbed and he wanted to wait and tell me when we got to his house? He'd told me he didn't want to talk at Greasy Ed's.

Lisa didn't say a word for a few moments. Her gaze went to a shoebox I hadn't noticed that was on the kitchen table.

"Porky Pig and Daffy Duck left that," she said in a voice that sounded old and tired, but she didn't answer my question.

The shoebox was tied with a piece of string. I got a knife. After cutting the string, I flipped the lid off the box with the tip of the knife. On the bottom of the box was a lock of hair held together with a small, green, beaded burette, a silver ring that looked like a skull, a thin gold necklace, and a white envelope.

Lisa covered her mouth with her hands and started to sob again. I figured the hair belongs to Kathy, the ring to Rick, and the necklace to Margaret.

"There goes everything you had convinced yourself you knew," my Guardian Angel said with a look on his face that made me feel more useless.

My mind was racing like a car at Indy that had gone out of control and was about to slam into the wall. I took the envelope out of the box and removed a sheet of 20-pound bond paper. Unfolding the paper I read: SAM WAS A BAD BOY. ALL I WANT IS WHAT IS MINE. YOU KNOW WHAT IT IS. YOU DO NOT HAVE MUCH TIME. CHILDREN AND SPICE AND EVERYTHING NICE. DON'T CALL YOUR FRIENDLY NEIGHBORHOOD POLICE.

"Poets they are not," my Guardian Angel said.

"The kids were taken one day before Sam was killed. They never made it to camp," Lisa said between sobs.

"Did Sheila know this?" I asked.

"Sam had to tell her. At least you would think he would have."

"Why did you lie to me about Sheila wanting the children back by a certain time?"

"I've been so worried I don't know half the time what I am doing," she said, but she didn't sound guilty.

"What do these people want?" I asked Lisa.

"I don't know, Roosevelt. I have no idea what dirty business Sam was messed up in. I never wanted this big house. I don't care about fancy cars. I like nice clothes. But believe me, I loved Sam."

She started to cry again. "It's not my fault, I swear."

I felt like a young bull that had just been castrated and was watching over the fence as the farmer was having a mountain oyster party.

I was now back to warming the bench after striking out so many times the coach had pulled me from the lineup. I have nothing to go on but a distant voice in the dark - a voice that should not have been at the neighbor's house.

"Roosevelt, you idiot, ask her if she is an undercover cop," my Guardian Angel said in a not so friendly voice.

"You ask her," I said, also not in a not so friendly voice.

I made Lisa and me another drink. It seemed like one of those nights when it would be good to get plastered, throw up a few times, sleep on the bathroom floor and start all over again in the morning.

I made the drinks extra strong. "I'll find those kids," I told Lisa.

She made a vain attempt at a smile.

After she sipped her drink, I told her, "I saw you go to Greasy Ed's the day he was killed."

She didn't seem overly concerned about the news. "Who killed him?" she asked casually, sounding like a homicide cop who had seen so many murders they no longer fazed him.

"There are no leads," I half lied.

"Sam owed him some money. He bet the horses through Ed. Greasy Ed wasn't the kind of guy you didn't pay. I found a slip on how much he owed and took it over and paid him. I've been there before when Sam made his bets."

I went upstairs to Lisa's room. The intruders had taken her pistol.

When I came back down, Lisa was going through one of her transformations from little Miss Sears and Roebuck to Cindy, The Seducer of Men. She has to have some form of chemical imbalance or it is her special way to fight stress.

"Finish your drink," she told me in a sexy voice, "I'll make us another one."

I gulped down the drink and handed her the glass. When she came back, she handed me the glass and stepped back and looked at me. "You were cute with nothing on but your cowboy boots."

"Are you going to be an idiot again?" my Guardian Angel asked me.

I didn't say anything.

Lisa put her arms around my neck. "I want you to take me to my room, take my clothes off, and then make love to me for about six hours," she purred.

"During very rare occasions Roosevelt is good for about thirty seconds?" my Guardian Angel said.

My body said, yes, my mind said, no. My male side said, yes, yes, yes, my integrity said no, no, no.

"Please, no integrity," my Guardian Angel cried and put his hands together like he was praying.

"I don't think it's proper right now," I told Lisa.

Lisa took her arms from around my neck, stepped back, slapped me and stomped out of the kitchen.

"Good work lover boy," my Guardian Angel said.

"She was my friend's wife," I said.

"That doesn't mean much in this modern world," he said.

True is true, but still.

When I woke in the morning to my surprise, my head didn't hurt much and there was no lump. I took a shower and put on clean clothes.

When I went to the kitchen Lisa was over her slapping anger, while I was in the shower she had made bacon and eggs and orange juice. "I thought you might be tired of health food," she said as she put the plate down.

"Do you think there is a tunnel between this house and the house next door?" I asked Lisa in between bites of egg.

"I saw you snooping around the tennis court," Lisa said.

"You can't even be sneaky anymore," my Guardian Angel said still bummed out at me for not sleeping with Lisa.

"I don't think so," Lisa went on. "If there is, I don't know about it."

100

I would have bet my last 10 dollars there was a tunnel between the two tennis courts but why I am infatuated with the tunnel idea I really don't know. I guess one has to be infatuated with something in life to make living bearable.

"We have to find whatever it is the kidnappers want. Sam had to steal something from them. They ransacked the house last night looking for a clue, but I doubt they found it," I said, feeling like a General who had lost the war and knew it, but was trying to rally his men so they would die for him and make him famous.

Lisa picked at her egg like the cholesterol would jump off the plate and bite her.

"Did you know about the address in Mexico hidden behind one of the photographs in your bedroom, and the phone number to Mexico hidden in Sam's den?"

"No," she answered, but she looked startled, and I was surprised she didn't say anything about me snooping around the house.

"That's your job, Roosevelt, remember?" my Guardian Angel said.

"What did you and Sam do in Mexico?" I asked Lisa.

"We first went to Mexico City. It's the most depressing city I have ever seen. You either have money or you have nothing. The air is so polluted you could put L.A. air in bags and sell it to them and they would think it is pure. We then went to Puerto Viarta. And then, for some reason, we went to some ugly little town just south of Arizona."

"Nogales," I butted in.

"Nogales, that's it. I walked around and looked at cheap trinkets while Sam went off to do something."

"Did he seem nervous or anything out of the ordinary?"

"He was really nervous. So nervous he wouldn't eat anything and just drank."

"Where did you go after Nogales?"

"We came home."

"Do you remember Sam ever seeing anybody in Mexico?"

"As a matter of fact, I do, we ran into Salvador Moralis at a nice restaurant in Nogales. He came over to our table and sat with us for a while and even told the waiter he was picking up the check."

"First she doesn't know Moralis, then she does, and then she does again," my Guardian said, shaking his head.

I don't miss as many things as he thinks I do.

"Did you bring anything back with you?"

101

Sam bought a set of luggage. But, no, I didn't buy anything. It's all junk. Oh, yes, we bought Rick that silver ring that is in the box."

"I bet you carried the set of luggage through customs," I said, my image of Sam the peaceful hippie was vanishing quickly. "Do you know where the luggage is now?"

Lisa thought for a moment. "I don't. You know I've never seen it since."

"I don't want you to go anywhere, do you understand. I also don't want you answering the door while I'm gone."

Lisa nodded her head. I don't think the idea of being tied to a chair again excited her. Now, being tied with silk scarves might be a different story.

I went to my room and got my notebook and pistol. Back in the kitchen, I set the pistol on the table. "Do you know how to use this?" I asked Lisa.

"I'm a good shot," she replied, like shooting things was her hobby.

I should have asked her why a city girl like her is a good shot and how she knew how to operate a 9 m.m.? "If somebody wants to kick in the door, put them on the path to enlightenment."

For some strange reason I felt like kissing Lisa on the forehead and telling her I wanted meat loaf for dinner.

Matilda started right up as usual. I drove to a wooded park not far from Lisa's. Sitting there I read my notebook as joggers ran by and ladies in pairs pushed babies in strollers while discussing the price of Similac. Many of my clues seemed useless but I didn't discard them. There are many useless things in my life that have proven to be useful later on. I do know one thing for sure though, the only person I trust is myself.

"You don't trust me?" my Guardian Angel asked, seemingly offended.

I laughed.

"You are a smarter man than people think you are," he said.

I stopped at the nearest pay phone. I was using so many pay phones I felt like a dope dealer. Godzilla answered the phone for the Outer Limits. Business is probably so good she never went home or her husband told her not to bother.

"I'd like to reserve number 28 for this evening," I said, knowing I was knocking women's lib back another ten years.

"You can either put this on your credit card or pay cash, but you must come down to our home office," Godzilla informed me.

It didn't take long to get to the Outer Limits. Godzilla took my money and asked if I wanted a receipt. I always take my receipts, why, I don't know. I either lose them or end up tossing them away and don't need them until the IRS wants to know why I deducted 37 note pads. I figured I could deduct Sheila as a business expense, after all, I was after information. "I would like to meet the lady at the Ramada Inn bar by the airport at 7:30 tonight."

Godzilla smiled at me, her, 'she will be there, you lousy going out on your wife jerk,' smile.

Back on the street, I wondered how many bananas Godzilla ate a day.

From the Outer Limits it didn't take me long to get to Police Headquarters. It was a large building made from imposing blocks of granite - government tries to give the image that it will last forever. The jail was on the top floor. It's strange that prisoners and governments go together.

"You shouldn't be doing this," my Guardian Angel warned.

Policemen in-groups have always frightened me, it's something about people all dressing the same. The police seemed to be infatuated by my long hair and beard and probably thought I was an undercover agent with the D.E.A. - police salaries being about $34,000 a year, they figured I was stealing more than they made and gave me dirty looks as I walked by.

Detective Owens's office wasn't what I had imagined. I had imagined a small grubby office, littered with paper, no windows, and a secretary that would scare an attack dog.

Instead, the office was large, the secretary was young, pretty, and very professional. The chairs were even comfortable. There were stacks of new magazines, none of which were catalogs for police uniforms or bulletproof vests.

On the walls of the receptionist office hung three prints from Ducks Unlimited.

I only waited five minutes when the secretary smiled at me and pointed to the door.

Detective Owens was sitting at a large wooden desk, polished almost to a glass shine. It was neat, with nothing on top but a phone and a small computer with a pen and pencil set next to it. Owens was framed by a large picture window. There were two chairs in front of his desk and no other furniture. A print of a man fishing was on one wall and several citations for winning shooting matches - both rifle and pistol. In his office, Owens looked like the closer at a car lot who was going to try to sell me undercoating and an extended warranty that would cost more than the car.

To my surprise, he smiled at me like I am his long lost cousin. "Hippie, got a joint?" he laughed.

I sat down in one of the chairs, which made me several inches lower than Owens - a childish power play to make one feel inferior - but sad to say it worked.

"Got anymore women you want to pass around?" I said.

"Not funny," Owens replied gruffly.

I was glad I had him back in his normal mood.

"How's life?" I asked.

"I've got seven months until I retire. Seven more months and then I'm going to go somewhere where it's warm all the time, play golf, and fish."

Owens doesn't look old enough to retire. But, retirement is something I've never thought of. I don't have enough quarters on my social security to get a loan for a TV set.

"Seven more months and it's the big twenty-five," Owens said, but not proudly.

"Are you going to invite me to your retirement party?"

"By then you will probably be dead," Owens said in a tone of voice I didn't like, like he was trying to tell me something - something I should be listening to.

"I was in the neighborhood and thought I'd stop by. I haven't been able to find out anything. If nothing comes up within a few days I'm going to get out of here," I said.

"You haven't followed Moralis around?" he asked me. For some reason, it sounded like a double-edged question.

"You'd like that," I said, "Moralis would put me in a garbage can with his chicken bones."

Owens seemed to relax. "We haven't found out anything about Sam either, no suspects, no real motive. If he was working with Mexicans and they wanted him killed, they had some guy come up out of Mexico, put the final touch on him, and the killer went back to Mexico."

"How about Moralis?"

104

"We can get about as close to Moralis as a little league kid hitting as many home runs as Mickey Mantle."

"It's frustrating," I said.

Owens, after being a cop for almost 25 years, could care. When he went home at night he didn't sit around the kitchen and worry about how many unsolved cases were on his desk. He knew that fewer than 10% of all crimes get solved, and like he said, he only had seven months left.

"You get any squeeze off Lisa yet?" Owens asked, sitting forward in his seat like I would make a video and sell him one.

"Lisa isn't an orange," my Guardian Angel said.

"She looks good but is about as cold as a snow cone," I told him.

Owens was disappointed in me.

"You ever find out anything about Greasy Ed?" I asked.

"We know he ran a small time book but nothing that was worth our time. We have no idea who killed him. We know you didn't, you couldn't shoot that good."

Owens laughed at his own police humor joke.

"I've been hearing a lot of noises late at night at the neighbors. Have there ever been reports of anything going on with the Browne's?" I asked as casually as a guy trying to bum a cigarette.

Owens left eyelid jerked and he scratched his nose. Then he smiled like he had just won my last 10 bucks in a poker game. "The Browne's are a wealthy and respected family in Des Moines. They also give large amounts of money to the policemen's fund and are active in many charities around town."

"Al Capone fed the homeless," I said. "That didn't stop him from killing 7,000 people."

"You watch too much TV," Owens said.

"I don't watch TV," I replied. "Even with the few brain cells I have left my mind won't function that low."

Owens looked at me like I was a coffee stain on his only clean white shirt and I knew it was time to go.

"I was just stopping by," I said. "I thought I would try and see you one more time before I get out of Dodge."

"This is Des Moines," my Guardian Angel said.

I looked at Owens's shooting awards. "You must be a good shot," I said. "Police competition has to be tough."

"I am a great shot," he replied proudly.

105

I held out my hand to shake and to my surprise, Owens shook my hand.

As I was about to open the door Owens said to me, "Nobody wins them all, Roosevelt."

I wanted to tell Owens the same thing, but I kept my mouth shut.

The secretary was out of the office. I stopped at her desk, and quickly took one sheet of the paper out of the printer to her computer, folded it and put it in my pocket.

I needed time to think and asked directions from a little old lady who was downtown to pay a traffic ticket how to get to the main library.

Libraries are holy to me. The rows and rows of books are symbols of man's futile attempt to feel permanent. Libraries are also quieter than churches, and you don't have to put money in boxes that have candles all around them, or have to listen to people preach at you.

When I got to the library I went to a small cubicle used for private reading. I tore out all my scribbled pages from my notebook. It was time to really get organized and nail this puppy down.

"Why would anybody want to nail a puppy down?" my Guardian Angel asked. "Petting puppies is much nicer."

An hour later, I had written all my clues in the order that I think they should be written. I also wrote a list of questions that I have to answer before I can solve the case.

"You could try calling information and see if they could answer your questions," my Guardian Angel said.

"Funny, funny," I said.

Back at the house, against my orders, Lisa was gone. She had also moved the shoebox that had been our uninvited guest's gift and I didn't see my pistol. I had a momentary fear that Lisa would shoot somebody with my gun and blame it on me. I could see 12 men in a jury box taking my word over hers about as well as I could see me donating to the police fund.

I went to my room and took all the notes I had received from the kidnappers out of my suitcase and lay them on the bed. I set the sheet of paper I had stolen from Owens's office next to them. They matched, it is perfect edged computer paper in 20 pound.

"That paper is more common than trees," my Guardian Angel said.

"It's why we don't have many trees," I said.

I read and reread the notes, looked at the type, they all matched. I put everything back in the suitcase and took a shower. I have a date in a few hours with Patricia, good old number 28. It was a surprise party.

CHAPTER NINE
STUPID AGAIN

I got to the Ramada Inn early and went to the bar, got a beer and sat at a corner table. I could see who came in the door but they couldn't see me. It was a perfect table for people to meet who are doing something that makes them paranoid - like two middle management guys from the state department.

The bar had already had happy hour and all the appetizers had been gobbled up by the businessmen who were getting ready to go to their rooms, take a shower, and after calling the little lady at home, watch a dirty movie.

By my watch it was 7:15. The waitress came over to my table. She was wearing a long black dress and a white blouse that was so starched she could have been in the Navy. She was about as excited to be serving drinks as a recently divorced airline pilot flying a plane full of marriage counselors.

None-the-less, she gave me her 'young lady to middle aged man' smile. I ordered another beer and tried to ignore the loud laughter from another table. There are times in life when nothing is funny.

At 7:35 Sheila walked confidently into the bar. She was dressed like a businesswoman who had done well. She sat at the bar.

"Oh boy, Roosevelt, she looks nice," my Guardian Angel said. "But she is not going to like your surprise."

Sheila ordered a drink and seemed perfectly at ease. I would think that a lady working for an escort service would be scared to death - murdered and battered prostitutes aren't crimes the police take much interest in - no publicity.

I let her take a few sips off of her drink before going over. "Hello Patricia," I said cordially.

Color rushed into her face - a sunset red. "You jerk," she grimaced and started to stand up.

"Surprise, surprise," my Guardian Angel said waving his arms around like he was at a kid's birthday party.

I held her arm firmly. "I paid for you. I don't think your boss would like me to call and say you walked out merely because you didn't like my face."

A momentary flash of indecision darted through her eyes, before she decided the game was up, and she reluctantly relaxed. I released her arm. "I have a table in the corner," I told her, moving to her side so she couldn't walk toward the door.

I pointed at the corner table and she headed toward it like a robot with rust in its knee joints. Gentleman that I am, I carried her drink for her.

The waitress came over. "The lady and I will have a bottle of champagne, whatever is the cheapest," I ordered, adding to Sheila, "just for old times."

"She'll never ask you to see her body paints again," my Guardian Angel said sadly.

Sheila and I sat in silence, like a couple who had lost the spark and had given up on trying to communicate.

After the waitress opened and poured the champagne, I held up my glass to toast. Sheila, more like an obedient dog, held up hers. We clinked the glasses lightly together. "To truth," I said.

"That's funny," my Guardian Angel said.

I know Sheila's champagne went down like warm vinegar. She must like vinegar. She drained the glass and held it out for me to pour more. After drinking half of it she said, with no animosity in her voice, "So little private eye has been on the job?"

"It's amazing, isn't it?" my Guardian Angel said.

"Why did you try and shoot me the other night?" I asked her.

"What in the blazes are you talking about?"

I shook my head and said, "I know you shot at me the other night when I left your house."

Sheila hesitated, as though constructing an alibi. "I could have killed you," she said. "I only wanted to scare you in hope you would leave town."

"Not a good alibi," my Guardian Angel said, but adding, "I thought you thought Lisa shot at you."

"You came close to my head for trying to scare me," I said to Sheila.

"I told you, I could have killed you. I was raised on a farm, remember? I was shooting rabbits in the head from 50 yards when I was 10 years old. My daddy used to call me crack shot Anne."

"Thanks for missing," I said.

"Up your nosy nose, Roosevelt," Sheila snapped. "I should have blown your brains out, because of you....you..."

I finished her sentence. "Because of me, your children are in mortal danger. You thought by me being around the kidnappers might get jumpy."

"I thought, you thought, the kidnapping was all a lie," my Guardian Angel said, bewildered.

"Sometimes I think, what I think, but I don't know what I think, and what I say means nothing," I said to him. "But I still think it's a lie."

"Lisa told you about the kidnapping," Sheila said, sounding upset. "I told her to leave you out of this."

"I wanted to go to the police but she said no," I said.

"You don't have kids so you have no idea what it's like."

"I would have liked to have children," I said.

Sheila's strength went down like the old Berlin Wall. "Oh, Roosevelt, it's all so messed up."

I patted her hand gently. The fact she had tried to kill me was just one of those things in life one has to get over.

"You are one messed up person," my Guardian Angel said.

"What was Sam up to Sheila?" I asked.

"I need something stronger than this bubbly water," Sheila said.

I waved to the waitress. Sheila ordered a whisky and water. I ordered a beer.

When the drinks were brought back, Sheila drank half of hers in one gulp.

"Whiskey drinking bad shot Anne," my Guardian Angel said but was still impressed.

I sipped my beer and waited for Sheila to tell me her story. The fact she was a part-time hooker didn't concern me. Everybody has some form of vice in them. Besides, prostitution really does no harm - if it does we should ask Canada, Germany, Norway, and Sweden, why they have so little rape.

"Sam was an idealist, you know that," Sheila began, then finished her drink. I raised my hand and pointed for one more. "When he came back from New Mexico, he told me he had met some guy who smuggled grass."

"Everybody in New Mexico smuggles grass," I cut in. "Without it, there would be no economy."

"You want me to tell you or not?" Sheila asked angrily.

110

"Let the lady talk, Roosevelt, haven't you ever learned? When a lady talks, even if you are not listening, you have to put on like you are," my Guardian Angel said.

The waitress brought Sheila's drink. What is it about booze that makes people want to run their head?

"As I was saying, this guy smuggled grass, and he knew some other guys who needed guns. They were going to save the poor people in Mexico. Sam believed him. Sam started to go to all the gun shows buying rifles and pistols. Back then, you didn't have to show an I.D. to buy guns. It was when people thought people committed crimes not guns. He would drive a trunk load of guns down to Tucson and the Mexicans would come up and pick them up. To Sam, it was like he was making the world a better place. It was all well and good for a while until Sam started to drive pot back from Tucson for them. He would bring it here and they had a man who would take it on to Chicago. It started to make me nervous and I started to get on him about it. Sam and I started to fight a lot. One time, after he got back from Tucson, I could tell the bottom was starting to fall out. It seems the good old revolutionaries really didn't care if they killed rich people or poor people. They had made a lot of money and instead of helping the people they were forcing poor people to grow their dope so they could buy more hotels. Sam was informed by the boss he was part of them now. By part of them, he meant forever."

I had heard all this before. The jails are full of people who only do illegal things because they need a little money. The big boys come on like ice cream and cake and everything is all roses. Suddenly, the ice cream turns to mud and the small guy goes to jail for 40 years and the big boys go find another sucker.

"They paid him well, didn't they?"

"We had money stuck in the ground, hidden in the attic, money was coming out our ears. Hippiedom became get all you can, don't look back, the commune was greed."

"Fishing with money will get you a lot of suckers," my Guardian Angel commented.

"What happened between you two?" I asked.

"I couldn't take it anymore. Sam bought me the Mother Goose store and the next thing I knew he made me the manager of a topless bar. The people who ran his life opened them to launder money and he said I had to work there, although the money is not bad."

"Who is the heavy?" I asked, not telling her I had seen her at the Pussy Cat Retreat.

"Maybe she saw you and left the note on Matilda," my Guardian Angel said. "Maybe she is the one who hit you on the head after your fruitless night on the river."

"I've never thought of that," I told him, "but it has possibilities."

Sheila answered my question. "Salvador Moralis is the guy I see every so often, but I know he's only a pawn.

"Do you have any ideas, Sheila, who tells Moralis what to do?"

Sheila shook her head.

I didn't believe everything she had told me but like all lies, there's a degree of truth in them. I do believe Moralis works for somebody. It seems there is always somebody bigger or stronger.

"That's true until it comes to God," my Guardian Angel said.

"Do you have any idea what happened for Sam to get killed and the kids kidnapped?"

Sheila drained her drink. "Sam told me he was going to steal a lot of money and after he did he would come by the house with the kids and we would disappear."

"Were you seeing him after your divorce and he remarried?" I asked.

"It's a daytime soap," my Guardian Angel said, "but at least the plot is good."

"Sam married Lisa on a whim. He confused sex with love. It didn't take long for him to find out the difference. He didn't hate her, he just made a mistake. It wasn't three weeks after they were married that he was knocking on my door like a lost puppy dog. I loved him, Roosevelt, I hope you believe that."

"I don't think Sam told Lisa anything about what he was doing," I said.

"Sam wasn't a hateful person and I hate to say it, but, I think Lisa really loved him."

"To want to do such a desperate thing as steal money, Sam must have been in trouble."

"He took a lot of money and put it on a deal - some of it I think he borrowed. I don't know what happened, but I know everything went sour and he lost all the money."

"Sam ever mess around with heroin?"

"Sam would never mess with heroin," Sheila said, like heroin was a four-letter word.

"The heroin business is an easy business to get killed in," I said.

She seemed taken back by my statement. Then said, "When Sam bought the big house, he told me he had to buy that particular one, but he didn't tell me why."

On a hunch I asked her, "You ever know a big guy who ran a restaurant called Greasy Ed's?"

"No."

My mind was whirling as fast as a Frisbee in a tornado.

The waitress came over and Sheila ordered another round. When they arrived she half smiled at me. "I bet you wonder why I'm working for an escort service?"

I wanted to tell her, "Not really," but when a person starts to bare their soul, they'll tell you whether you want to know or not.

"Is there a job opening for Guardian Angels?" my Guardian Angel asked.

"When Sam and I divorced, I had the store and the money from the bar coming in. The store has never made money. It's more like a writer, an act of love, or an obsession. Moralis knew I needed money and told me about the escort business he owned - he told me that some people liked middle-aged women and I could make extra money. It seemed exciting."

"With all the insurance money you are about to get, you don't have to do that anymore," I told Sheila.

"I have three more months on my contract. You don't break a contract with Moralis."

"Have you and Lisa been in contact a lot?"

"She keeps me posted or stops by."

"You overlooked the idea they might be in contact," my Guardian Angel told me.

Why do people always harp on one's shortcomings?

"Doesn't it seem strange that the kidnappers have never contacted you?" I asked Sheila.

"What if they don't even know about me?"

"Answer that one famous private detective," my Guardian Angel said.

I couldn't and it bothered me.

It was close to 9. I felt tired and my head was starting to throb.

"Whoever the kidnappers are they know about you," Sheila said.

The statement shocked me, but I didn't show my shock.

Sheila seemed to sag like a leaf on a tree during a hot summer day. Her lower lip started trembling and tears dripped from her eyes. "I'm so afraid," she cried softly. "The poor kids."

After all of Lisa's crying I am growing immune. Sheila's tears didn't faze me.

Sheila had her quiet cry and then looked at me, her dark penetrating eyes, now only empty pools, "I'm truly glad I didn't shoot you, Roosevelt. You're my only hope."

Hope is truly a four-letter word and is used far too often. I have hope. Hope there is never another war. Hope that the United States will truly live up to its promise. Hope that one-day we will not be chained to the oil companies. Hope that before I die, I will catch a trout over 24 inches long. Hope that the Japanese won't eat up all the whales. Hope the I.R.S. gets a soul. Hope that Middle East people and Christians learn people don't have to believe the same to get along.

"The first time I came over to your house, you told me you hadn't been on horses in years, yet hanging on your clothes line was a pair of riding britches and on the porch was a pair of riding boots."

"They belong to Margaret. I cleaned the boots and washed the pants."

"Where does she ride?"

"She rides at the Browne's. They're never home, but Manuel lets her ride whenever she wants."

"Well isn't that cozy," my Guardian Angel said.

"You go home now," I told Sheila. "I'm working on a plan and will come by soon and see you. And don't ever go back to the Pussy Cat Retreat."

"I'll have to," she said.

"Not after tonight you won't," I said.

"Roosevelt, now don't do anything rash," my Guardian Angel said, sounding worried.

It was time for me to take some definite action. Since I'm not a cop I don't have to pretend that I always follow the law, which, sadly, many police don't either.

"Will you come home with me tonight?" Sheila asked, looking like a lost kitten.

"Of course he will," my Guardian Angel said, giving me a pleading look.

"I have things I have to do," I told her.

"You are a disappointment," my Guardian Angel almost cried.

"It's Lisa," Sheila muttered, sounding more hurt than angry.

"No, it's not Lisa," I told her.

I escorted Sheila to her car - the legal way - and watched her drive away. I went back to the lobby and called Lisa. She answered the phone on the third ring, sounding out of breath, and tense.

"Where are you Roosevelt? I don't like being here alone."

"Somewhere between Mars and limbo."

"Don't be funny, it doesn't suit you," Lisa said.

"He was telling the truth," my Guardian Angel said.

"I'm calling to tell you I'll be late."

"He's such a nice boy," my Guardian Angel said.

"I'll wait up for you," Lisa said.

I didn't tell her by late, I meant really late.

I left the Ramada and watched a jet take off from the airport. I had more than a few hours to kill and decided to take a drive in the country. Where, I didn't know, but at times in life it's good just to head out, let the road be my guide and see what life will bring me. From Florida, it has brought me a load of grief, a knot on my head, and shot at twice, but life isn't always so fickle, it does have its moments.

Within thirty minutes I was driving by farmhouses, scattered about a mile apart, with their lights still on. They reminded me of isolated channel markers. I thought of the men and women inside watching their TV's who, from day to day, know what they will be doing. I've always shied away from the routine in life, but in truth I have found nothing better. I've spent my time like a pair of dice, which on any roll, can crap out.

"One day, Roosevelt, with a little luck, you might crap in," my Guardian Angel said with a chuckle.

I stopped at a small rest area on a two lane black top road. I looked at the stars, but in the humidity of the Midwest, they didn't twinkle, but seemed to fade in and out like they didn't know if they wanted to shine or not. I know that somewhere in the vastness is a world filled with beings that, I hope, are not as messed up as we are. I've always thought we look and dream about space because we know, deep inside, that one-day we will destroy this world of ours. We need a place to go.

Hopefully, the survivors will not be the ones who were the cause of our destruction.

In the darkness, I heard a night bird singing and could picture the lonely little bird sitting on a branch, singing to try and be brave or wake up a friend who would come over and talk to him.

I dozed off in the front seat and didn't wake up until close to 1 o'clock. I felt refreshed, not good, but refreshed. I went back over my conversation with Sheila and tried to pick out what parts had been the truth by remembering her body language as she talked.

"Remembering went out of your system thirty years ago," my Guardian Angel quipped.

Back in town, I went to the friendly all night Walmart and bought two, five-gallon plastic gas cans. The clerks at the store looked like bleached out zombies who only draw life from fluorescent light bulbs.

At a gas station, where the attendant working inside wouldn't remember if a three headed monster had been in, I filled the gas containers and picked up two packets of their free matches. I read the inside of the match covers, for two bucks I could get four ball point pens that cost a nickel each to produce - even matches, in this world of ours, have a scam.

By the time I got to the Pussy Cat Retreat, it was closing time. By 2 a.m. in Iowa, people have to be out of the bars. It gives them a chance to go home and get some sleep so they can get up and get drunk again. It was 2:10 and a few drunks were still inside wishing they had enough money to take one of the girl's home. The girls were waiting for their boyfriends who have never had a job in their lives, and wouldn't, as long as the little lady never lost her figure, and when she did they would trade her on a younger model.

I drove by and continued driving for another 30 minutes, then I turned around. When I drove by again, the parking lot was empty and all the lights were out. It was sleepy time in dreamland, but Tinker Bell doesn't live at the Pussy Cat Retreat.

I parked Matilda a block a way, and taking one of the gas cans, ran as fast as I could to the rear of the lounge. I poured gas all over the back of the building and placed the plastic container next to it. I lit a match, tossed it at the building and ran. The heat from the fireball was so hot on my back it felt like I had fallen asleep in a tanning booth. The gas can would melt in the inferno, leaving no trace. By the time I got to Matilda, night had turned into daylight. It reminded me of a firefight at night with the flares hanging in the sky like falling stars. If anybody saw me driving away, I doubted they would tell the police. Even in bad neighborhoods, topless bars aren't a source of pride. That is, unless your wife works there. Several blocks away I stopped and waited for the blare of the fire truck sirens. It didn't take long. When they drew close, I made my way to The Pussy Cat Retreat II. Within five minutes, it also, was a ball of flame.

"Mr. Moralis won't like this," my Guardian Angel said.

"Nobody gets everything they like," I replied.

True to her word, Lisa was waiting up for me. I was too tired to discuss what I had been up to. She was little Miss Sears and Roebuck and went off to bed happy that she was no longer alone.

I felt good. I had done a good deed for society. I wondered how many topless bars and pornography stores I could torch before I got caught. I know if I got caught, I would ask for a jury trial and my defense attorney would get as many women on the jury as he could. They might even award me damages for mental stress and blame the topless bars. It was their fault I had to burn them. If they wouldn't have been there, there wouldn't have been any temptation.

"What about 1st amendment rights, oh old ex-hippie?" my Guardian Angel asked.

"Life is a dichotomy," I said.

I jotted in my notebook. I had gained some interesting information tonight. I know certain things for fact. I have a cornerstone to begin my house of destruction.

Lisa was still in bed when I got up in the morning. I went to the pool and marveled once again at the expense of the tile floor. I took four laps in the pool in my birthday suit, dried off and went back to the house. I will have to start getting back in shape. I have been lazy in Iowa, not jogging or lifting weights. About the only thing I have been lifting are drink glasses.

"You could put more ice in your drinks," my Guardian Angel said.

Lisa was making orange juice. "Sit down, we have to talk, I told her."

She handed me a glass of orange juice and sat. For some reason, she reminded me of a canary sitting on its perch, chewing on sunflower seeds with the husks spilling out of the birdcage onto the floor. Maybe swimming does funny things to me. "When the kidnappers call, you're going to have to ask them what they want. Cry, do anything, but tell them you have no idea what they want."

"Why didn't you think of this before?" she asked me, suddenly she was a smart canary.

"I also need your help this morning."

She perked up like a teenager who found out his parents would be gone for a few days and were going to trust him to stay alone.

"I have to get into the Browne's house. As far as I know they're still not home. Their helper, Manuel, is. I want you to go over and keep him occupied while I break into the house."

"What do you mean by, keep him occupied?" she asked, giving me an, 'I don't just sleep with anyone look.'

I winked at her, but didn't bother to answer her question. I don't know many women that have any trouble keeping a man occupied, especially when they want to.

We ate a light breakfast of toast and jelly and more juice.

After eating, Lisa went upstairs. She came down after having changed clothes. What she was wearing wouldn't be called lewd, but it was on the high end of the provocative scale. The short pants were not quite respectable, but passable. The blouse was one of those kinds that ties in the middle and comes off in less time than it takes to put on. She was wearing a pair of sandals with a thong between the big toe and second toe.

"In the 14th century we called shoes like that belly slappers," my Guardian Angel said.

"Give me about twenty minutes," I'll try to keep him down by the corrals," Lisa told me.

Lisa reminded me of Cleopatra as she strutted confidently out of the house.

Twenty minutes later I made my way next door. Inside the gate, I cut toward the Browne's house, using the trees and bushes as cover. I didn't see anybody anywhere. I felt safer in the daytime than at night. During the day, I could see anybody coming up on me.

The house was easier to get into than I thought it would be. One window was not latched. The house had an unused smell to it, like it had been empty for more than a few weeks. There was a thick layer of dust on everything. If the Browne's were coming back, I would have thought they would still have had a maid keep the house clean - I doubt very seriously if Mrs. Browne cleans her own house.

Why I wanted in the house I really didn't know? It is another one of those things I do in hopes of falling, by accident, into the truth.

"When you fall you always hit your head," my Guardian Angel said.

The inside of the house dwarfs Lisa's. Each room was richly decorated with real paintings hanging on the walls. Downstairs, there were three living rooms, each with a fireplace. I figured these were used for entertaining. The kitchen was the size of a small house. The refrigerator was off and was empty. A calendar on the wall hadn't been turned from last month. There was no fresh food in the cupboards and very few canned goods. There wasn't even a bag of stale potato chips.

There were six bedrooms. I could find nothing of any interest. In the master bedroom there was a picture of the Browne's. They are a good looking couple, older, refined, and confident.

Going out the window I could hear Lisa laughing down by the corrals. I made it without incident back to Lisa's.

As I waited for Lisa to return, I have no doubt in my mind the Browne's will never come back to Des Moines. I also have no doubt they would never be found.

Lisa didn't come back to the house for another three hours. I didn't see any straw on her clothes. She threw her arms around my neck and kissed me like I was the last man on earth. She then went to her room, and came back wearing a blue bikini. "Let's go swimming," she said, not bothering to ask me if I had found anything at the Browne's.

"I'll be in charge of the lotion," my Guardian Angel grinned like he had just eaten the last meatball.

We sat by the pool with a cordless phone between us. "When was this pool built?" I asked Lisa, wondering why she wasn't interested in what I had found at the Browne's.

"It was all here when we moved in," Lisa replied. "But Sam put in the tiles all by himself."

I looked at the 500 or so tiles. "How about the potted plants?"

"We bought them from a greenhouse," she said and held up a bottle of sun tan oil for me to take.

I shook my head.

The phone rang.

"Phones annoy me," my Guardian Angel said trying to grab the bottle of lotion.

"Maybe it is Manuel thanking her for a lovely morning," I told him.

He scowled.

119

"You have to tell me what you want," Lisa said, sounding like she was about to cry.

Lisa listened for a few seconds and then hung up. I took note that whenever the kidnappers call, their calls are short enough there is never enough time, that if the calls were being monitored, they could be traced. "What did they say?" I asked.

"They'll let me know what they want," she said, but no longer like she was going to cry.

"Did they say how?"

"We'll get a special delivery letter tomorrow."

I went back to the house and called a friend of mine in El Paso, Texas. He had been a cop in Florida and was now a big shot in the Border Patrol. Done with catching illegal aliens, he sits in an air-conditioned office and drinks coffee all day. I only call him when I need something. And he owes me. I tailed his wife for a week and took pictures of her going into a house she rented with a man. The house had been easy to break into and plant a camera in the bedroom. It saved Melton about half his paycheck in alimony, when, after seeing the interesting pictures, his ex-wife decided she could take care of herself.

"Melton," I said.

That was all I had to say. "What do you want?" he asked dryly.

"I need a rundown on two people who went to Mexico. I have a feeling they might not be coming back."

"I wouldn't go to Mexico for all the drug money in the bank in Guatemala," Melton replied.

Take advice from people who know I have always believed. "Their names are Bill and Connie Browne," I said.

I gave Melton the phone number and hung up. There was no need to talk old times. What I knew about his ex-wife had done in our relationship. Man, reduced as he is in our society, still has pride, and somebody who has seen pictures of his wife with another man is not someone you keep close ties with.

It only took five minutes for Melton to call back. "What are you doing in Iowa?" he asked me.

"Eating sweet corn," I replied, "and trying to learn how to grow good tomatoes."

"Your two people went to Mexico a month ago. Their rented car was found last week on a side street in Nogales. There's been no report of them returning to the states."

"Thanks," I said. I knew there would never be a report of them coming back into the states, unless it was in body bags.

Lisa came in.

"Did you see anything unusual at the corrals?" I asked her.

"There are six stalls inside and three of them are locked is about all."

"I wonder why people would lock empty horse stalls." I said more to myself than Lisa.

"Manuel seemed nervous too," Lisa went on.

I knew what I would have to do tonight. "I'm going over tonight and break into the corrals," I told Lisa.

She seemed frightened, but said, "What for?"

"I'm bored," I lied.

"You think bored, live in my sandals," my Guardian Angel said. "Morals, looking for love, what can be more boring?"

I went to my room and put on an old pair of Levi's, a black T-shirt, and my tennis shoes. I wrote in my notebook.

"The writing is all good and all," my Guardian Angel said. "But I think you should consider doing some rewrites."

When I went back to the kitchen, Lisa had just hung up the phone. She smiled at me in such a way a jolt of fear shot through my chest. "Careful is what careful does," my Guardian Angel said.

Lisa had made me a tuna fish sandwich. I ate it slowly. I don't know why, but I felt like it might be my last meal.

"It's a lousy meal to go out on," my Guardian Angel said, "at least Jesus had wine."

CHAPTER TEN
MONEY MONEY EVERYWHERE

With a few hours to kill before I was going to sneak over to the corrals at the Browne's, I took out of my suitcase and put the kidnap notes, the key to the tennis court, the card with C'est La Vie Mother Goose on it, and my notebook on the bed. Lisa gave me the shoebox the kidnappers, or whoever they were had left and also a photograph of Sam.

I set out the ring, the hair, and the gold necklace next to the other things. I opened the kidnap notes so I could read them. I moved the objects around until they were divided into two separate groups. I set the photograph of Sam in between the two displays. I have all the pieces to the puzzle, now I have to figure out what it is a picture of.

"You're really fishing for straws," my Guardian Angel commented dryly.

"You're not being much help," I countered.

"I'm not the famous private detective. I'm only a mere Guardian Angel whose advice is seldom taken," he said looking hurt.

"Don't give me that pious junk," I told him.

He looked insulted but sometimes people and Guardian Angels have to be insulted.

I gazed at all the objects, but after twenty minutes I had to admit my Guardian Angel was right - no revelation jumped out at me. I put the key to the tennis court in my pocket and everything else back into my suitcase, took out a penlight, and locked the suitcase.

It was 9 o'clock and still too early, but I was ready to go sneak around the Browne's.

At 10, I was restless. By 11, I felt like a businessman on an important trip whose plane had been snowbound in Chicago and he was going to have to sleep in the airport.

At 11:30 we received the special delivery letter, early. Lisa was putting on nail polish and I was pacing around the kitchen when the rock came through the window. Lisa jumped and screamed. I didn't run outdoors. I had been bushwhacked once. I ran to my room to get my pistol, remembered I had given it to Lisa, and ran back. Lisa was standing in the middle of the kitchen, with my pistol in both of her hands, with the hammer pulled back, aiming at the door. I took the pistol from her shaking hands, in my mind I could see her pulling the trigger and Lisa and I doing a Mexican hat dance trying to dodge the ricocheting bullet.

I lay the pistol on the table and picked up the rock. If anybody was going to crash through the door they would have already made their entrance. A note was tied to the rock. Typed on 20-pound bond paper it stated - THERE IS A MILLION IN CASH THAT IS MINE. I WANT IT. I WILL GET IT. FIND IT SOON OR THE KIDS WILL DIE.

When Sam stole, he didn't steal pocket change.

My Guardian Angel whistled.

Lisa, after reading the note, almost fainted. I helped her to her bed and put the pistol on the bedside table. "Are you sure you don't want to call the police?" I asked her.

She shook her head.

"Are you sure she almost fainted?" my Guardian Angel asked.

"I am not sure of anything," I answered and went back to my room.

I put the rock and the message inside my suitcase.

"Getting into your suitcase is becoming a regular ritual thing." my Guardian Angel said.

"Sam, you idiot," I said. "You should have known better than to steal money from gangsters."

"What if Sam didn't steal any money?" my Guardian Angel asked.

The 'what if' rang in my ear like my Guardian Angel had slapped me.

"What if Sheila and Lisa are in cahoots and are just using you?" my Guardian Angel asked rubbing his chin like he was Sherlock.

I didn't like the question. But it was a good question.

I went to the kitchen and swept the glass off the floor. Taking three carrots out of the refrigerator I broke them into small pieces and put them in my pocket.

Outside, the moon was waning and I couldn't see my shadow as I headed toward the corrals.

"I could tell you, you might get killed doing this," my Guardian Angel said. "But I suppose it would be a waste of time."

"It would be."

I made my way to the chain link fence and followed it to where I knew it would get me close to the corrals. I stopped and waited quietly for a few minutes. I didn't hear any unusual noises around me. I climbed the fence as quietly as possible, with as much ease as a middle aged man can, but going over the top I slipped and landed with a thud that, in my ears, sounded like Mt. St. Helens blowing her top.

"Good job graceful one," my Guardian Angel said but with a tone in his voice that he had enjoyed watching me fall down.

Rolling away from where I had fallen I hid behind a tree. I could hear the horses stirring, but there was no other noise. I continued on until I saw the lights from Manuel's house. Through a window I could see him sitting in a chair and watching TV.

I made my way to the corrals. A horse stirred as I walked into his paddock. "Good boy," I whispered, holding out a piece carrot.

He snorted nervously, but smelled the carrot and took it. I stroked his forehead and listened to his contented chomps. The other two horses, knowing they were missing out on something, came out of their stalls into the paddocks. I gave them each a carrot. For thoroughbreds, they weren't jumpy at all. Most thoroughbreds are as high strung as a fifth grade music teacher.

I didn't try to go through the door to the horse shed, but slipped in with one of the horses. Like most horse stalls, it had a double door where one could leave the bottom shut but the top open or the other way around. I opened the bottom door, stepped into the run, shut the door, and moved quickly to the far end of the horse barn and knelt down.

I didn't hear anything and made my way along one wall until my hands slid across a door. I touched two padlocks - one for the bottom door and one for the top. They were, to my luck, combination locks. It takes a soft touch to open them without the combination, but I am good at it. It took me five minutes to unlock the lock on the top door. The top door swung open on hinges that hadn't been oiled since the crusades. A horse snorted and pawed the ground.

I crawled over the top of the bottom door and moved around the room slowly. I didn't want to turn on my penlight. The stall was as dark as a cave a bat would love. There was nothing in the stall. I went back over the bottom door, locked the top door and moved to the next one.

It took me longer to open the lock. My hands were sweating and my breathing sounded like a moose trying to be quiet in church. I finally opened the lock. The stall contained saddles, bridles, and a few tools. As I fumbled around, I knocked over an aluminum shovel.

"A good burglar you're not," my Guardian Angel said.

124

The shovel was so loud I went over the door as fast as I could, locked it, and stood by one of the stall doors that a horse was in hoping Manuel had not heard me.

The silence was deafening, all I could hear was the deep even breathing of the horses. After a few minutes, and satisfied Manuel was not coming, I found the last locked stall. It took me even longer to open the lock but I finally succeeded. I slid over the top of the bottom door. The stall was filled with hay bales. Manuel must have thought they were baled gold to keep them in a locked room. Sliding one of the bales over I reached under it and felt wood, I ran my hand over the wood and traced the outline of a box. Moving other hay bales, I discovered 10 boxes, each about 3 feet long and a foot and a half wide. I took the penlight out of my pocket and cupping my hand around it, turned it on. Stenciled on the boxes in black letters was – 'M-16, ARMY ISSUE - 1 DOZEN.' Manuel wasn't stocking up on M-16's to hunt deer.

"Sam's reputation is going down hill fast," my Guardian Angel said.

After moving all the hay bales back I crawled out of the stall, locked the door and made my way back outside, feeding the last of my carrots to a horse.

Standing by the wall to the horse barn Manuel's TV was still on but the lights were off.

I made my way until I hit the chain link fence and followed it until I got to the rear of the Browne's tennis court. I went around the tennis court until I came to the gate, took the key out of my pocket - it unlocked the gate.

Why would both tennis courts have identical keys if there is no tunnel? But, why would there be a tunnel if the guns were stored in the horse barn? What is this tunnel thing I am hung up on anyway?

"All you old hippies always got hung up on something trivial," my Guardian Angel said, giving me a look like old hippies were lower than diaper rash.

I moved quickly around the inside of the tennis court, listening for a hollow sound. The only hollow sound was my head. I had just locked the tennis court when a car turned into the driveway. "Dive, dive," my Guardian Angel yelled.

The car headlights barely missed me as I dove behind a tree. I saw the darkened figures of two men. One of them was smoking a cigarette.

I recognized the two men from the funeral as they got out of a new Cadillac. The man-riding shotgun had to be Moralis. They went inside the house without knocking.

Making my way quickly I went around the Browne's house, through the trees, to the back of Manuel's house. "Not a good idea old peeping tom," my Guardian Angel warned.

I sat with my back against the wall underneath Manuel's window. The window was partially open, and the curtains were not closed. I could hear men arguing, but I couldn't make out what they were saying. I also couldn't take the chance and try and peek in the window. If I did, it would be a stupid imitation of a pop up target at a carnival and the prize wouldn't be a cheap stuffed animal.

The men seemed to have resolved their disagreement because I heard laughter. I was about to give up on my vigil when the phone rang. I could make out Manuel's voice when he answered it, but that was all. He hung up and I heard the men walk out of the house and shut the door. Creeping to the corner of the house, I watched one of the men drive the Cadillac over by the horse barn without turning on the headlights. The three men stood by the sliding door to the barn and talked in hushed whispers. About ten minutes later a delivery van pulled into the driveway and parked by the horse barn. I couldn't make out what was painted on the side. The men loaded the M-16 cases quickly into the truck. As soon as the truck was loaded, the driver drove off. He didn't want to sit around and ask how everybody's family was or where they were planning on going on vacation.

I could no longer see Manuel, but the other two men were standing by the car. I was so intent on trying to hear what they were saying that I didn't hear the person come up behind me until a twig snapped.

"Oh, oh, I was napping," my Guardian Angel said with about as much guilt as a twelve year old boy who had been watching his older sister make out with her boyfriend.

I fell flat against the ground and rolled to my right. A slug from a silencer equipped pistol slammed into the ground right next to me. I kicked out, catching the man in the knee and he stumbled. In that one second, with him thrown off balance, I jumped to my feet and ran. Everything happened so quickly I was not able to see what the man looked like. My attacker hollered for help. I darted to my right. I saw little flashes of fire, heard no noise until the bullets hissed by my head like a convention of mad hornets.

126

I cut toward the river. Two slugs zapped into trees around me. The men didn't holler to each other, but they were getting close. When I got to the river, I dove in and started swimming for all my might. Bullets zipped into the river around me. I dove under the dark, muddy water.

The current was stronger than I thought it would be and the water colder. I swam, in God knows what direction, until I thought my lungs would burst, and shot out of the water gasping for air.

Treading water I spun around in circles. The river had carried me a lot further than I thought it would. I let it take me and after what I figured was over a mile I swam to the opposite shore. Crawling up on the bank, I felt like a seal that instead of flippers had feet. Looking at my watch it had stopped running. I took it off and tossed it in the river. They don't make cheap watches like they used to.

"Sorry Roosevelt," my Guardian Angel said, but not sounding as sorry as he should be.

"You miss one more time and God and I are going to have a talk," I warned him.

"God wouldn't talk to you if you were the last men alive on earth," he retorted.

"Are you sure?"

There was no answer. He wasn't sure.

Cleaning myself up as much as possible I made it to a street.

The street was as deserted as a Stephen King novel, but miraculously a cab rounded a corner. I took a twenty out of my pocket and began waving it. If it was New York the driver would have gone by me like I was his mother-in-law, but since this was Des Moines, he stopped, looked at me and said. "Mister, you don't go swimming with your clothes on."

Luckily, he didn't want to talk as he drove. He let me off a block from Lisa's house and I gave him the twenty and tipped him ten more. "Anytime you want to go swimming at night you let me know," he said with a smile.

I went to the house and tip toed into Lisa's room. She looked like Sleeping Beauty after she had eaten the whole apple.

After taking a shower, I went to the kitchen and made myself a gin and tonic - it was almost 5 in the morning. Time flies when you're getting shot at.

I then went to bed and slept until ten. Lisa was outside pulling a few weeds out of the flowerbeds. She had on a special outfit for gardening, green shorts, a green blouse with yellow flowers on it, matching cotton gloves and was wearing a wide floppy brimmed woven hat. "I'm going to sell this house and I don't want it to start looking sloppy," she told me, tossing a dandelion into a paper sack.

I wondered how she could go from worried to normal so quickly.

I told her the whole story of my evening, including finding the guns in the horse stall.

"It's hard to believe Sam would get mixed up with people like that," was all she said and went back to weeding.

"Weeding is a very important thing in modern America," my Guardian Angel said.

"I think the money the kidnappers want is hidden around this house," I told Lisa. "We had better start looking for it."

"I have a question for you, Roosevelt," my Guardian Angel said. "Why did the fantasy kidnappers wait so long to tell you what they wanted?"

"I don't have the faintest idea," I replied.

"I didn't think you did," he said.

"Then why ask?" I said.

"Stupidity is a subject I am trying to get a handle on," he said with a big grin.

Lisa and I spent the next four hours searching the property. I tapped and examined closely every tile in the swimming pool, none of them would move, and all the mortar matched. I poked into every potted plant with a stick. I walked over every inch of the property looking for a place where the money could have been buried, dug where I saw a dead blade of grass, or anything that could have been construed to be disturbed ground and found nothing. I climbed up trees. We went all over the house - took the back off of the TV, undid frozen meat, looked under the refrigerator. I tapped walls and the backs of closets. I took off heat duct panels and peered into them. If Lisa would have had a breadbox, I would have searched it. We even searched all the cars, by search I mean search - took off the door panels, and bounced the tires for uneven weight. When we were done, we both felt like we had taken a cram course in searching from an F.B.I. SWAT team. But we had flunked, we hadn't found a thing - we had been swatted.

We were sitting in the kitchen, drinking a glass of instant iced tea when I had an idea. "I won't be gone long," I told Lisa. "If the kidnappers call ask them to come over and look for the money."

"Is this another one of your useless ideas, or does this one mean anything?" my Guardian Angel asked.

"You who have been slipping in his duties had better get a better attitude," I told him.

"I'll work on it, but it's tough," he said.

Neither remorse nor guilt bothers my Guardian Angel too much.

I drove to the Small Business Bureau. Like most city agencies, the lady working at the front desk was hired because she was naturally rude. "You will be called," the lady told me in a dull monotone.

I don't know why I have to be called, because four of the six people sitting at desks behind her weren't working - unless looking around is considered working.

After about twenty minutes, my name was called and I was directed to a metal desk where the sister to Miss Rude worked. She didn't smile. I sat in a metal folding chair. I felt like I was about to get booked into jail. "Yes," she said with as much enthusiasm as it takes to blow my nose.

"I need to know the name of the person who owns a restaurant called Greasy Ed's. I'm going to file a lawsuit."

She tapped away on her computer for a few minutes. I take it she couldn't spell greasy or Ed's.

Finally she wrote something on one of those little yellow pads with glue on the back of each sheet, the ones that only stick to the refrigerator for about three minutes, and handed it to me like she was handing me the keys to the city. "Good luck," she said.

I didn't look at it until I was outside. Have you ever read a book that has a sex scene so disgusting in it you have to read it again? My throat went dry and my ears started to ring.

"This is not good," my Guardian Angel said.

Alisa Wrench, glared back at me from the little yellow piece of paper like it was written with radium.

I felt like a dill pickle that as a child had been promised he would grow up to be a sweet pickle.

I drove to Greasy Ed's and it wasn't for the chili. The sign has been freshly painted. The interior was clean and the posters of scantly dressed women were gone, replaced by country prints. The tables had new red plastic table clothes, each with their own salt and peppershakers and a bottle of Tabasco. Harold was standing behind the counter talking to three black men who were eating fried chicken.

"Hey," Harold said to the three men with a big smile, "This is the guy who gave me the free chili and beer. Sit down, dinners on me."

I sat at the counter and the three men looked at me like I must be lost. "Ease up," Harold told them. "He's ok."

With Harold's words, they half smiled at me letting me know it was ok to sit at the counter, but only once.

Harold brought me two pieces of fried chicken, a leg and a breast, with a side of slaw. He poured me a draw. The chicken was delicious, the slaw superb, and the draw, ice cold.

Harold looked at me and said, "Man, old Greasy Ed getting blown away has sure been good for me. Little lady who owns this place gave me the job and told me to fix it up the way I wanted."

"Lady is cute, short, dark hair," I was about to go on but Harold cut in.

"For a white girl, she's hot," he smiled at me rolling his eyes toward the ceiling.

The three men laughed.

I finished eating and reached in my pocket for some money. "No, no, foods on me. You were like the reaper that brought me good luck," Harold said.

I tossed a ten on the counter. "Buy these guys a beer then."

As I walked out, I heard one of the men say, "Nice enough guy for a honkey."

"Is a honkey related to a donkey?" my Guardian Angel asked.

"Almost," I replied.

I sat on the bench outside the cafe. It had also been painted. I thought to myself. Self, you could have stayed a hippie. You could have found you an earthy girl who liked to can and weave. You could have had five kids that would run around and not need haircuts or shoes. You could have eaten whole grains and fruits until you were so healthy your body would drop dead from too many vitamins. Your lady wouldn't gripe if you didn't have a job as long as you weeded the garden. You could have picked up pocket change by growing organic vegetables, never paid taxes, never shaved at all or cut your hair. God, I thought, where did I go wrong?

"Life is all decisions, and you have been short on the right ones," my Guardian Angel said.

While I drove back to Lisa's I wondered why she would volunteer to give up her insurance money. I suppose she still has the house. I figured the house would sell for at least $700,000. The way things were going I can't see anybody in this whole scenario that wasn't going to benefit. I am going to have to go back to crime solving 101. I am missing something that has to be obvious. I also have to get my priorities straight - am I trying to solve a murder, solve a kidnapping that is, or is not, a kidnapping, both, or subconsciously, am I trying to find meaning in my life by doing everything backwards? Or, am I getting so confused by having to word my conversations with everybody to make them think I think they are telling me the truth, that now, I am lying to myself and can no longer discern what the truth is?

"Roosevelt, that was one good thought, and even though confusing, it makes sense," my Guardian Angel said seemingly impressed.

"Thanks, it's about time you gave me a compliment."

"Don't let it go to your head."

Going up the steps to the kitchen door I still felt I know a few things even if they don't have a pattern.

"A pattern to you is a tie dyed shirt," my Guardian Angel said.

Lisa was sitting at the kitchen table, her arms were wrapped around her, her knees were crossed and she was bouncing her foot a mile a minute. She looked like she had gulped six cups of espresso.

As soon as I shut the door she blasted out of the chair like the first cannonball fired at Fort Sumter. She started jumping up and down like a high school cheerleader at a basketball game. "Roosevelt, Roosevelt, Roosevelt," she said over and over again.

Grabbing my hand she pulled me upstairs to her room. I felt like a little boy being potty trained and had said number 2 for the first time. Locking the door behind us, she got down on her knees and from underneath the bed pulled out a black plastic bag and set it on the bed. She stepped back and pointed at it and once again started jumping up and down.

I opened the bag - "Lord, Lord," is all I could say.

"I'll be," my Guardian Angel said, starting to jump up and down. "Let's go to the islands, forget the kids, forget Sam."

I turned the bag upside down and watched the stacks of money fall out. I had no doubt there was one million big ones. "Where did you find it?" I asked, looking at the pile of money and wishing I was a crook.

"When you left, I went back outside to weed. I remembered Sam planting a bush a few weeks ago. It had completely slipped my mind. He

131

planted a bush and put that bark stuff around it. Well, there were a few weeds popping through. One of them had a big old root. But I was determined and when I got to the bottom of the root, I saw black plastic."

"The old buried under the bush bit," I said. I didn't say, you dizzy idiot, how could you forget him planting a bush when we were looking for the money?

"Maybe she did not forget," my Guardian Angel said with a sly smile.

"Roosevelt, we have to celebrate," Lisa said.

She put the money back in the sack and stuck it under the bed. I could think of no better place for it, except in the trunk of Matilda.

We went to the kitchen and Lisa got a bottle of champagne out of the refrigerator, Dom something. She poured us two glasses, set the bottle in ice between us, and we toasted.

Lisa looked as happy as a cowgirl who had just been elected Rodeo Queen and was sleeping with a champion bull rider. Her champagne tasted a lot better than the stuff I had bought for Sheila.

By the time we were finished with the bottle we were both laughing over stupid little things.

Suddenly Lisa turned into little miss sexpot. "Roosevelt, I want to put that money all over my bed and make love on it."

"What a great idea," my Guardian Angel said doing a little jig.

It did sound like fun, but, Sam, my old friend, his ex-wife, I couldn't.

"I'm sorry," I said to Lisa.

"You're not a good capitalist," my Guardian Angel said like a banker who had just been caught stealing points.

Lisa scowled at me and went to her room. Giving her gorgeous fanny a few shakes as she did.

"Oh, Roosevelt," my Guardian Angel cried. "You break my heart."

CHAPTER ELEVEN
TEDDY BEAR BREAK-IN

In the morning Lisa and I counted the money. She didn't seem to be bothered that I hadn't slept with her.

"She isn't, but I am," my Guardian Angel pouted.

Lechery can be a strange thing.

The money was all in 100's and in stacks of $10,000 so it was easy to count. We locked it in the trunk of the Mercedes. Now, all we had to do was wait for the kidnappers to call.

"Kidnappers who aren't kidnappers can't call. The proper thing to say is, we are waiting for the liars to call," my Guardian Angel said. "Plus, it might be kidnapper and not kidnappers."

"Is it at all possible to trade you for another Guardian Angel?" I asked him.

"You'd miss me. I am one of a kind."

Lisa was happy, but I suppose finding a million bucks is a mood elevator. Even if she has to give it back she is rich for a little while.

"Don't you think we should call Sheila and have her come over? She'll really be relieved at the news," I said to Lisa.

"I don't want her around," Lisa said. "When we get the kids we'll take them over to her. It'll be a surprise."

"When the kidnappers call back, you tell them I'll talk to them," I told Lisa.

"Do you think that's a good idea?" she asked me, but not in a tone like it worried her, but more like it bothered her.

"I can handle it."

"I forgot that one kidnapping case made you famous."

"Famous, famous for what? Being a fool," my Guardian Angel scoffed.

He was right. If I was really famous I would not be making $100 a day it would be $1,000 a day and no less, plus expenses.

"I have to be gone for a while. Do you think you can handle it here with all the money?" I asked Lisa.

"I'll lock the gate. When you're about to come back, call and I'll open it," she said, not a least bit nervous.

"Roosevelt, if she is not an undercover cop," my Guardian Angel said, "I will become as moral as you."

"Don't ever mention her being an undercover cop to me again," I said, slightly agitated.

He shrugged his shoulder in a way that let me know he thought I was an idiot.

As I drove away Lisa shut Eric the Red. I hoped Sheila wouldn't be home.

I stopped at a store and bought a box of dog treats.

My luck holding, Sheila's car wasn't in the driveway. The man who had been mowing his yard the first time I went to Sheila's was again at it. If people didn't have to mow yards in the Midwest there would be enough gas reserves to last an extra hundred years.

I parked in the driveway and waved at him. He waved back.

The back door was locked but, like most houses, a rear window was cracked. I was in the house as quick as a fly at a barbecue. I had two dog biscuits in my hand, but surprisingly, the dogs didn't greet me with a chorus of yips. I was playing one of my long shot hunches again - it only takes hitting one to make all the effort worth it. I went to the phone in the kitchen with the note pad by it. Scribbled on the note pad were three numbers with out of state area codes. I wrote them down.

I went to the bedroom and opened the drawer to a bedside table that had a phone on it. There was a sheet of typing paper with three numbers on it, also with out of state area codes. I quickly wrote them down. "Yapper attack," my Guardian Angel warned.

I started back for the window when the two little dogs darted from the basement, each one grabbing a pant leg. They growled and twisted their heads like they thought they were bulldogs. I held the dog treats down to them but they liked my pants legs better. I made it to the window with the dogs attached to me like Lampreys to a Lake Erie trout. By the window, I bent down, looked at both of the beady-eyed little Tasmanian devils and barked as loud as I could. They let go of my pant legs as if my pants were made from cat food and darted into the living room like I was going to bite their heads off.

My Guardian Angel laughed.

As I was about to go out the window I thought I heard a noise in the basement, but I decided it would be better to leave while the getting was good. I was getting into Matilda when the man across the street shut off his mower and came over. "I haven't seen Sheila in two days," he said, looking at Matilda fondly.

He was in his late 60's, a short, plump guy, bald, with a round happy smile. I could see him and his wife taking care of the grand kids every weekend and loving every minute of it.

"It's not normal for her to be gone and not tell somebody. My wife normally feeds the dogs when she is gone," he said.

I could tell he was genuinely concerned.

"She was supposed to meet me," I told him, knowing that any minute Sheila would drive in and he would spill the beans that he had seen me go to the backyard.

"I've seen you here before," he said. "This old car is hard to miss. You want to sell it."

"Matilda isn't for sale, she and I have been through a lot of good times," I told him, while patting the top of the car like Matilda would roll over and let me pat her stomach.

I got into Matilda, trying not to be rude, but after breaking into someone's house it wasn't really the time to chitchat. "When you see Sheila tell her I came by," I said, and started the engine.

I backed out of the driveway and waved at the man as I drove away. He waved back, wishing I would have sold him the car. He probably had a grandchild in college, or he wanted to take Matilda's body off the frame and put it over his lawn mower.

I drove to Sheila's store. It was early afternoon but the store was closed.

I sat in front of the store for twenty minutes feeling tense and ill at ease. Finally I couldn't take it anymore and drove back to Sheila's.

Going by Sheila's house the living room curtain moved. There was still no car in the driveway.

I drove around the block and then parked in Sheila's driveway. The neighbor was not outside. I saw smoke coming from his backyard from a freshly lit barbecue.

I went to the front door and rang the doorbell. The two dogs started to bark like they were going to tear apart a goldfish. I suppose they only bark when the doorbell rings and not when somebody breaks in. I rang the bell one more time and the dogs stopped barking like somebody inside the house was making them be quiet.

I went back to the car and wished the neighbor would invite me over for a barbecued T-bone. Two blocks from the house, I turned around once again. When I drove by the house the curtain moved again.

"Do you think the house is haunted?" my Guardian Angel asked.

135

"Haunted by treachery," I said.

I stopped at a drug store about a mile away and bought a six-dollar watch with an authentic plastic band. It was guaranteed to last longer than a Rolex and run under water up to a depth of ten feet. I called Lisa from a pay phone next to the store and after I hung up I wrote down the pay phone number.

Lisa was waiting for me by the gate. She locked the gate behind me. I waited for her and she got in Matilda for the short ride up the driveway. "This is a funny little car," she told me. She reminded me of a college coed who would find it interesting to try and do it in the front seat of a Volkswagen - something to reminisce about when she was 80 and slightly tipsy on bourbon.

Lisa was as chipper as a robin with two lovers. She busied herself around the kitchen making sandwiches - the kind with the crust cut off the bread. She served the sandwiches on one plate and handed me a napkin. I suppose anything served without silverware is called finger food. "I really admire how you've gone through all of this," I told Lisa. "Sam getting killed, the kids kidnapped, some people would have cracked up and not been able to function."

"I don't care what you say, she is an undercover cop," my Guardian Angel said.

Why is it that my Guardian Angels cannot get off his high horse especially after I told him to never bring up the subject again?

Lisa nibbled on her sandwich like a not too hungry chipmunk and said, "My father always told me one had to flow with the punches. Live day to day. I've always done that. There's nothing one can do about what happens in life except get up in the morning and go on."

I was impressed. She sounded like an old infantry trooper. "Tell me some things about Sam's son, Rick," I said, it seemed like a good finger food topic.

"He's a good boy. The normal 14 year old, " Lisa started, seemingly relaxed. "Last year he hated girls and now all he wants to do is look at Playboys." She laughed a pleasant knowing laugh. "He keeps one under his bed."

"How does he do in school?"

"He's not a great student, but good enough. He does have problems getting along with kids, but he isn't a sissy."

"How about Kathy?" I asked. By now I had eaten 5 sandwiches, finger food doesn't go far.

136

"Kathy is well adjusted and outgoing. Put her in a room with anybody and she will get right in on the conversation. She is like a furry rabbit, everybody wants to pick her up and say how cute she is."

Lisa's little chipmunk mood changed slightly. "Now Margaret is different. She never really came to grips with the divorce. She and her mother were very close and I think she resented me. At times she can be sullen and moody. Sam went out of his way for her but it was as though she hated him for leaving Sheila. She very seldom stayed here but preferred to stay with Sheila. The only thing she is really interested in is competitive shooting. She got a lot of awards."

"The two rifles in Rick's room aren't his, are they?" I asked.

"No, those are Margaret's, Rick cleaned them for her."

"Interesting," my Guardian Angel said raising his eyebrows.

"What do you think of the kids?" I asked Lisa.

"The kids were getting to the age they would be gone soon and I could handle it."

"I wouldn't want to be a kid now, but I suppose each older generation has said that from the beginning of time," I said.

"You still are a kid, Roosevelt. That is one of your best features," my Guardian Angel said.

Lisa cleared away the table. I thought back to the first time I had talked to Lisa about the kids and how she told me Sheila had lost custody and that the kids were all well adjusted. I remembered my first visit with Sheila and her denial of losing custody. I thought about Sheila telling me they had gone to camp and they had called her, and Margaret running off with her boyfriend. I thought, and I thought, and I thought. I have heard a stupid man is a happy man. I am indeed stupid but I am not too happy.

"Happiness is purely a state of mind," my Guardian Angel said.

"I can argue that, but I don't have the time," I said.

When Lisa finished cleaning the table I asked her for a photograph of each of the kids. She brought me three school photographs that sell for about as much money as it takes to set up a photography studio. I went to my room, taking the cordless phone with me.

"You could get a cell phone," my Guardian Angel said.

"Cell phone conversations are by law public transmissions and the government does not need a court order to tap them," I said.

"You are not a crook. What does it matter?"

"Governments can change. Don't ever forget that."

In my room, I took out all the collected puzzle pieces from my suitcase. I set them out once again in two piles and put the photographs of Sam and the kids between them. I then wrote on two separate sheets of my notebook paper, Sheila and Lisa. I tore the pages out and set them above the photographs and stepped back and looked at them.

If you have ever looked at a 3-D picture you know you are supposed to look with each eye straight ahead and then the pictures will mold into one. I un-focused my eyes and let the different parts of the puzzle swim around. To my surprise they all became clear, as clear as a Colorado trout stream in September - a stream that although pretty, is as polluted as the St. Lawrence River.

I took the phone numbers I had copied at Sheila's out of my pocket and looked at them like they held a truth I really don't want to know. Sometimes the truth is the thing we least want to know. Lies only deceive - truth hurts.

The first number I called was a toy outlet called Stuffed Treasures. Strike one.

The second number I called had been disconnected. Strike two.

The third number was another toy outlet called Teddy Bear Express. Strike three, batter out.

The fourth number I called had rung six or seven times and I was about to hang up when a man answered, "Lake Placid Music Camp, Carl speaking," he said as cheerfully as a man can, whose kid's parents keep calling at all hours to find out how little Mary or Johnny are doing and if they have taken their vitamins.

"Carl, I hate to bother you, but I was just wondering how Kathy Wrench is doing."

I received the answer I thought I would. Base hit.

The fifth call only rang twice. "Colorado Outward Bound," a crisp voice answered, the man had obviously been in the military, has a barrel chest, and arms that are so muscled he can't scratch the back of his head.

"You toughened up Rick Wrench yet?" I asked.

The man laughed like that was the stupidest thing he had ever heard. I knew he could make a squirrel tough. Once again I received the answer I expected - men on first and third, with one out.

On the sixth call, I once again was about to hang up when the phone was answered by a young woman. She sounded healthy, which I knew she was since she worked at a swimming camp. "I understand that a Margaret Wrench was in your camp and she ran away?"

The cute sounding little mermaid told me everything I wanted to hear. Home run, three runs score.

I rearranged the photographs and notes with a heavy heart. It was like I had hit a home run off of Nolan Ryan in his last major league game, running home I wanted to apologize and tell him it had to be an accident, but I also wanted the ball.

I looked at my puzzle one more time and put everything back in my suitcase. I went upstairs and knocked on Lisa's door. "Come in," she answered, like I was the bread and she was the jelly.

She was lying on top of her covers wearing a silk see-through black teddy and reading a book. She looked like a page out of Victoria's Secret. "Come to join me big boy," she smiled.

I smiled back. I like Lisa, she has her own way about her and I can't blame her for anything. "No, not tonight," I said like an apology.

"You're about as much fun as burnt toast," my Guardian Angel lamented.

Lisa didn't lose her smile. "Just looking, huh?"

"I came for my pistol."

She took the pistol out of her bedside drawer - handling it like she'd been born with a pistol in her hands. I took it. "Don't hurt yourself," she chided.

"You are one lovely creature," I said.

"I won't blow away," she told me as I left.

Back in my room, I took my pistol, broke it down and wiped off all the parts. I took all the bullets out of the clip and wiped them off. I don't want to leave any brass lying around with my fingerprints on it. I know, that soon, the 9 m.m. will see some action.

"If you would have gone to Colorado and gone fishing I guarantee you trout do not try to kill you," my Guardian Angel said.

"If I get killed, what will you do?" I asked him.

"Hopefully, God will assign me to someone who is not so moral," he replied.

"I hope he assigns you to a preacher," I said with a chuckle.

I didn't sleep well. I tossed and turned like the night before an operation in Nam, but I wasn't afraid. It was about 4 a.m. when I decided on a course of action and then fell into a deep sleep.

The phone rang at 6:30 and woke me up like a cannon going off next to my head. I picked it up as quietly as I could. "Do you have what I want?" a disguised female voice said, but didn't sound threatening at all.

"You're going to have to talk to Roosevelt," Lisa said in a tone that left no room for argument.

There was a pause as if the caller had been thrown off guard. "I'll call back in ten minutes. Have him answer." The caller hung up.

I was dressed before Lisa burst into my door. She hadn't bothered to put on a robe and looked like the angel of the morning in her black teddy. "I heard," I told her. "Why don't you get dressed and I'll meet you in the kitchen."

"Don't get dressed and meet us in the kitchen," my Guardian Angel said.

I didn't know Lisa could get dressed, put on lipstick, and comb her hair so quickly. When the phone rang, I let it ring five times before I picked it up.

"Roosevelt," the disguised voice said. "There had better not be any tricks."

"I won't talk on this phone. Call me in twenty minutes at this number. It's a pay phone. I advise you to call from a pay phone," I said in a voice like an Army sergeant who wouldn't take anything from anybody, including the colonel. I gave the person the number and hung up.

Lisa looked at me in shock. So much shock, she couldn't think of anything to say. "Trust me," I told her.

"Oh boy, we're in for it now," my Guardian Angel said shaking his head.

"You're coming with me," I told Lisa and grabbed her hand.

"But what about the money?" she protested.

"Nobody will steal it," I said, and pulled her out of the house, feeling like a biker telling his lady she had to work at a topless bar.

About to get into Matilda, Lisa looked at me as if I was an idiot. "Aren't you going to take your pistol?"

"Not this time," I answered her.

When the pay phone rang, I answered. "It's really a nice morning, isn't it?"

"Stick it, Roosevelt."

"No, you stick it," I said angrily. "Now you listen and listen good. I'm going to tell you how this all is going to go down. If you don't want to do it this way I'm going to take the money straight to the cops and tell them everything I know. I promise you."

The caller was thrown off guard and I pressed on. It's important that once you have the initiative to not let up. "I want Rick to be let go as a sign of good will. He'll be at his mother's house in no more than two hours. You'll then call me at this number at straight up noon. Not one minute before and not one minute after." I hung up the phone.

"I don't know what you are up to, Roosevelt, but I don't like it," my Guardian Angel said.

Back in the car I asked Lisa. "Are you hungry?"

She nodded.

We ate at a sawdust joint by Wavlin Golf Course. The inside walls were decorated with paintings of golfers. I had a large breakfast of sausage, bacon, hash browns, three eggs and choice of toast - it was called Double Bogey Murder. Lisa drank juice.

I ate everything and Lisa looked at me like I was some kind of animal to be eating at a time like this.

After breakfast I drove to Sheila's house. Her 1998 blue Taurus with the dent in the door was in the driveway.

"You stay put," I ordered Lisa as she was about to open her door.

"You won't sleep with her but you will order her around," my Guardian Angel said like he had written a book on how to handle women.

Lisa's hand moved away from the door handle like it was a bottle of cheap perfume.

I hadn't even knocked on the door when Sheila stepped out on the porch looking as if she didn't know if she was happy, sad, or disgusted. I looked deeply into her eyes, and asked. "Is he here?"

"Thank-you, Roosevelt," she suddenly sobbed, throwing her arms around my neck and hugging me like one of her stuffed toys.

"I'll be," my Guardian Angel said in surprise.

I let her hug me for a short while and then I stepped out of her embrace. "You have to stay here. I don't care how long it takes, or how nervous you get, don't go anywhere. Don't even use the phone. If I have to call, I don't want the line to be busy."

Sheila nodded her head like a dog watching his master eat popcorn.

"I want to see the boy for just a minute."

Sheila was about to protest but I walked by her and into the house. Rick was sitting on the sofa looking like the roughest thing he has been through lately was he was forced to eat a Wendy's.

He looked at me nervously, moved his tennis-shoed foot around in a circle, and grinned shyly.

I walked over and jostled his hair lightly. There was no need to bother the boy. Sheila watched me with her arms crossed in front of her stomach. Rick looked at her as if saying, what do I do Mom?

I left the house without saying anything more. "Rick is there," was all I told Lisa.

Lisa looked at me with a look on her face I couldn't read.

"Undercover cops are good at that," my Guardian Angel said.

Lisa and I drove around town killing time until noon like a young couple that had had a spat. Neither of us spoke or looked at each other.

At straight up noon the phone rang. "Roosevelt, it's your turn," the voice said.

"Listen, punk," I said. "It's my turn when I say it's my turn. You have one hour to have Kathy at her mother's house. Then you call me back at 3."

I hung up before the person could reply.

At 1:15 I drove back to Sheila's. This time I had to ring the doorbell, listen to the two dogs, and wait for the door to open. Sheila looked stressed out. "Is she ok?" is all I asked.

"Please save Margaret," Sheila begged.

"I'll be," my Guardian Angel said.

It's fun when I surprise him twice in one day.

I had a lot of things I wanted to tell Sheila but I kept my mouth shut.

"Kathy is there," I told Lisa, getting back in the car.

"You really are good at this," she said, like the words were forced.

"Before this is over you'll find out how good I am," I told her.

She leaned over and kissed me on the cheek. "This is fun," she beamed.

"About as much fun as cleaning fish," I told her.

We didn't have time for a sit down lunch so we gobbled down some taco's that tasted like ground up old shoes with ketchup on them. But, at least the price was right, six for a dollar, cheaper than I could have bought shoes at a Good Will store. If it would have been the late

142

60's, every vegetarian hippie in the town, when he needed a meat fix, would have eaten there.

The phone rang at exactly 3 o'clock.

Before the person could say anything I began. "You will have Margaret at the airport in two hours. She will be standing in front of the United Airways' terminal. I will drive into the parking lot and park where I can see her. I will be in a 1993 blue Mercedes. When I see Margaret I will then get out of the car, walk to Margaret, and she and I will go inside the terminal for exactly fifteen minutes. There will be a suitcase in the back seat with what you want."

I said everything slowly and deliberately, feeling like a star witness for the defense that had been rehearsed for three days on how not to make a glove fit.

"What did they say?" Lisa asked when I got back in the car.

"They said they wanted to trade you for Margaret until they had the money. I told them ok."

Lisa looked like she would faint. "Only joking," I laughed.

She punched me in the arm.

"That's a good one Roosevelt. I like that," my Guardian Angel laughed.

Lisa and I drove around and took in the sights for over an hour. After driving around in so many circles and U-turns I knew Lisa didn't know where we were I parked in a strip mall. "Show time Lisa. Let's get going."

I got out of the car and opened the door for Lisa. She looked confused, but didn't say anything.

We walked through a quiet residential neighborhood. The houses were neat and comfortable. A few people were walking their dogs and people were in their yards watering flowers or talking with their neighbor. "Where are we going?" Lisa finally asked.

I didn't answer her. There is a time for answers and a time to keep quiet.

"Where are we going?" Lisa asked again, sounding impatient, almost spoiled.

I still didn't answer her.

After another half a block, she asked me again. "Where are we going?"

"We are the surprise at a surprise party," I said.

"Shouldn't we have brought a present," she said.

143

"That's a good one," my Guardian Angel said.

After another two blocks we went down an alley. The alley was lined with garbage cans that reminded me of lonely old men bundled up in winter clothes.

Lisa and I were standing on the side of Sheila's house when the front door opened. When Sheila and Margaret were about to get in the Taurus I stepped out. "Now isn't this a nice family reunion," I said.

"Roosevelt, you are one sly monkey," my Guardian Angel smiled.

CHAPTER TWELVE
TKO

When Margaret saw me she screamed. Lisa screamed. Sheila screamed. It was a screaming contest and whoever screamed the loudest got a free trip to the throat doctor. "Watch out for Sheila," my Guardian Angel screamed - he hates to be left out.

Sheila was carrying a small handbag and started to swing it at my head. Out of reflex I punched her in the forehead with a short jab, but harder than I intended. She hit the ground, legs splayed out, arms outstretched like she was trying to make an angel in freshly fallen snow, stone cold out. "That wasn't very nice," my Guardian Angel said giving me a disapproving look.

"I didn't mean to cold-cock her," I said.

Margaret started to cry little girl tears and plopped down on the ground like her whole world had collapsed. I felt sad for her.

Lisa looked on in utter bewilderment and then bent over and looked at Sheila. "Good punch," she said to me.

In truth, it had been a good punch. I had never hit a woman before in my life, but I didn't feel overly guilty.

Lisa helped the crying Margaret to her feet and I bent over and helped up the now moaning Sheila. Inside the house, Rick and Kathy were sitting on the floor of the living room watching TV and didn't get up. They needed a dose of good manners.

By now Sheila was getting a small bump on her forehead. I helped her into one of the kitchen chairs and told the sobbing Margaret to sit in the living room.

Lisa looked at Sheila like she wished she had been the one to give her the goose egg. None-the-less, her feminine side came out and, playing Florence Nightingale, she wet a dishtowel and handed it to the now fully awake Sheila.

Sheila put the wet towel on her forehead and said, "Roosevelt, you'd mess up a ham sandwich."

"Roosevelt would forget the ham," my Guardian Angel said.

Lisa started to laugh. She laughed so hard her sides started to hurt. She held her sides and laughed, got the hiccups and still laughed.

I didn't think anything that happened was gut wrenching funny, but I didn't say a word. There is so little laughter in this world I hate to stop it when it occurs.

The TV in the living room started to bother me. I don't know why it is, but coming into a house and seeing kids' sitting in front of a TV has always bothered me. I can look at their young shiny faces, filled with life, and hope, and dreams, and when sitting in front of the boob tube I can see their brains running out of their ears and onto the floor. "Turn off the TV and go to your rooms," I ordered the kids.

Rick and Kathy looked at me to see if I was serious, and when they realized I was, they went to their rooms.

Margaret looked pleadingly at me and I could tell she wanted to tell me something. "Don't worry, hon," I told her tenderly. "Everything is going to be fine."

I saw a flicker of reassurance in her eyes and she smiled fleetingly at me before going to her room.

"See if there's anything to drink in the icebox," I told Lisa.

"Please," Lisa said. "You've really been pushy today."

"Please," I said, knowing I had been rude and crude, but it has been one of those 'men have to be men' sorts of days.

"Men have to be men, don't make me hurl," my Guardian Angel said sticking his finger down his throat.

Lisa put three beers on the table. I opened one and pushed it to Sheila. She grabbed it like it was the last bottle of water in Death Valley and drank half of it.

I took two large swallows and wish I had a case. I felt like drinking as many beers as I could and then passing out and dreaming about peanuts.

Lisa pulled a chair away from the table and sat. I looked at her. She looked at me. I looked at her some more. She looked at me. And then we both smiled. They were warm smiles. Smiles like two old lovers have for each other after they haven't heard from each other for years, and a phone call arranges a quick meeting at a bar. The bar is small and only has a few people in it. A piano player is playing sad songs and wondering why he never got his big break. The couple has a few drinks, feel close, and talk about their kids, avoiding conversation about wives and husbands. They discuss the circumstances that took their lives in different directions and when their time is up they kiss goodbye.

146

"You should try writing cheap romances," my Guardian Angel said. "People make fortunes with that kind of dribble."

My Guardian Angel has never read a touching novel - all he reads is trash and would not know what a good literary romance was.

Sheila broke my trance. "Roosevelt, how did you figure it out?" she demanded - one beer made her brave or it was the knot on her head.

"How did you figure it out?" Lisa asked.

"How did you figure it out?" my Guardian Angel asked, more perplexed than either Sheila or Lisa.

"Is there anymore beer?" I asked, wanting to keep them in suspense and savoring my thought of literary romances.

Lisa got me another beer and opened it. I always seem to talk better when I'm trying to get pie-eyed.

"At first I figured that whoever killed Sam also kidnapped the kids," I started. "I kept trying to put it all together but the more I tried, the more I got confused. It didn't make any sense that a kidnapper after money would kill the only guy who would know where the money was. So I decided there really was no stolen money. Sam had made a lot of money and hidden it and his murder was a separate crime. The first real clue I had that the kidnapping was a sham was when I came to see you the first time, Sheila. You were cooking a large pot of spaghetti sauce. People who are eating alone don't cook large pots of spaghetti sauce."

"Good, better than good," my Guardian Angel said.

"But, what really cemented it down was the fact the kidnappers knew who I was and the caller was female. Only five people in town know my name - two of them are now dead - the three remaining were Owens, Lisa, and you, Sheila."

"Impressive, Roosevelt," my Guardian Angel said with about as much conviction as a second string quarterback telling the starter he was doing a good job.

"Another tip was the notes on the twenty-pound typing paper. What I noticed in the ransom letters was that each letter said 'I', not 'we'. And whenever the kidnapper would call they always said 'I want', not 'we want'. It would be hard for one person to kidnap three kids and be able to watch them."

"That was my idea, don't forget," my Guardian Angel said.

He was trying to steal my thunder.

I looked at Sheila. "The first time I met you, you told me the children were away at camp and that Margaret had run off with her boyfriend. Lisa told me they were kidnapped. You had sent the first kidnap note and were trying to cover your tracks."

I took a sip of my beer. "The next time I met you, Sheila, you told me Sam had stolen some money, but in an earlier conversation you told me that Sam would never do anything that would harm his family, which is evident, he set up everybody he loved or had loved with enough insurance to be comfortable for the rest of their lives. I can't see Sam stealing money that would jeopardize anybody. I think he was holding money for people."

I tried to pick my next words carefully. I didn't want to see Sheila and Lisa rolling on the floor trying to scratch each other's eyes out. I always believe in fair fights and right now

Sheila wasn't at her best form. I looked at Sheila. "You told me that after Sam married Lisa he would still come over and see you. He knew his marriage to Lisa had been a mistake."

Lisa's eyes bulged out and she started to stand up. "Hold it, please," I said.

"Let her go," my Guardian Angel begged. "It will be better than ladies mud wrestling."

"Were you sleeping with Sam?" Lisa demanded, trying to imitate a Gestapo agent.

"Yes I was, you wife stealer," Sheila snarled as much as a person can snarl who has just recovered from being knocked out.

Lisa glared at Sheila, but she couldn't really say anything. The one time outside lady had been outsided by the lady she had one time outsided. Life is a karma nightmare when it comes to sex in America. Lisa then did the unexpected. She laughed and shook her head like she should have known all along and sat back down.

"Only an undercover cop would not be angry," my Guardian Angel said.

I went on with my story. "I figured then, Sheila, that you knew how much money Sam had hidden and Lisa knew nothing about it. I also figured Sam was really going to take the money and run off with you. Sam was making some big bucks and it wasn't from running 30 or 40 pounds of pot. It was from running guns and heroin."

Sheila chewed on her lip like a lady waiting for the cops after she has rear-ended a car full of nuns.

"You're smarter than you look," Sheila said.

148

"But then Sam was suddenly killed and you had to try and figure out a way to get the money. You didn't want Lisa to stumble onto it by accident and you not get a dime. So you came up with a hair brain idea that in your greedy little mind sounded good. You would fake having the kids kidnapped, call Lisa, and hope she would get so frantic she would find the money. You would make the switch and everything would be fine in Fairy Tale Land."

"Roosevelt, you old sly dog," my Guardian Angel said.

"So," I continued, "about the only thing that messed it up was, by complete accident, I show up as uninvited as a statewide outbreak of corn fungus."

Sheila was not a happy camper.

"You left the note on Matilda in front of the Pussy Cat II, didn't you?" I asked Sheila.

"It wasn't the tax man," Sheila snarled.

"She must have seen you inside, also," my Guardian Angel said which put a few questions in my mind I don't have any answers to, but I pushed them away for the time being.

"After Lisa found the money I broke into your house, Sheila, and wrote down phone numbers that you had by your phone. I heard a noise in your basement when I broke in and saw your curtain move when I drove by - it had to be your kids. When I called the phone numbers they happened to be to the camps the kids were at. I learned Rick and Kathy had been home for over a week. Margaret had never shown up.

Lisa took a deep breath. "Sam never told me the kid's were going to camp. I suppose since he was planning on running off with bimbo there was no need to tell me."

Sheila did not get upset over being called a bimbo.

"The night I went to the river and conversed with the mosquitoes, I figure it was you, Sheila, and an accomplice, who broke into the house. What with the masks on Lisa wouldn't have recognized you. Whoever the accomplice was and whoever hit me is still a mystery."

"I hit you," Sheila smiled like a pickpocket who boosted a billfold with $500 in it. "I was leaving and by chance I saw you walking along the fence."

"I knew it was someone shorter than me because the angle of the bat was up," I said, paused, and then grinned. "I guess now we're even."

"I should have killed you," Sheila sneered, not going along with the even idea. She no longer reminded me of an old fun loving hippie who had inhaled too much incense.

"Who helped you break in?" I asked.

For some reason Lisa flinched at the question.

"I won't tell you," Sheila said. I knew she wouldn't.

"I have no doubt you were trying to kill me when you shot at me the night I came over, Sheila. You just missed. When you told me you were trying to scare me away, I knew that was a crock. The bullet came too close to my head. I told you I could forgive you for that but Matilda, that's a different matter."

"I don't think Sheila shot at you," my Guardian Angel said, "or Lisa."

"Who could it have been?" I asked him.

"It's another mystery," he said.

There is always someone to rain on a parade.

"What are you going to do now?" Lisa asked.

"I could file charges on Sheila for shooting at me, but then I don't think I could prove it. I don't think there's a charge for trying to steal money that is illegal money, and I don't think there's a charge for saying you kidnapped your own children, although you didn't, for the purpose of extorting money that was illegal money. You could try to pin a case on Sheila for breaking into your house and destroying everything," I said.

Lisa shrugged her shoulders, like saying, what for.

Sheila, strangely, didn't look frightened.

"I can't see any good coming from getting hold of the police. I think we have all been through enough," I said.

Sheila didn't say thank you, you are kind, thanks for the break, nothing. Instead she proved to me that the old non-materialistic hippie days, were for her, long gone and forgotten. "What are you going to do with the money?" she asked.

Once someone gets bitten by the greed bug, it's hard to get rid of the virus.

"You keep it Roosevelt and let's you and I get out of here and go buy an island. If you owned an island you would have no trouble finding a woman," my Guardian Angel said, adding, "one that would not need many clothes."

"You and Lisa are going to help me do what I have wanted to do all along?" I said to Sheila.

150

And to my Guardian Angel I said. "I want a wife that loves me for me, not for what I have."

"You had better get a dog," he said, frowning.

"What have you always wanted to do?" Lisa and Sheila asked in unison. A million dollars can make allies out of any enemy.

"I'm going to catch the person who killed Sam and I'm going to make sure Moralis and his people don't see anything but concrete and steel for the rest of their lives," I said.

"God," Lisa said, "I almost forgot about Sam getting killed.

Greed is stronger than love.

Sheila's face showed a momentary flash of fear.

"You still haven't told me what you're going to do with the money?" Sheila said.

"Keep it Roosevelt. Keep it, don't buy an island, you and I can go to Tahiti and buy a grass house by the beach and lay around looking at near naked babes while you sip on exotic drinks," my Guardian Angel pleaded.

My Guardian Angel has a one-track mind.

Lisa didn't say anything but from the neck up she looked like a question mark.

"When it's all over you two can split the money minus my share," I said to Sheila and Lisa, like a million is only pocket change.

My Guardian Angel moaned, fell to his knees, and prayed to the money god.

If Lisa and Sheila had been basketball players, they would have high fived each other. With the cash and Sam's insurance they are fat cats. I can see Sheila buying a store the size of a Walmart, putting nothing but stuffed animals in it and using it as a front for an escort service.

I can see Lisa running around town all day trying on clothes. She would have the before breakfast outfit, the breakfast outfit, the after breakfast outfit, the brunch outfit, the after brunch outfit, the lunch outfit, on and on, until the before bed outfit, the bed outfit, and the when she couldn't sleep outfit.

I can't see either one of them single for long. I have noticed that not too many rich people are single. Money has a way of erasing many character flaws, especially when the character flaw says, "You want to get a job?"

"How about you? How much of the money is your share?" Lisa asked, giving me a don't be greedy look.

"You two can give me what you think is fair."

They both looked at each other and I could tell what was fair to them was to me lousy wages.

"When it comes to money you have a tendency to open your mouth before you think," my Guardian Angel said.

I stood. I was tired and wanted more to drink but not in Sheila's kitchen. "You rest up and I'll be in touch," I told Sheila. "And don't worry, I don't carry grudges."

Sheila didn't know what to say.

Lisa and I went out the back door.

"How about we buy a bottle of gin and get some tonic and limes and go to my house, get naked, and drink?" she asked me before we got to the car.

"I like you Lisa, but I've told you before, Sam was my friend."

"You are a nice man," she smiled.

"If I was alive you could get me naked," my Guardian Angel said to Lisa.

I stopped at a liquor store and bought gin and tonic and limes. Sitting in the kitchen over two tall drinks I felt empty, solving part of a crime at times is anticlimactic.

"Who do you think killed Sam?" Lisa asked me.

"I don't know," I lied. The truth being I didn't want to tell her who I think it was.

The rest of the evening we talked small talk until we both staggered off to our rooms. I was about to fall asleep when my Guardian Angel whispered. "You did a great job figuring out the fantasy kidnapping, Roosevelt, and don't get me wrong, I don't want to erode any of your glory, but, and this is a big but, there are two things you forget to consider."

"Oh wordy one, what?" I asked.

"You forgot to consider the fact that Lisa and Sheila were in communication all during the fantasy kidnapping and that Lisa lied to you more than once."

I felt like I had eaten about ten pounds of rocks.

"You also keep ignoring me when I tell you Lisa is an undercover cop."

I ignored him again.

I slept late in the morning and when I woke up I took a shower. I dressed slowly and got out my suitcase. Laying all my evidence out on the bed I tossed aside the key, the pictures of the kids, and the kidnap notes.

I placed the two pieces of paper with Sheila's and Lisa's names on them side by side, with the photo of Sam underneath them. I put the card with C'est La Vie Mother Goose over the top. I wrote on a sheet of paper, Moralis, and lay it down. I put a blank sheet of paper on the bed and wrote on the bottom of it, Greasy Ed. I took the key I had tossed aside and put it with my new pile.

I stepped back and looked at my new and revised pile. I saw the picture the puzzle made. I felt like a soldier with a little hippie girl standing in front of me as I stood at attention. I want to move, I want to do anything, but I couldn't as she stuck a flower in my rifle barrel.

I put my notebook in my pocket, picked up all the discarded information and went to the kitchen. Lisa was not in the kitchen as I threw the old stuff away.

My project, after I eat, was to thin out my notebook and then put in motion the plan that had taken shape in my head a few days ago. I can hear the voice that answered Manuel in the dark the night I stood by the fence. The voice doesn't belong to a vampire, but it would love my blood.

When Lisa came into the kitchen, I wished I had never known Sam. She had on white shorts, very short shorts, a white halter-top that hid nothing, and a smile. Virgin white on Lisa is like real whipping cream on a homemade pie. I want to howl but there was no moon.

My Guardian Angel howled for me.

"Did you make coffee?" Lisa asked.

My lips would not move so I shook my head.

When the coffee was done she brought me a cup, sat down, and looked at her cup of coffee like it would tell her future. When we had finished our first cup, she poured us another one. Caffeine was replacing the gin and I felt better.

Lisa was drinking her coffee and I was looking at my notebook when I suddenly had a thought. "You and I should hide the money in a place that's not so easy to find and if anything happens to either one of us the other one will know where it is," I told Lisa.

I've never in my life met a woman that won't guard her money. A man will give a woman every dime he has. All a woman has to do is smile and a man will throw his billfold at her yelling, "Take it all, it's yours."

"We should hide the money," Lisa agreed with me.

After two cups of coffee, Lisa bounced out of her chair like a Dallas Cowboy cheerleader who had been asked out by the tight end. Lisa got the keys to the Mercedes and we went to the garage.

Lisa put the key in the trunk lock while I tried to ignore the way her short pants fit. When I tore my eyes away and looked in the trunk I felt like a steamroller had rolled over my foot and it hurt so much I couldn't yell. The bag of money had done a Houdini and disappeared from the inside of a locked trunk.

"This isn't funny," my Guardian Angel said.

I felt like a frog that had played chicken with an Oldsmobile. An Oldsmobile doesn't feel a frog when it smashes it, and all the frog goes is rib...there is no rib it...rib it...rib it...

I looked at the trunk again. I looked at Lisa. Lisa's eyes were the size of saucers that had never seen the bottom of a cup. I did one of the stupidest things I could do and ran my hands over the inside of the empty trunk, like maybe the bag had just done a momentary disappearing act to scare me.

My mind started racing. There was no way Sheila could have taken the money.

Lisa. Who else but Lisa?

"You don't think I took it," she said, playing a perfect Harlow and reading my mind.

"Who else has the keys? Who else knew where it was?" I said, trying not to sound like a boxer who had just been hit with a low blow.

She looked at me like I was the skunk underneath the chicken house. "Me. You think I did it?" she replied, holding her hand to her chest like Scarlet O'Hara faking she would swoon, and adding, "You knew where it was? And I'm sure there aren't too many locks you can't pick."

"You're right about the locks, but I'm no thief," I said, but I knew I sounded guilty.

Lisa started to laugh. I thought everything was about as funny as getting shot. "You should see your face," she laughed harder. "You should have seen your face when you looked in that empty trunk," she laughed harder yet.

If she would have laughed harder she would have grown hair on her feet and turned into a hyena.

I wished I was a member of one of those remote tribes that live in the jungle, kills hyenas with blowguns, and cooks them on an open fire, hair and all.

"I hid the money again," she said, trying not to laugh so hard.

I wanted to grab her pretty little neck and shake her until her toenails fell off. Instead, I stood there unable to move my jaw to make a sound. I let relief overcome my anger and I chuckled kind of like a guy who has just lost his house and car on a poker hand.

My Guardian Angel was laughing so hard he was crying. "You really did look funny," he said.

I followed Lisa into the house and up to her room. "It's in the back of the TV," she said, pointing at the floor console.

I owe her one, and I swear I will get even.

"A man never gets even with a woman. They are always one step ahead," my Guardian Angel said like monks know all there is about women.

CHAPTER THIRTEEN
TO SPIN A WEB

When I got up in the morning I went over my notebook once again.

"This notebook thing you have is getting the better of you," my Guardian Angel said.

"Go back to sleep," I told him.

"You know I don't sleep," he said.

"Don't take everything so literal."

"Don't play mind games with me. Mind games are a twentieth century invention and I don't do well with them," he said.

I had to go through my notes as there is a lot of information I no longer needed - fake kidnapping ones own kids to try and get a million had been one thing, but, murder, guns, and heroin have a slightly nastier sting to them. And now, thanks to my Guardian Angel's good memory, I have to figure out why Lisa had been lying to me when she wasn't part of the fantasy kidnapping.

"It would be easier if everyone knew that people lied all the time then the truth wouldn't confuse the issue," my Guardian Angel said.

I didn't see Lisa all morning but shortly after two, dressed in a business like manner, she told me she was going to see her attorney. There were a few more papers to sign on the insurance. Within a few weeks, both she and Sheila would have more than enough money to not worry if the poor people ate cake - not counting the million minus my share.

Before Lisa left she kissed me on the side of the face like we were an old married people.

By 4 p.m. my notebook was done and I tossed my old pages in the trash. I now have 24 clues, but, I know some of them only have the remotest chance of meaning anything. I hope that at least half of my assumptions are based on the truth.

"If you are lucky, maybe ten percent," my Guardian Angel said.

I went to Lisa's bedroom, did my payback, and decided to go swimming.

I swam a few laps and bobbed up and down in the water for several minutes. I would hold my nose, sink to the bottom, let the air out of my lungs, and then come to the top.

When I was done playing six-year-old I sat on the edge of the pool and looked at the tiles Sam had set himself. I wondered why somebody would go through all the trouble and expense to tile around a swimming pool when he was planning on taking off with his ex-wife.

I walked around the pool and noticed for the first time the small windows just below the top of the pool cover. They hinged out for ventilation.

"Walking around blind is your style," my Guardian Angel said. "Plus, half the time you only see what you want."

I pulled a chair over to the vents and stood on it. I had a view of the driveway where Sam had been shot that any North Vietnamese sniper would have given his rice ration for.

"Lisa was wearing a bikini when she ran out after Sam was shot," my Guardian Angel said.

"My memory isn't that short," I replied.

I went back to my room and once again set all the clues I had out on the bed. I made a circle of all my puzzle pieces and put the address and phone number from Nogales in the middle. I know everything I can see is connected with Nogales except the murderer. There is still a lot about this case that smells worse than a can of cat food that had been out all day. After fifteen minutes, I could no longer take taxing my brain with different scenarios and went to the kitchen.

"Waking up in the morning taxes your brain," my Guardian Angel said.

I made myself a gin and tonic. Sipping the drink I realized Lisa always had booze and food around the house, but I had only seen her come into the house with groceries once - the mysteries of the modern woman.

"You know, Roosevelt. I don't want to sound like I am telling you what to do, but, I think you are drinking too much gin lately," my Guardian Angel said sounding like my Great Aunt.

"You are right. I'd better cut back," I agreed, Aunt's are always right.

I was pouring the drink down the drain when Lisa got back. She was happier than Bob Dylan after being told he could carry a tune. "I take it everything went well?" I said.

Lisa ignored me while she made herself a drink. But when she sat her smile was so big she could have rented it for a ski slope. "The attorney says it will only take a few more weeks to settle the money. In cases like this where it's a pure case of murder there is nothing to slow up the works."

"Murder can solve a lot of problems," I said.

"What do you think you are, a murder prophet?" my Guardian Angel said.

"Sheila will have full custody of the kids and when I sell the house I'll give each child a fourth. The attorneys are taking care of everything," Lisa beamed.

"That's nice of you," I said, truly impressed, but I wonder how much the attorneys are getting and looked to see if Lisa's skirt was rumpled or if there were any, "Ah yes, I can help you, you poor thing," paw prints on her blouse.

"I'll be so glad when this is over," Lisa said with a sigh, giving me a wry grin - becoming rich has its costs.

"If you were smart you would start courting her," my Guardian Angel said.

"Why? Because she is beautiful, sexy and rich," I asked him.

"Sounds like good reasons to me," he said, "even if she is an undercover cop."

Lisa held out her empty glass to me. I made her another drink. When I sat back down, Lisa looked at me in a strange way and I got a hint that I was becoming like a relative that has overstayed his welcome.

"You know, you have really been a big help, Roosevelt," Lisa said, running her finger up and down the glass and looking more at the glass than at me.

"You solved the kidnapping and you've helped me as much as anybody could."

"Time to pack your bag oh sleuth slayer," my Guardian Angel said.

"But now," she continued, hesitated, began again, "Now, Roosevelt, I think we should forget about everything and let the police see if they can find the murderer."

I was about to answer but Lisa got up and left the room. When she came back she handed me a medium sized manila envelope.

"It's not my birthday," I said. "The last time I got a present UPS delivered a wrong package. It was a shame because the shirt was too small."

"Open it anyway," Lisa said, like I was as funny as a flat tire on Monday morning.

In the envelope was a bundle of $100 bills and for a moment I felt like John Gotti before he died from cancer in the maximum security federal penitentiary.

"There's $5,000 there," Lisa said, like $5,000 would make me want to jump up and down on one leg for two days, which it did, but I kept my cool. I didn't want to ruin my image.

"What image?" my Guardian Angel said. "Take the money and let's boot scoot boogie out of this town."

"Is this my cut of the million?" I asked.

"No, that's a present from me to you," Lisa said.

I didn't say to Lisa, "No, that's too much." I said, "Thanks," and took the money and locked it in my suitcase.

"I don't think the police can solve this case," I told Lisa when I returned.

I could tell she was disappointed. "But I can with your help," I added.

"Roosevelt, I don't want to see you get hurt."

The mood in the kitchen was suddenly as dark as learning your mother in law was coming to stay for two months and is bringing her parakeet and her cat.

"I want to catch Sam's killer, Lisa, and I want to put Moralis away," I said.

Lisa looked at me with pleading eyes.

"You want to see the person responsible for his death put away, don't you?' I asked.

She bowed her head. "I do, Roosevelt, but, but," she stammered. "I think I'm falling in love with you."

"I can't believe it," my Guardian Angel said and plopped down in a chair.

I felt like a Muslim at a Jewish wedding.

"And feeling the way I do, I don't want to see you get hurt," Lisa continued.

"She doesn't want to see the old hippie, middle aged man, who she is so in love with she can't live without him, get hurt. How quaint," my Guardian Angel said, shaking his head like quaint should be a four letter word.

Little tears glistened in the corners of Lisa's eyes. I wondered why love is always such a bummer. Oh God, I thought.

"If you fall for this you are stupider than I think you are," my Guardian Angel said.

"My luck, a lady falls in love with me but she is not the love of my life," I replied.

"Lord Lisa, Sam has only been dead a few weeks. How can you love me?"

"Sam is dead. Dead for a week, a month, a year, what does it matter?"

"Lisa," I croaked, my vocal cords turning into viola strings. "You can't love me."

"I don't want to see you get hurt, Roosevelt, and I'm afraid if you keep working on this case you're going to join Sam."

Once again tears formed in the corners of Lisa's eyes.

"I feel it's my duty," I said.

Lisa looked at me like I was a dog who had shed on her new sofa. "Duty," she blurted. "You were in the army, you would think you would have had enough duty to fill the Great Lakes."

"We all owe our country," I said. "If we didn't have enemies duty would not be an issue."

She gave me a dirty look.

"Want another drink?" I asked. I've always had a knack for changing the subject.

She handed me her glass like if her finger happened to brush mine it would rot and fall off. Love is fickle.

I made her drink strong.

After I gave Lisa her drink she looked at me seriously. "I'm glad you didn't give in to me just because I'm pretty. I like strong men."

"I like you, Lisa. And truthfully I don't know why I feel so strongly about finding Sam's killer and getting Moralis and his bunch."

"I think it's because people like him are what killed you old hippies off," Lisa said.

"We did ourselves in," I replied.

I looked away from Lisa for an instant and when I looked back she had transformed. Miss Sexpot radiated from her like steam from an overheated radiator.

"I'm going to go change," she said.

"You couldn't take that one home to grandma," my Guardian Angel said, "but Grandpa would enjoy the view."

160

"I know you're right," I said to my Guardian Angel. "I should get in Matilda and beat feet for Colorado and some trout fishing. Trout don't have any inclination in their little heads about wanting to run guns to Mexico or buy Peru. They don't swim in their cool clear water and dream about taking heroin to Chicago so junkies can run around town robbing little old ladies to get money for another fix. All trout want to do is eat flies – preferable one of my fake ones so I can roll him in flour and fry him."

"Poor little trout fish," my Guardian Angel said faking he was crying.

When Lisa came back she was wearing an ankle length, off white, silk nightgown that was as transparent as glass.

"Please, forget trout fishing, take her to her room," my Guardian Angel croaked.

"We have to be serious," I said to Lisa, about as forceful as the United Nations telling a country they had better watch out or they would send Bozo the Clown over to kick their rears.

"Ok, be serious," Lisa said, putting a hurt pout on her face.

"You are a real bummer," my Guardian Angel said.

"Lisa," I said, "I know that the Browne's in some way were connected with Sam. I think their usefulness is over and they have been killed and their bodies didn't get a Christian burial down in Mexico. Manuel is the gopher up here for the shipments of guns. The house is a holding area. I know Moralis is one of the big guys."

Lisa looked at me seriously. "I only have one question," I continued, "why do you own Greasy Ed's?"

Lisa didn't bat an eyelid in surprise. "Sam put Greasy Ed's in my name months ago. He never told me why and I didn't ask. I had all but forgotten about it."

Lisa was like a mob wife, just bring home the bacon, I don't care about you killing Johnny today.

"You put it up for sale already," I went on.

Lisa looked perturbed for one second and said, "What would I do with that place? My attorney said it was a good idea to sell. I met two men at the cafe who said they would run it for me, and I told them they could keep all the money until I sold it or if they could come up with a small down payment I would sell it to them."

I couldn't see any good reason to hang onto a restaurant that makes, at most, a couple of hundred dollars a day, and there was no

161

doubt Harold and no name was enjoying it. I hope they can raise the money.

"Is that all you wanted to talk serious about?" Lisa asked me after a few moments of silence.

"No, I have a plan," I said. "Manuel and his men have to figure you know something about what's going on. If you said you had a way to get a load of guns for them I think they would buy them. We could set it up and then call the police to make the nab."

"Is making a nab the same as making an arrest?" my Guardian Angel asked.

"How would that get Sam's killer, Roosevelt?" Lisa asked.

"A man has to have some secrets," I replied and winked at her.

"If Manuel ever thought I was up to no good they would kill me," Lisa said, with about as much emotion as if she was eating a lettuce salad.

"You make the initial contact, tell them I have the guns and you can step back."

"Why would they trust you?"

"Greed, good old greed."

Lisa ran her hands through her hair. She smiled a seductive smile. I tried not to look at her glass outfit.

"You are one hell of a man," she said as she left the kitchen.

"Roosevelt, Roosevelt, Roosevelt," my Guardian Angel said sadly.

When I was up and about in the morning Lisa was gone and I moved several things from my room and put them in Matilda's trunk. By ten I had showered and dressed and was headed down town. I hadn't seen Detective Owens in a few days and it was time for a visit.

At the police station I walked through the sea of blue shirted cops feeling like a tuna fish in a tank of barracudas. Owens's secretary smiled like an toothpaste commercial. "You're lucky, he's in," she said like I had just won the lottery.

"Roosevelt is here to see you," she said into the intercom.

I sat and thumbed through a Readers Digest. I had barely read the first joke to, Humor in Uniform, when Owens opened his door. "Come on in, freak," he said - about as happy to see me as ring around the collar.

Owens looked better than he usually did. His clothes were ironed, and he seemed relaxed, like he had recently returned from a vacation.

"Been traveling?" I asked.

162

"Two days in Mexico eating tacos and drinking beer," he beamed.

"Where did you go?" I asked.

"A little place called Nogales, just south of Tucson, they have a retirement development down there I'm thinking about. Nice homes, swimming pool, good security, and only a hop and a skip back to the United States."

"Not good," my Guardian Angel said.

"I've never been there," I told Owens.

"I thought every old hippie in the country had been all over Mexico trying to see where all the bud is grown that gives them Alzheimer's at 40."

"It's not grown in the desert," I replied.

"What gives?" he said curtly. "I thought you were leaving town?"

"He's not smart enough," my Guardian Angel said.

"I think I've stumbled onto something about the Wrench case," I said, lowering my voice, like the walls might have ears, which I'm sure they do, but they are called bugs, and I don't mean the kind that crawl on you and leave little red welts.

Even with all his years of being a cop Owens's face drooped for an instant.

"Sam was involved with a group of men who were running guns to Mexico and bringing heroin back to the states," I said, watching Owens as intently as a robin watches a worm.

"How do you know this?" Owens demanded, far too urgently.

I took my time before answering. "You told me," I said, telling him only a half-truth.

Owens, looked at me strangely and then smiled. "I did, I remember now, the first time you and I had a little chitchat at the truck stop."

"I think I can get inside and crack the case," I told Owens as somber as a Priest saying High Mass.

His smile vanished from his face as quickly as a lady puts makeup on the dark circles under her eyes. "And I'm not going to tell you how," I said, before he had a chance to ask.

I could see the gears turning in Owens's thick skull. "You'll get killed," he said.

"Someday, but I want to know if I get in you will come in and make the arrest."

"Buddy boy," Owens said, "if we arrest Moralis and his boys, the mayor will let you marry his daughter."

"I'd rather have cash," I replied dryly.

"You must be sleeping with Lisa by now," Owens grinned, visualizing me rubbing my skinny freak body all over the young delicious Lisa.

"No, Roosevelt has been going through an attack of morals," my Guardian Angel said.

"I didn't learn them from you," I told my Guardian Angel.

I didn't respond to Owens's question. My non-sex life is my own business. "I need your home phone number, who knows when I might have to call," I said to him.

Owens took one of his cards out of his pocket and wrote his home phone number on it. "You know you're jumping into a pit full of snakes," he said, handing me the card.

"You never know who a snake is," I replied, taking the card and leaving the office without saying goodbye.

Driving away from police headquarters my Guardian Angel said, "You be a fool, Roosevelt."

I can't argue the point.

CHAPTER FOURTEEN
AS THICK AS MUD

Lisa was buzzing around the kitchen like a 1950's commercial for Spic and Span. She was cooking something that smelled so good I made Pavlov's dog seem like he had dry mouth.

I sat at the table and before I could say, "What's for dinner?" she took a small pitcher of martinis out of the refrigerator and two chilled martini glasses.

I don't really like martinis.

She poured us a drink and put three small olives on a plastic toothpick in each glass. "What are we celebrating?" I asked.

"We're celebrating me becoming a crime fighter," she beamed like the little train that said it could.

"Are you sure?" I asked.

"Sure I'm sure or I wouldn't have said it," Lisa said.

"Roosevelt, I don't trust her, even if she is an undercover cop," my Guardian Angel said.

"She is not an undercover cop," I stormed, "and what does trust have to do with it?"

"If you consider your death as no big deal than it doesn't mean much," he replied.

The first martini tasted bad, but after the first one my taste buds were numb.

Lisa had baked chicken stuffed with wild rice, steamed asparagus and a tossed salad. After two martini's, she could have served me the kitchen table with ketchup on it. I'd have scraped the ketchup off of the table and eaten the table without even sprinkling on some salt.

I ate my food so fast you would have thought I had been in a Weight Watcher's program for five years. When I finished, Lisa had barely eaten half her chicken and was nibbling on a piece of asparagus like a rabbit with sore gums. "I like your idea," she told me. "I think Manuel will welcome me with open arms."

"Who wouldn't but good old Roosevelt," my Guardian Angel said giving me a look like I am lower than gum on the bottom of a chair.

"Don't be too pushy with him," I said to Lisa.

"You and I would make a good team," Lisa said. "When this is all over, I could take some of my money and we could set up our own detective agency."

I was trying to think of a nice way to say, no way, when I was saved by the phone. Lisa answered it, looked at me with a quizzical look on her face, and handed me the phone. "It's for you, some Border Patrol guy."

"Roosevelt," Melton, my Border Patrol friend from El Paso said, "are you in the business of saving women now?"

"I'm trying to save myself," I replied truthfully. "How's the business of catching people down on their luck?"

"I called in reference to your inquiry about the Browne couple," Melton replied, ignoring my sarcastic remark.

By the tone in Melton's voice, I knew the news wasn't good.

"I just got a report - they found them two days ago stuffed in the trunk of a car about 50 miles from Juarez. They each had been shot in the back of the head. The way it looks they were baking in the trunk for about a week. Some guy stealing the tires from the car was so repulsed by the stink he contacted the authorities."

The news did not surprise me, but it didn't make me feel good. It was obvious Moralis and his people have no qualms what-so-ever of getting rid of people. The life expectancy of a person messing with heroin is about as long as a radio operator in the infantry, a little less than 20 seconds in actual combat.

"Thanks for calling," I said, there really wasn't much else to talk about.

"The Browne's were found dead in Mexico," I told Lisa. There was no need to tell her the circumstances.

Lisa didn't even gasp or stop nibbling on her asparagus. She was as calm as if she had done the killing and was lying to the jury.

"Strange," my Guardian Angel said.

I took Owens's card out of my billfold and called his home number. When he answered the phone, he sounded bothered. "It's not your friendly extended warranty auto insurance salesman," I said.

"When they kill you, I won't have to talk to you anymore," Owens chuckled.

Owens was about as funny as two bodies in the trunk of a car.

"Listen, I was wondering if you have had any breaks on the Greasy Ed killing."

166

"Roosevelt, I'm not on the clock."

"The men in blue are public servants, ready to put anything aside at any moment for the public good," I said.

"We haven't found a thing. There isn't even any word out on the street."

"Any idea what caliber the gun was?"

"It was a 32, we know that much. At last count there are about 7,000 of them in town."

"Thanks," I replied. "You can go back to an exciting night of watching cop shows."

Owens was about to say something not very nice when I hung up.

"Lisa's missing pistol is a 32," my Guardian Angel said.

"I wish I didn't know that," I replied.

"Do you think the same people who killed Sam killed Greasy Ed?" Lisa asked, finally finished with her asparagus.

"I really don't know," I replied. "I was only fishing."

"How can you fish without a fishing rod?" my Guardian Angel asked.

Lisa cleared the table, rinsed the dishes and put them in the dishwasher. I've always thought it is weird that before dishes are put in a dishwasher they have to be washed off.

It's like taking a shower, getting out of the shower, drying off and turning around and getting back in.

"I'm going to go over to see Manuel," Lisa said.

I was amazed at how calm she was. "Are you sure you're ready?" I asked. "Don't you think I should brief you?"

"I don't need any help on how to handle men, Roosevelt."

"I don't trust her but I like her style," my Guardian Angel said.

"I'm going for a ride but won't be gone long," I said to Lisa.

Lisa looked at me like she didn't care if I jumped in a lake and she needed me as much as she needs acne. She left without even touching up her makeup.

As soon as the door closed, I picked up the phone. "Hey Owens," I said when he answered.

"Roosevelt, how'd you like your nose put on the back of your head?"

I ignored his remark. "I heard two of Moralis's topless bars got torched last week."

167

"How'd you know that? "It wasn't even in the paper," Owens demanded, sounding like he'd been caught off guard.

"A little bird told me."

All I could hear was Owens's breathing over the phone.

"I was wondering if you have any leads as to who might have done it."

"In Iowa we investigate fires at topless bars about as much as we investigate who stole a kid's bike. But, we figure some Bible thumper burned them."

I felt hurt, hard work without recognition is hard to take.

"Roosevelt, don't call me again until you need help," Owens warned.

I know I have him confused and wondering what I am up to. It's always good to keep the police confused.

"Is a bible thumper someone who punches a bible?" my Guardian Angel asked – modern terms at times throw him.

"No, it is a religious person who tries to make people believe like he does and lives his life by a literal translation of scriptures," I replied.

"Didn't they call that the Inquisition?" my Guardian Angel replied looking afraid.

As I drove away, I wondered what Sheila was going to say when I knocked on her door? I don't think it will be, "Hi Roosevelt, I missed you."

I didn't realize it was so late in the evening when I got to Sheila's. I'd been so wrapped up in my thoughts I hadn't noticed the sun was about to set. Rick and Kathy were in the front yard and when they saw my car they ran into the house as fast as a covey of quail darting across a dirt road being chased by an overweight house cat. I hadn't made it more than half way to the front door when Sheila came out. She stood, her feet spread apart and her arms folded across her chest, like a big league home plate umpire who was about to tell me I was out, when I had plainly been safe, but he didn't like me because I was making 82 million a year and he wants to see if I will get mad so he can kick me out of the game.

"Turn around and get out of here," Sheila ordered.

"I only want to talk," I replied in a subdued voice.

She took a menacing step toward me and I backed up. Since she didn't have a purse, I couldn't knock her in the forehead. "Please, Sheila, let's talk."

"What do you want to talk about?"

"Free love and rock and roll," my Guardian Angel said hopping up and down like an old hippie chick dancing to Blue Cheer.

"I need your help to find out who killed Sam," I said to Sheila.

"Why don't you just get out of town and go somewhere and bother somebody else," she said, but without quite as much hate in her voice.

"It wasn't my fault I got lucky and caught you," I said. "Give me a few minutes and let me explain."

"You sound lame," my Guardian Angel said.

Margaret was looking out the window. She looked worried. Children should not have to be worried. They have a whole adulthood to worry.

"You want to see Sam's killer get caught, don't you?" I pressed on.

"The only reason you can catch your butt, Roosevelt, is because it's on top of your shoulders," Sheila replied.

"I've told him that before," my Guardian Angel said.

I didn't say anything. The longer I remained silent, the more she seemed to relax, until, she shrugged her shoulders and said. "We can sit in the backyard. Would you like a beer?"

The martinis were still buzzing around my head like two honey bees locked in a car. "No thanks," I said. "I'll take a glass of iced tea or water though."

"You go around, I'll be out."

As I rounded the corner to the backyard, the porch light came on. There were four chairs on the porch. I sat in one. Within a few minutes Sheila came out with two glasses of iced tea. She handed me one and sat in the chair next to me. We were sitting no more than a foot apart.

"Cozy for somebody who has tried to kill you," my Guardian Angel said.

"So, just exactly how are you going to find out who killed Sam?" Sheila asked me, but there was a tone to her voice that I couldn't place - somewhere between apprehension and guilt.

"I'm going to get myself in with Moralis and his boys, hopefully, something will come up."

"You had better stay away from them, Roosevelt," she said, sounding concerned. "Those boys are tougher than you have ever seen."

I was about to answer her, when she added. "And you had better watch out for Lisa."

169

"It's too late," my Guardian Angel said.

"Thanks for the warnings," I said to Sheila. "But I was wondering if there was anything else you might be able to tell me about Moralis that would help me."

Sheila sipped on her iced tea and gazed out past the end of the porch light. "In life there is no black and white," she said, not really to me, but to the night. "What you see and think, or what you have been told is more often than not, at best, a half-truth. But then, sometimes, lies are told to help you, not hurt you."

For a moment I thought I was back in philosophy 101 which I had flunked.

"You flunked basketball," my Guardian Angel said. "But Sheila is trying to tell you something. All you have to do is figure it out."

"Moralis is as mean as they come. He was born in Mexico and got his green card about 20 years ago. He married an American girl and became a citizen. Since then he's set up a small empire taking guns to Mexico and bringing out drugs. He used to bring in grass but he no longer messes with the small stuff. His heroin supplies at least five major cities and at the least he's bringing in over 5 million a year in profit for himself. He's a major mover and a major killer. If you cross Moralis you've signed your death warrant."

Her statements confused me and she sounded like a cop.

"Maybe she is an undercover cop like Lisa," my Guardian Angel mused.

"Does anybody have an idea where Moralis gets his heroin?" I asked Sheila — Sheila is a cop like I am the president.

"There's more heroin in Mexico than Fords in Detroit," Sheila said. "I understand more people are growing poppies now. Heroin is easier to ship and brings in more money. Hippies smoked pot and thought they saw the light. People now days want to see the darkness."

"It's a tough world," I said.

I could tell Sheila wanted to tell me something. She pursed her lips, weighed her thoughts and sipped on her tea. "Roosevelt," she finally said. "Let me give you some advice, get out of here. Move somewhere where a few old hippies have retreated and sit around wondering where the good times went."

"I saw some kids wearing peace signs the other day," I said. "And a guy with bell bottom pants on."

Sheila laughed, a pleasant but sad laugh.

I laughed.

"We must have looked funny," she said. "Think about Mr. and Mrs. America when they saw the first freaks walking around - it was no wonder they were upset. We were so young and simple - life was going to be peace and love. We didn't know that free love meant herpes and the clap. We thought life was good if you lived good. We didn't know life isn't good. Everything is out to get you, wear you down, and tear you into little pieces until you don't want to bother to try and put yourself together again. And then, when you are worn down, you look around and you're old. Your hair is turning gray, your back hurts, your feet hurt, and your fingers are swelling. And what have you done? Nothing. Nothing at all except pass the days thinking you were doing something, when in all truth, you were doing nothing."

"We got the ball rolling," I said. "There are people concerned with the environment, nature groups, government watchdog groups, concerned people."

Sheila smiled ruefully.

I handed Sheila my glass. "No hard feelings," I said, standing.

"Us old hippies weren't brought up to hate."

I was a few steps away. "One other thing, Roosevelt," Sheila said. "Thanks for burning the Pussy Cat Retreats."

I started to say it wasn't me, but by the look on her face I knew it wouldn't do any good.

"You are not a good pyro," my Guardian Angel said.

I drove away from Sheila's feeling bone weary tired. I felt like going to the country, laying down on the ground and looking up at the stars and searching for answers. But now, I know the only thing I would get out of it is ticks and chiggers.

I turned on the overhead light in Matilda and took out my notebook and looked up Moralis's home address. It didn't take me long to drive by his house in West Des Moines. It wasn't a house, it was a mansion, a mansion with a locked gate and security cameras and guards. Moralis was living in a castle, a castle that I hope is made out of glass.

When I got back to Lisa's, Lisa still wasn't back. There was a martini left in the pitcher and I poured it in a water glass. I guess one knows the circle is getting close to completion when an old hippie is drinking martinis like his dad used to do.

171

"Life is nothing but knuckle balls and change ups and trying to keep swinging the bat even though you have never hit the ball," my Guardian Angel said.

I waited for Lisa until my eyes could no longer stay open and then went to my room. I was so tired I didn't go over my notebook. I usually fold my clothes when I take them off but I let them fall where they would and crawled into bed like a drunken sailor. As sleep overcame me I could see Lisa looking at me and smiling while she pointed a large and menacing looking pistol at my face. "Roosevelt," she said, "I told you to get out of town."

I woke up and looked at the ceiling. I felt empty. I am a dreamer without a cause. I can't stop pollution, hate or corruption. I can't help the Cubs win.

"Life is being strong," my Guardian Angel said.

"Life is trying to love each other," I said.

"Only those who have been lonely can truly love," he said.

I slept again.

I woke up when the bedroom light came on. If somebody had been trying to kill me I would have already been dead ten times. Lisa looked at me like I was the ugliest thing she had seen in her life and curtly said. "Get up Roosevelt, it's time for you to start making your money."

She must think a 100 bucks a day is too much for getting shot at and beat up.

I crawled out of bed feeling like the martinis had taken over my feet. Lisa was sitting at the kitchen table. Glancing at the clock it was 1 a.m.

"It was easier than you would have thought," Lisa said. "When I told Manuel Sam had told me everything the only thing he said was he figured as much. When I first told him I had confided in you, he seemed to get angry but when I told him you were broke and needed money and could get him some guns, he came around."

"Things are going too smoothly," my Guardian Angel said.

"He wants me to bring you over this afternoon and talk. You can take it from there," Lisa said.

My Guardian Angel started slam dancing on my chest and hollering, "no, no, no."

My brain screamed, "no, no."

My feet knew which direction they should go. But my mouth said, "Good work. What time do we go?"

172

"Two."

I wanted to ask her why she didn't wait until a reasonable hour to tell me, but I didn't.

"You could also ask her what she has been doing with Manuel for all this time," my Guardian Angel said.

In the morning I felt good and after cleaning up went to the kitchen. There was a note on the table from Lisa - "Back by noon" - is all it said. There were no little X's meaning love and kisses.

I made myself two soft-boiled eggs and ate them with white bread and drank 4 cups of coffee. Feeling restless, I went back to my room and took the $5,000 Lisa had given me and went outside and hid it in the door panel of Matilda. I chuckled, thinking about what I have in the trunk.

Back in the house, I wished I had a small pistol I could hide in my boot, it wouldn't be wise to carry my 9 m.m. to talk to Manuel.

The rest of the morning I went over my notebook and added a few scribbles.

"Roosevelt, your entire notebook is nothing but scribbles. It would make a real private detective blush," my Guardian Angel said like he was embarrassed.

Lisa came back shortly after noon. She looked as fresh and happy as a new bride before her honeymoon. All she said to me though, was, "I hope you know what you're doing?"

"I never know what I'm doing," I told her.

"You're honest, at least," she said.

"Honesty in this world is called being a sucker," my Guardian Angel said.

For close to an hour I paced around the kitchen. It was strange, I felt nervous, nervous is normally not part of my vocabulary. Lisa was in her room - probably putting on her, Roosevelt is going to get his outfit.

At two Lisa came downstairs. She didn't say a word as she walked to the door, opened it and nodded for me to follow. I felt like a young calf that had been fed milk and kept in a pen so small I couldn't turn around and was about to become veal for some rich overweight banker in Omaha.

"Chicken is a poor man's veal," my Guardian Angel said.

The door closing behind Lisa and me rang like jailhouse doors that would no longer open. It was a beautiful day. Somewhere in the mid-eighties and the humidity was low. A few white clouds floated across

173

the sky. Lisa and I walked through Eric the Red and up the street. A man driving a deep blue B.M.W drove by and honked. Lisa waved at him like he was her long lost brother.

When we turned into the gate to the Browne's, my Guardian Angel said to me, "It's been fun but after they kill you would you ask God if he would assign me to be Madonna's guardian angel."

I didn't answer him and wondered why I hadn't reenlisted and done another tour in Vietnam - at least then I would have received hazard duty pay for doing stupid things.

When we knocked on the door to Manuel's house, the knocks reminded me of the bell in the Tower of London ringing after another of good old George's wives heads had hit the pavement. Manuel answered the door. "Come on in," he said, and smiled at me like a large cane spider smiling at a fly.

Lisa sat on one end of a brown leather sofa and I sat on the other. "Would you like a beer or something?" Manuel asked, being the good host.

Manuel had on a pair of $600 lizard skin boots with a matching lizard belt. The type of boots a hired hand could not afford to buy.

"I don't want anything," Lisa said.

"I'll take a beer," I said.

Manuel got me a San Miguel beer and one for himself. He sat across from Lisa and me. "To our future profits," he toasted, raising his beer to me.

I tipped my beer at him and drank deeply and waited for Manuel to make the opener. When one is in strange territory it's always best to play second fiddle.

Manuel looked me straight in the eyes for a few seconds. I did not lower my gaze. After our initial male test, he broke the ice. "Lisa informs me you have a desire to make some money."

I could see no reason to beat around the bush. "I can get you guns," I said, wondering where I could get guns.

"I don't want shotguns and pistols," Manuel replied, his tone now icy. "I need automatic rifles, or rifles that can be switched easily from semi to auto."

"I have a friend in the Army who can get M-16's, several cases at a time."

"And how much do you want?" Manuel said calmly, but I knew he was impressed.

"$800 each," I said without hesitation.

Manuel laughed.

I took another drink from my beer before saying, "Guns are funny to me, too."

Manuel's mood changed as quickly as fall turns to winter in Canada. "Listen," he ordered. "You're nothing to me, only if we can do business."

I stood and looked at Lisa. "Let's get out of here, he only wants to play tough guy and I know he doesn't play tennis."

I caught Manuel off guard. I was supposed to show fear and bow to him. Most crooks, after they've made enough money, are only in the game because they like to scare people. They think fear is respect - fear isn't respect - if they wanted respect they would get a real job.

Lisa was in shock and started to speak. "Shut up," I ordered her.

Manuel jumped out of his chair like he was ready to tear me apart. I glared at him. "You come at me Manuel and I'll stuff your eyeballs down your throat before you can say, "Bless me Father for I have sinned. I ate fish on Friday."

Lisa jumped up. "Cool it, Manuel," she said calmly. "Roosevelt has enough Karate belts to wallpaper your house."

Manuel sat back down slowly and then grinned at me. I wondered why he had followed Lisa's order. "I like men who are not afraid," he said.

He was telling the truth. Men who are afraid in crime are like virgins at a biker party.

"$800 is too much," Manuel said as Lisa and I sat back down.

"$800 is a steal," I replied.

My dad always told me to never undersell when it's a sellers market.

"When can you deliver?" Manuel asked, knowing he wasn't going to Jew me down.

"Two days and I'll bring you two cases. You have the money. I'll talk to nobody but you. Lisa will come over and you show her the money. Then I will bring the guns over. If it all goes well we can do five cases a week from then on."

"Don't call me on the phone," Manuel said.

"Do I look like your grandmother?" I answered, like what he had said was the dumbest thing I had ever heard in my life. Crooks talking on the phone want to go to jail.

"You ready?" I asked Lisa.

Lisa followed me like a trained poodle that had been clipped to look like two balloons and had a ribbon between its ears. Manuel didn't bother to get up as we left.

"Good job, Roosevelt," my Guardian Angel said. "I always told you you'd make a good crook."

Lisa didn't say a word until we were in her kitchen. Then she got right to the point. "Where are you going to get the rifles?" she asked.

"That is a problem," I said.

"You don't get M-16's in a box of Cracker Jacks," my Guardian Angel said.

Lisa shook her head and walked out of the kitchen like there was no doubt in her mind I am a lost cause.

I went to my room and once again went over my notebook. I looked at the photograph of Sam and the key to the tennis courts. I wished I could hold them up to my head and they would talk to me. After reading through my notebook several times the sun was going down. Time had flown. I'd grown older and didn't even know it. I felt as tired as I used to when I was in college and cramming for finals. I blame a lot of things in my life because of my bad grades, not studying had nothing to do with it.

I lay in bed with the bedside light on looking at the ceiling. I don't know how many ceilings I've stared at in my life. Ceilings have always been an infatuation for me, people disenchanted with life look at a lot of ceilings. Ceilings are the lonely part of a room, they spend their entire existence always close to the party, but ignored.

I turned off the light and wondered about Manuel. It seemed to me he had taken the bait too easily, but I also know the criminal mind is a devious mind, kind of like the mind of a C.I.A. agent or the President's speechwriter.

I gazed into the darkness, looking at the shadows that crept across the walls from the faint light filtering thorough the windows. Life is all shadows, even when the sun is shining, it is shadows. Truth is something that happens by accident. I wished I was living in a log cabin high in the mountains. I didn't have electricity, but read by kerosene lamps and heated and cooked with wood. I didn't owe my soul to the utility companies, or the taxman, and didn't dream about reaching 65 and retiring by some golf course in Phoenix and fooling myself my life's efforts had all been worth it. I know that no matter what happens there will still be guns going to Mexico and junkies roaming the streets of the world. Junkies are sad human beings. I was almost asleep when I had a feeling I was missing something important about Sheila, something I should know. I felt like my mind was nothing but a blob of silly putty.

"Is anybody in Iowa my friend?" I asked my Guardian Angel.

"Only me, Roosevelt."

"You're not always nice to me," I said.

"I tell you the truth."

"Why are there so many lonely people?" I asked him.

"I really don't know."

"It's sad isn't it?"

"Very," he said.

CHAPTER 15
TO BE A THIEF

In the morning I shot out of bed. I had a problem. I had to find two cases of M-16 rifles and I know I can't call up the N.R.A. and say, "Hey guys, lend me some automatic rifles, I want to go deer hunting with my buddies and need some real fire power."

If I had time I could run an ad in Soldier of Fortune Magazine, stating I wanted to start a revolution in Idaho and needed automatic guns. I would have so many guns within a day I would make Lewiston my capital.

I heated up a cup of coffee in the microwave, swilled it down and headed for the door. As I opened the door, Lisa came into the kitchen, freshly showered, with a large blue towel wrapped around her. Ladies in towels have always excited me. But I waved goodbye and jogged to Matilda.

"If I had my choice between guns and a sexy lady I'd take the lady," my Guardian Angel said, "even though they are both dangerous."

"That's why you're on the bottom of the list for Guardian Angel assignments," I replied.

"No Guardian Angel likes a sarcastic human being early in the morning," he replied tersely.

My Guardian Angel has never learned to laugh at himself.

The Headquarters for the F.B.I. in Des Moines isn't a massive building. There aren't many crimes against corn and soybeans to warrant a large office. Most of the heavy hitter stuff in the Midwest centers in Kansas City and Chicago. I think the reason gangsters like Kansas City and Chicago is because the weather is bad most of the time and people don't go outdoors.

I went to the reception desk in the Federal Building. A woman, in her forties, who looked like a librarian, smiled at me. I didn't see a listing on the pegboard behind her for snitches so I said. "I need to talk to an agent. I want to report a crime."

"Go to the second floor, room 204, that is our investigative department. I'm sure they can help you," the lady smiled.

Smiles too early in the morning have always bothered me. Nobody can smile in the morning unless they're trying to cover something up - something the F.B.I. is good at.

I don't know why, but every F.B.I. office I've ever been in has a secretary working the front desk that looks like she came right out of a potato field in Russia and has about as much humor as Manual Noriega when they told him he was getting 50 years of free room and board in the United States.

This one was no exception. "I wish to report a crime," I told Mrs. Stuttgart - as her nameplate read.

"What type of crime?" she asked me, like I talk in incomplete sentences.

"I'll only discuss that with an agent."

She raised her lip at me like a Doberman pincher about to bite my arm off and said curtly. "Take a seat, it shouldn't be too long."

"I don't know why you are doing this," my Guardian Angel said.

"It will work," I said, giving him a sneaky smile.

I was thumbing through a year old Outdoor Life when a man in his late twenties came through a door. He stood over me like I was a street punk who didn't have the brains to do a crime that was worth his time. He was tall, over six feet, with blond crew cut hair, blue eyes, and had on black trousers with a white shirt and a blue tie. His holster didn't have a pistol in it, which, in my opinion, was about useless. "I'm Agent Price," he finally said, like I should bow down and kiss his polished shoes.

"Bob Roosevelt," I said, standing and not bothering to shake hands. "You lose your gun?" I asked.

He didn't smile at my remark. "Would you follow me please?"

In the office were six military style metal desks. Four other men were standing by the drinking fountain like the drinking fountain was evidence in a case that was so important they couldn't let it out of their sight.

Agent Price sat behind his desk and gazed at me like the only thing keeping him awake was the fact that in 20 years he would get a good retirement. He shuffled a few papers around and finally said, "You have a crime to report?" in a tone like I'd come to the Federal Building to report that my neighbor's dog kept pooping in my yard and I wanted the owner's house put under surveillance.

"Have you heard anything about the Sam Wrench murder?" I asked.

Price perked up a little. "It's a state case," he said, far too casually.

To be a Federal case, a body has to be dragged across state lines or a person has to dust somebody who is important. The Feds like good press - they have had enough bad press.

"For your information, Sam Wrench was involved with a man named Salvador Moralis," I said.

Hearing Moralis, Price was suddenly all ears.

"Moralis is a gun smuggler and heroin dealer," I went on. "He cleans his money through an escort service and topless bars."

"They burnt down," Price said, but I could tell Price was wondering how I knew all this.

I also wondered how he knew the two topless bars that burnt down belonged to Moralis?

"By chance, I have a way to get in with one of Moralis' men. I've already made contact and set up a deal to deliver two cases of M-16's," I said casually.

"Excuse me," Agent Price cut in, "but I need another agent to hear this story as you tell it."

"I won't talk to more than one person at a time. No tape recorders, no nothing, understand?" I stated with no trace of weakness in my voice.

"I don't think I can do that," Price said, leaning back in his chair in a power move.

I stood. "Then I'm sorry to have bothered you," I said, and I started to walk away.

"Hold on, please," he said quickly. "Tell me your story."

I stopped, looked at him for a few moments, and sat back down. I hadn't broken a law and there was no need to let the Feds bully me. They are servants of the people. At least they're supposed to be. But, at our present rate they'll soon be our masters, pass a few more bills to take away our rights under the name of fighting crime and see what happens in 50 years. Big Brother will become Big Man Who Puts Yoke Around Citizens' Neck.

"As I was saying, I can get in with these people. All I need are two cases of military M-16's."

Price coughed. "I think you should start at the beginning."

"Let's you and I go to a coffee shop and talk. I don't feel comfortable here," I told him, looking over at the other agents.

Price had his coat on quicker than Batman starts his car. He and I left the office without him saying goodbye to his buddies. As we walked to a corner coffee shop, I thought I saw Sheila's 98 blue Ford Taurus parked across the street in a space reserved for Federal Employees only. But, there are a lot of Ford Taurus's around, and I couldn't see if the driver's door had a ding in it.

The coffee shop was filled with pretty secretaries and men in suits with cell phones on their belts. Twenty years ago the only people that wore cell phones were drug dealers, now, everybody and their mother have one. I think they make people feel important or most people are dealing drugs these days. We sat at a table by the window. I had no doubt that if I would have stayed in the office my conversation would have been tape-recorded. Price hadn't had enough time to wire himself so I felt free to talk. I in no way want to put myself in the position the Feds could try and use me by trumping up some charge. In fact, if I had had time, I would have hired an attorney to approach them and get down on paper what I wanted to do and state in writing that there would be no ramifications against me.

"Why don't you start at the beginning," Agent Price said, smiling like I was the key to his next promotion.

I was about to start when the waitress came over. We ordered two coffees. He drank his with cream and sugar. I figured he was a graduate of some prep school and probably drank herbal tea before bed - real men drink their coffee black. But, years ago, I believed real men smoked only non-filtered cigarettes - now, those that did, are dead real men.

I told Agent Price everything I had stumbled onto about Manuel and Moralis, including the murders of the Browne's and Greasy Ed, and the fact I had been there when Sam was killed. I mentioned Lisa and Sheila casually but didn't bring up anything about the fake kidnapping or the money. I informed him of my hunches. "So," I said to end my story, "now all I need are two cases of M-16's and you boys can step in and pinch these low lives."

Agent Price looked at his cup of coffee like it was going to jump up and spill itself all over his nice white shirt. "I'll have to check with my superiors. We can't go around giving out M-16's to every guy who comes in off the street with a story to tell."

I was going to say, "The government gives them to every right wing government in the world so they can kill civilians," but, instead, I said. "Run me through your computers. You'll find I'm a private detective from Florida. I also solved a case that made TV."

Price's face lit up like he had just won $3,000 on Wheel of Fortune. "I thought I'd heard of you, I saw you on that TV show."

"How many times are you going to be able to milk your 15 minutes of TV time?" my Guardian Angel asked, about as bored as a six-year-old kid watching Gone With The Wind.

"45 minutes, you always forget the two reruns," I said.

Price, like most agents, probably watched every crime show on TV, but I had a suspicion he had heard of me since I've been in town. Why I thought this I don't know?

"I'll meet you back here in two hours," I told Agent Price, wondering if he wanted my autograph.

"How much do you want if we bust them?" Price asked.

"Nothing. But I won't testify in court."

Price was impressed with me wanting nothing.

"You can give me a confidential informant number and tape my testimony if you want, though."

I stood up and tossed five dollars down on the table for the coffee.

Headed toward Matilda, I again looked at the 98 blue Ford Taurus parked in the Federal Employee parking lot, but didn't go across the street to see if it belonged to Sheila. Federal parking lots are not the best place in the world to go snooping around.

I watched Agent Price hurry back to the Federal building. I was sure that within five minutes the whole floor would be buzzing and they would be trying to find out everything they possibly could about me. I trust Feds about as far as I can throw a Mac truck. Like Mac trucks, Feds have the tendency to flatten things.

I decided to go and see if Sheila was at work. There were a few questions I wanted to ask her.

When I entered the Mother Goose Margaret was behind the cash register checking out two older ladies who were cooing like pigeons over three stuffed animals they were buying. "They are so darling," Margaret said.

After the ladies left Margaret saw me and her smile turned into a look of fear and apprehension. "There's no need to not like me," I said. "I only want the best for you."

I had never really looked closely at Margaret before but she is a very pretty girl. She is tall, well proportioned, with graceful hands, she has deep, dark eyes like her mother, but she didn't look like either Sam

182

or Sheila. Her eyes kept darting from me to the floor. "How are things going?" I asked.

"Not too bad, Mr. Roosevelt," she replied, like I was a guidance counselor and she had gotten in trouble for smoking in the school parking lot.

"Is your mother here?"

"No, she won't be in today," she said sheepishly.

"It's too bad about your father," I said.

"I didn't like my father," Margaret said distantly. "He ran away from my mother and us."

"In time you might understand," I said.

"I try," she confessed. "But I don't understand."

I felt a deep sadness in her and a loneliness that could not be touched.

"Tell your mother I came in. Tell her I came by to say good luck and I hope things work out for her. I'm going to be leaving soon. There's nothing more I can do."

"I'll tell her," Margaret said.

I started to leave. I stopped suddenly and turned around. "Do you still shoot in competition?" I asked.

"No, I gave my rifles....." she caught herself.

Driving away from the Mother Goose I felt ill at ease.

I drove around aimlessly for about thirty minutes and then stopped at a fast food fish restaurant where they take cardboard, bread it, deep fat fry it in lard, and serve what they now call fish with malted vinegar. I was eating when an idea hit me so hard I left the restaurant without finishing my cardboard.

I telephoned Detective Owens. "Hearing from you thrills me as much as my ex-wife calling," Owens said.

"You have to meet me in the parking lot of the Kmart down on Army Post Road," I told him as seriously as a mistress telling her sugar daddy she needs a diamond bracelet to keep her image up.

"Roosevelt, you think all I have time for is running around and talking to you?"

"Who else would you rather talk to?" I replied, like he had hurt my feelings.

"Twenty minutes," Owens answered and slammed down the phone so hard a lady driving by in a Buick jumped.

Driving towards the Kmart I felt cagey.

"Don't feel so cagey or you'll get locked in your own cage," my Guardian Angel said.

Kmart parking lots are not the most interesting places to be, unless you like screaming kids and dodging shopping carts that are left all over the lot with the sole purpose in their lives to dent your car.

I was standing in front of Matilda looking like a bored dad waiting for the Mrs. and the kids when Owens drove by. Unmarked police cars are so obvious it's like painting an elephant pink and thinking nobody can tell it's an elephant.

Owens found a parking spot about 50 yards away. I went to his car - as out of shape as he looked I didn't know if he could walk that far. "This had better be good," Owens said.

"Yeah, I know," I said. "You're missing Days of Our Lives."

"You watch it too?" Owens asked with a look of excitement, like he had finally found a bosom buddy to confide in.

"Not in a few weeks," I lied.

"You won't believe what is going on when you start watching again," Owens said and started to fill me in.

"No, don't," I cut in. "Don't ruin it for me."

Owens gave me a knowing look.

"I didn't call you to talk about the soaps," I said. "I have a chance to get in with Moralis and his boys like I told you."

Owens looked at me like our friendship was over.

"I met with Manuel and told him I could get him two cases of military M-16's."

Owens stiffened like he had just got a shot of penicillin.

"I told Manual I would deliver the guns tomorrow to his house. When I do, I think you should be in the area. I feel confident Moralis will show his face and you could get both of them for possession of automatic weapons."

"How did you get the guns?" he asked suspiciously.

"We all have our secrets," I replied.

"You call me just before you make the delivery and we will make the arrest," he said.

"Make sure you tell your boys I'm a good guy."

"You must have really liked Sam," Owens said, looking at me like he was trying to read my mind. I know he has a hard time reading the newspaper so I doubt if he can read my mind.

184

"I hadn't seen Sam in over thirty years. I hadn't even thought about him. I really don't know why I'm doing what I'm doing. I know that it isn't for justice. I know justice is about as fair as Tiger Woods playing golf with me for Matilda. I think I'm doing it for a lost dream. Who knows?" I told Owens.

"I gave up on dreams years ago," Owens said and got in his car.

I got to the cafe by the Federal Building fifteen minutes early. The 98 blue Ford Taurus was gone from the parking lot. Since the lunch rush was over, the cafe was nearly empty and the waitresses were lounging around the front discussing finger nail polish.

One finally walked over to me so slowly she could have made it faster if she had crawled. I ordered coffee and she looked at me like I was the dirt she sweeps under the carpet - if I only wanted coffee why didn't I stay at home. Of course, I was not wearing a suit and don't have a cell phone so I am a second-class citizen.

My coffee looked like it had been perked three days ago and heated up in the microwave.

I was on my second cup when Agent Price came in the front door. He looked like the model for a poster advertising, "You Too Can Be An Agent."

There was nobody with him but I figured this time he was wired.

Agent Price sat down opposite me. A waitress came over to the table so fast her sneakers left black marks on the floor. He only ordered iced tea, but the girl grinned at him like he had ordered a five-course meal and was going to tip her so much she could take two weeks off and go to Hawaii.

"What did your boss say?" I asked.

The girl returned with the tea. Price put sugar in it, stirred it so long I thought the bottom of the glass would crack, took a sip, looked at me and said, "Roosevelt, we want you to get out of town so fast nobody will remember you were here. We have an ongoing investigation into Moralis and his crew and you could only mess it up."

I was completely taken off guard. I started to protest but Price looked at me so intently I knew it was no use. "I really don't want you messing things up. We'll get them, rest assured, it's only a matter of time."

I couldn't think of anything to say. I couldn't think of any argument to bolster my case.

"I'm sure if you want to hang around, we can dig up some charge to keep you in our well-maintained detention center for a few weeks. Conspiracy to buy automatic weapons might do for starters."

"You can buy this round," I said and left the restaurant as fast as my cheap booted feet would carry me.

"It's not smart to get the F.B.I. after you," my Guardian Angel said like he was telling me something I didn't know.

It wasn't hard to spot the car that followed me when I drove away. I drove around, making U-turns, driving through parking lots, until I felt I had lost the tail. I know it didn't matter - it wouldn't take a genius to know where I was staying. I also wondered what else the Feds know about me that Agent Price hadn't told me. I had a feeling they know a lot more than I think.

It was close to 6 p.m. when I got back to Lisa's. To my surprise nobody was home. I went to Rick's room and opened the closest. The two 22 match rifles that had been there the last time I looked in his room were gone. But looking in the other kid's rooms all their belongings were also gone. I suppose Lisa took their things over to Sheila's.

I went to Lisa's room and opened the drawer to her bedside table. The 32 Berretta was back.

"Greasy Ed didn't like 32 caliber pistols," my Guardian Angel said.

I went outside and it felt like 200 pairs of eyes were watching my every move. In Vietnam while on operations I used to feel there was a set of eyes behind every tree - eyes that controlled fingers that controlled triggers on rifles that controlled my life.

I walked the complete inside perimeter of the chain link fence, toured the swimming pool and looked inside the tennis court. I walked around the house and stood on the patio and looked at the large brick barbecue pit. While standing on the patio, I heard a car drive into the driveway of the Browne's house. But I didn't want to take a chance and sneak up to the fence and get caught spying. Looking over the vast grounds I went over the many strange facts about the case. Sheila is the ex-wife. Sheila was sleeping with Sam after he got remarried. Sam said he was going to take the money and run away with Sheila. Sam hadn't told Lisa about the million or the fact the kids were away at camp. Sheila tried to fake a kidnapping to get the money. Lisa found the money. During all this time Sheila and Lisa were talking. Both women had tried to seduce me. Greasy Ed was killed in the restaurant Lisa owned. Sheila, although soon to be rich, tried to get her paws on the money, worked as a manager for a topless bar, ran her own business, and also worked at an escort service. Lisa didn't work. Margaret was disillusioned with Sam. Rick and Kathy could care. Lisa owned a 32 Berretta - the caliber of gun that had killed Greasy Ed. Sam was killed by a 243. Margaret owned two 22 rifles. Matilda had been shot by a 22. Moralis was one of the big boys but Sheila said he wasn't the top dog. Manuel was from Nogales and the address and phone number I had found was from Nogales. I can't see Sam messing with heroin or messing with guns. I was welcomed with open arms by Manuel after only an introduction by Lisa. Lisa knows more than she lets on. The F.B.I. rejected my plan even though I was a shoe-in for them. And there was the voice in the dark. The voice that sends chills running down my spine every time I think about it. The whole mess was a can of alphabet soup with no vowels.

"Not unless you spell like you do," my Guardian Angel said like he was an English Professor at a private college.

I was so deep into my thoughts I didn't hear Lisa until she was standing by the barbecue pit. She was dressed like she'd been to a luncheon with the governor and was trying to seduce the governor's aid.

"I don't think I can get the rifles," I told her, sounding like a little boy whose baseball had gone into the backyard of a house with a dog so big it ate kids for snacks.

"Sounds like a real problem," she said far too casually.

Women have a way of getting to the bottom of things quickly and simply.

"Do you think B.B. guns would work?" I joked.

"No, but I bet a case of grenades would do the trick."

"I know there's a tunnel running between these two houses. Where it is I don't know, but I'd bet my last pair of underwear there is."

"Why would there be a tunnel?" Lisa asked.

"Why is the sky blue? Why is the moon round? I said.

Lisa shook her head.

I, in truth, have no idea why a tunnel between the houses would mean anything or would facilitate any crime. When I had seen the guns at Manuel's they were stored in the horse barn. If there is a tunnel, one would think they'd store them in the tunnel.

"What are you going to do about getting the M-16's?" Lisa asked. "If you don't, your plan is worthless." She didn't care about any tunnel.

187

"I'll have to sleep on it," I said.

"What good will that do?"

I shrugged my shoulders. "I don't know," I confessed.

She laughed like my sister used to laugh when I fell down and skinned my knee. "I tell you what. Let's go out and eat Chinese food. Maybe the waiter will tell you how to buy some M-16's," she said.

It sounded like a good idea to me and besides, I like Chinese food. It was also the first time a woman had ever asked me the famous line men know by heart, "Do you like Chinese food?"

I took a shower while Lisa got ready. I'd been ready for at least twenty minutes when she met me in the kitchen.

Lisa drove Sam's Lincoln, which gives me the willies. The restaurant was small, tucked back in a strip mall, with only a few people. We ordered a Flaming Volcano to drink. It's a large drink, with every kind of rum there is mixed in punch, so you can't taste the rum. Two of them are strong enough to make any sailor know he had better not try to swim back to his ship. It comes with two straws and there's a tiny volcano of sterno burning in the center.

"Greasy Ed's sold today," Lisa told me, her face flushed from drinking.

"Who bought it?"

"The two guys I let run it. I guess they've turned the old dump around."

"You didn't cheat them did you?" I asked, remembering the good chicken Harold had served me.

"I gave them a great deal, you should have seen their faces, pure joy."

The thought of Harold and Mr. No Name having the place made me happy.

We ordered Almond Chicken and Beef with Snow Peas and another Flaming Volcano. The Chinese waiter smiled knowingly at me when I ordered the second drink. The Chinese think a lot about what turns a man on. They have wiped out half of the animals on the face of the earth because they think bones and gall bladders make their sex drive stronger - they should give everything a break and try good old booze or learn the forgotten art of foreplay.

By the time the food came we'd drunk half of our second Flaming Volcano and Lisa had the giggles.

"I think looking at your face is making her laugh," my Guardian Angel said.

The food was delicious.

By the time we were done eating and had finished the second drink Lisa was blasted. She looked funny drunk and had a cute pixie smile plastered on her face like one of those fake tattoos.

As I drove home Lisa was singing. "Roosevelt got no guns, Roosevelt got no guns, but Roosevelt he don't care, Roosevelt he get guns."

It was a catchy tune.

"I doubt it will make the top ten," my Guardian Angel said. "But she might sing it at your funeral."

Driving through Eric the Red Lisa was no longer singing. She was looking at me like all I am to her is a sex object. "Why won't you sleep with me?" Lisa asked.

"Because he's dumber than a wonton," my Guardian Angel said.

"Years ago I made a vow I would only sleep with a woman if I loved her," I told Lisa.

"But I love you," she whined.

"No you don't, Lisa, you don't love me or need me," I said.

We were about to go into the house when my Guardian Angel yelled, "You are about to need a bulletproof vest."

I flinched and a bullet slammed into the side of the house missing me by no more than two inches. I hadn't heard a sound - the weapon had to have a silencer and also a starlight scope. I grabbed Lisa as two more bullets zipped by. I dove, carrying Lisa with me, behind the barbecue pit as a bullet hit where we'd been standing. Another shot ricocheted off the top of the barbecue pit.

Lisa curled into a fetal position and started whimpering.

I wished I was in the Army and had my radio - within five minutes there wouldn't be a bush or any living thing within five hundred yards of me, let alone some idiot who couldn't shoot straight.

After about ten minutes, Lisa still hadn't moved and there had been no more shots. I slowly inched around the barbecue pit, and then, throwing my life to the wind, stood up. There was no shot, life is a crapshoot.

"It's ok," I said to Lisa.

Lisa got up and to my surprise, she was no longer afraid, but as excited as a girl who'd just been on her first date and only had to kiss the guy. "Roosevelt," she said, "there's nothing boring about hanging around with you."

"That is all a matter of opinion," my Guardian Angel said.

Lisa and I made sure the doors were locked and all the curtains were closed. I didn't feel like standing by a window and seeing how full the moon was.

"Do you want to call the police?" I asked Lisa.

She thought for a few moments, and then to my surprise said, "I don't think so. Not with your plan with Manuel. It might mess things up."

Smiling at me, and looking like she had just made the freshman cheerleader squad, she pranced off to bed.

"Thanks for the warning," I told my Guardian Angel.

"It's my job," he said casually.

I didn't like the tone in his voice.

"If I get killed do you think I could be a Guardian Angel?" I asked my Guardian Angel.

"It takes a certain type of person. I don't know if you qualify."

"God might listen to you," I said.

"God assigned me to you because he doesn't like me," he said.

"Do you think the shooter was trying to kill me or Lisa?" I asked.

"You. Who would want to kill a fine looking woman like Lisa?" he said.

"Sheila," I replied.

"Oh," he said

CHAPTER 16
INTO THE PIT

First thing in the morning I went outside and examined where the bullets had hit the house. All that was left were small fragments of lead and copper. By the chipped bricks there was no doubt the bullets were not fired from a 22 rifle. The rifle had been a big one, intended to leave big holes that a Band-Aid wouldn't patch.

I searched the woods and discovered a set of footprints. The person had worn tennis shoes. I followed the prints to the back of the fence, to the beach where I had spent the evening waiting for the fantasy kidnappers. A boat had been dragged on shore and there were footprints where the shooter had pushed the boat back into the water. He or she had medium sized feet, and are heavy - as the imprints were deep in the sand.

I retraced the route the person had taken but found nothing, no matches, no cigarette butts, no gum wrappers, and no shell casings. There now have been four attempts on my life. Three is a charm was not a saying I wanted to think about on my way back to the house.

"Maybe Agent Price is in with the crooks," my Guardian Angel said. His statement scared me.

"Maybe Manuel is not really a crook," he said.

"How can you come up with such garbage?" I asked him.

"Every possibility must be examined," he said, which was true.

When I got back to the house Lisa was scrambling eggs. As she put a plate before me she said, "I don't think Manuel or any of his people shot at you."

"Why?" I asked.

"I don't know. Call it a woman's intuition."

"I think she is right," my Guardian Angel said.

"What are you going to do now? You don't have the guns and Manuel will write you off like some flake," Lisa said.

"I'll have to go over and try and buy some time. I can tell him there has been a delay, but to be patient."

Patience is something most crooks don't have. They have a weird code where everybody is a thief and liar but one is supposed to always tell the truth and be on time. My word is my bond deal. It's like a vampire telling you he doesn't like blood, he only wants to suck on your toes.

"What should I do if you don't come back?" Lisa asked, but not sounding worried, like she was expecting me not to come back.

I had a passing thought that Lisa had ice in her veins and not blood.

"Then Lisa is a cool operator," my Guardian Angel grinned.

"If I don't come back my midnight you call Agent Price at the F.B.I. Tell him I didn't listen to his advice and he had better get his men to the Browne's house quicker than The Rifleman saving Will," I told Lisa.

"You've been to the F.B.I.?" Lisa asked in alarm, like an old hippie who had run out of food stamps.

"I had too. Where else could I get the guns? But Agent Price informed me they had an investigation going on against Moralis and his men and for me to get out of town before he dreamed up some charge to put me in jail."

"You should get out of town," she said.

"What, you don't love me anymore?"

"It's hard to love a dead man," she said simply.

"Listen to her, Roosevelt," my Guardian Angel said.

I can't argue with her or my Guardian Angel's logic.

"Since I know you won't listen to me, do you want me to go over and see Manuel before you do?" Lisa asked.

"I don't think it would do any good," I replied.

"I still think I should go over first," Lisa said. "It might make it better for you."

I shook my head. "You stay here in case you have to call Agent Price."

Lisa started to protest but I went to my room.

"How can you trust Lisa to call Agent Price if you get in trouble?" my Guardian Angel asked me.

"I shouldn't," I replied.

"That is the smartest thing you have said in a long time."

"Do you really think she is an undercover cop?" I asked.

He nodded but said nothing.

I looked out the window for a while and tried to make sense out of what I was about to do, but it didn't work. My mind filled with futility and stupidity I went back to the kitchen and looked up Agent Price's phone number and wrote it on a piece of paper. Lisa was not in the kitchen. I called Agent Price. The secretary forwarded the call and Price answered on the second ring. "This is Roosevelt," I said.

"Roosevelt, you're trying my patience, you should be somewhere in Nebraska by now trying to find a field of ditch weed."

"I'd like to be, but my car is broken down and it will take a few days to get it fixed."

Price didn't reply as he knew I'd told him a bold faced lie.

"That excuse is so lame a 16-year-old kid wouldn't try it," my Guardian Angel said.

"Listen, I thought you guys might reconsider," I told Price.

"Keep away from Moralis. Stay away from the Browne's house. I won't tell you again. You could mess up a lot of hard work and long hours on your crusade to vindicate an old friend. Understand me, Roosevelt?"

I hung up the phone without saying goodbye. But I felt weird, something was going on, I hadn't told Agent Price anything about going to the Browne's house.

"Roosevelt, Oh Roosevelt," my Guardian Angel said. "You're leading me right to another assignment."

I looked for Lisa, but she wasn't in the house, so I went out to the pool, but she wasn't there either. Going back to the house I remembered I'd forgotten to ask Lisa when she had taken the kid's things over to Sheila's.

"There is a possibility Sheila had come by and picked their things up," my Guardian Angel said.

Lisa was walking down the driveway. She had been over to see Manuel as sure as Coca-Cola hates Pepsi.

"I told you not to go over there," I said angrily to Lisa.

"Roosevelt, I know you don't love me, no matter how strongly I feel for you, and since you don't love me, you aren't going to tell me what to do." Finished, Lisa huffed away like I was some construction worker that had whistled at her and she was as interested in me about as much as a southern bell likes a Yankee.

I followed her into the house for no other reason than to be doing something. Lisa was ignoring me, but I told her. "Thanks for trying to make it easier for me."

She didn't say anything.

"What did you tell Manuel anyway?" I asked.

"I told him there was a holdup, but that it wouldn't take long and that you would be over later and tell him all about it."

"What did he say?"

"Nothing, he really didn't seem concerned at all. In fact, he seemed remote, like his mind was on something else."

"Here is Agent Price's phone number," I told Lisa and gave her the piece of paper.

I started for the door when Lisa said, "Listen, Roosevelt, no hard feelings, ok?"

I gave her a faint smile.

"You should really reconsider what you are doing Roosevelt," my Guardian Angel said.

Throughout my life I have had a tendency to ignore good advice.

Going through Eric the Red, I felt like I was the last of the French Army returning to Paris after Napoleon botched whipping Russia. Only, in my case, there were no disillusioned French people throwing rotten eggs at me.

Manuel wasn't by the corrals, but the horses were contentedly chomping on timothy and didn't bother to look up as I walked by.

I knocked on the door to Manuel's house. To my surprise, there was no answer. I knocked one more time, waited, and there was still no answer. Manuel's truck was parked out front so I figured he had to be around, besides, Lisa had said she had talked to him.

I turned around and Manuel was behind me. Caught off guard, I jumped slightly. Manuel laughed, but it wasn't a laugh of mirth. It was more like a Roman Emperor laughing at a Christian who was about to be lunch for a lion that particularly likes lean, slightly olive colored, meat.

"Come on in," Manuel said, more as an order than a cordial greeting.

I followed Manuel into his house. "It is not good when you say things and then cannot do them," he told me with an edge to his voice.

"I came over to apologize, Manuel. I want you to tell your people I will produce. I promise."

"Promises mean nothing to me," Manuel said. "Promises are for little girls and people in love. I'm only interested in results."

I started to leave. "You are not going anywhere," Manuel said in a threatening voice. "There is a man coming that wants to talk to you and he said if you come over to keep you here."

I could put a hurt on Manuel so quickly he wouldn't be able to remember he was a Mexican. But there was no need. Now I had to play it by ear - what will happen will happen without me wasting a brain cell.

"If you wasted any more brain cells you couldn't count to three," my Guardian Angel said holding up three fingers.

"Why didn't you tell Lisa you wanted me to wait?" I asked Manuel.

"Why tell a woman anything?" he asked.

"Some questions answer themselves," my Guardian Angel said.

I sat on the sofa and Manuel sat in a chair as far away from me as possible. "Lisa tells me you were in Vietnam," he said, Manuel must be into hostage small talk.

"I did my bit," I replied, letting Manuel know by my tone I was not a happy camper.

"It was a strange war," he said. "I know several men who were over there. They are all crazy now, life means nothing to them. What does life mean to you?"

"Life is a search for good," I replied, not really wanting to get into a conversation about life. "And all wars, no matter their reasons, are bad for humanity."

Manuel looked closely at me. "Lisa told me you were an old hippie who is now a private detective. Why after all the years of being a private detective do you suddenly want to get involved with something like this?"

"Lisa talks too much," my Guardian Angel said.

"Money," I said. "It's only money. I'm running out of time and there aren't too many jobs out there for 62 year old, over the hill, hippies."

"Be like most old freaks and move to Oregon or New Mexico and sell crafts?"

"Why did you get involved?" I asked, not wanting to admit what he had told me was what I should do in life.

"Roosevelt, if you are from Mexico and not born rich, there is only one way you can ever get ahead, crime. The system is set up to keep you down. Unlike America, there is no middle class in Mexico. In Mexico there is only the have and the have-nots."

"Big business and the government are trying their best to make it that way here also," I said.

"America is very treacherous," Manuel agreed. "In Mexico, you know who are the crooks, but here, the people you least expect are the crooks, and crooks a lot of times are the good guys."

195

"You've been here long enough to understand," I said.

"I have been here long enough to miss my country, but I know there is no need for me to go back. I could not pick lettuce and tomatoes now and be satisfied. I have seen too much."

I looked at Manuel's lizard boots and his gold bracelet. He saw me looking at them. "They are nice, no. In Mexico I would never be able to buy such things."

I thought about all the Mexicans in the country slaving away picking crops and washing cars, mowing yards, doing jobs that most people will not do, and yet, they were making more money than they ever dreamed they could back in their own country - that is, when the people they work for pay them.

"What time is this mystery man coming?" I asked.

"As soon as it is dark."

"I wonder if it's Dracula?" my Guardian Angel said.

I looked at my watch, dark was close to six hours away. I didn't say anything. I know leaving and coming back wasn't in the scenario. But, I also know, that if I was smart, I'd K.O. Manuel, beat feet for Matilda, and floor her all the way out of the Midwest. Whoever the person was who was coming to see me isn't the love of my life I've been searching for.

"Since we have a long time to wait, do you have anything to drink?" I asked Manuel.

"Beer," Manuel answered.

Manuel went and got us a beer.

"Years ago I used to go down to Zewantanao, Mexico," I told Manuel. "There was a hotel there that for five bucks I got a room and breakfast. When I ate, the parrots would fly out of the jungle, circle over the ocean and come and land on the table. They liked the butter."

"Did you go there with a woman?" Manuel asked.

"Yes, I thought I was in love, but it did not work out."

"That is too bad. Maybe one day it will."

"I caught a Roosterfish and there was a family that lived on the beach. They cleaned the fish and cooked it on an open fire. For a sauce, they cut up limes and chili peppers and basted the fish with it. For cooking the fish I gave them a dollar and half of the fish."

"I know of this place," Manuel said. "Now there is a big hotel that costs $300 a day. There are fishing boats with American Captains. All the locals have been driven away."

"Down in the Banana Republic," I said, holding my beer up to Manuel in a toast.

"At least you old hippies didn't want to change anything in Mexico," Manuel said sadly.

We finished our beers and Manuel got up to get us another one. While he was gone I thought about $300 motel rooms and I was sad.

"The first time I came to America, I ran across the border with my brother and jumped on a train in El Paso," Manuel said, after he came back with two more beers. "We rode all the way to California and spent the summer sleeping outside and picking everything from oranges to cherries. I had never seen a land with so much and so many people who had cars and nice clothes. As a child I had no shoes. We mostly ate beans and when we did eat meat, it was because my brother and I would steal it. My father was a good man but poverty made him a drunk. My mother did her best, and prayed for us, but she died when I was 12. I was 13 when I started picking fruit. Who is to say what is right and wrong Roosevelt? Is it right for most of my people to starve? Is it wrong for me to make money and send it back to my family so they do not starve?"

"Laws are written for the rich," I replied. "The only thing we must follow in our life is our heart."

Manuel laughed, a deep, resounding laugh. "You would have been a good Mexican. God was playing a trick on you when he made you white."

"God was playing a trick on me when he made me," I said.

"No doubt," my Guardian Angel said.

"You know you did not have to get mixed up in this garbage," Manuel said, "Being a hippie did not enlighten you that the pursuit of money is the pursuit of hell."

"I know all about hell," I said. "Hell is war, and believing in the wrong things. Hell is living your life in a way you know you're cheating yourself. And hell is doing things that harm others."

"At one time I could have liked you. Now it is all business. And in business there can be no like or dislike, only business," Manuel said solemnly.

"Business is not a good thing," I said.

"I have things I must do," he said. "I trust you can find the refrigerator if you want more beer. And please, do not try and leave."

Manuel left the house. I finished the last of my beer and got up and got another one. The way I felt, I could drink a case. I had no desire to look around the house. I doubt Manuel would leave me out of his sight if there was anything in the house that was important. I also felt, if I tried to make a break for it, Manuel would put a slug in me.

I drank three more beers and watched TV. I hadn't watched TV since I'd been in Iowa. Nothing had changed in the world. There were still about 20 little wars going on, most over whose God is the best God, the economy was shot, and after 30 years, the D.E.A. proclaimed they were winning the war on drugs - the drug economy had only generated 24 billion this year - down 3 billion from last year.

Manuel came back at 8:00. We did not talk. It was dark. At exactly 8:30 a car drove up and stopped in front of the house. Manuel looked at me, with no mirth in his eyes or trace of friendship. When I gazed back into his eyes, he and I both knew we were fully capable of killing each other if the need arose.

I stood when I heard the knock on the door.

"You should have headed for the hills," my Guardian Angel told me.

When Sheila walked in the door, I flopped back into the chair like somebody had hit me in the knees with a ball bat.

"Roosevelt," Sheila said, smiling like I was her long lost brother. "It's my turn for the surprise party."

My tongue lay on the bottom of my mouth like a dead fish. I glanced at Manuel and he was pointing a large chrome plated pistol with a silencer at my chest. I didn't know what caliber it was, but, by the size of the hole in the barrel, it was big enough to blast a hole in me to drive a Sherman tank through.

"Boy have you been barking up the wrong tree," my Guardian Angel said.

I regained a small amount of my composure, "I take it you didn't come over to deliver Avon products," I said to Sheila.

"No," she said, with a wry smile on her lips.

"Get up," Manuel ordered, waving the pistol at me.

I stood. The pistol, Mr. Blow Big Hole In Old White Hippie, had a persuasive voice that wasn't worth arguing with.

"Now turn around," Manuel ordered.

After I turned, Sheila came up behind me, pulled my hands behind my back, and snapped on a pair of handcuffs. She wasn't rough and she wasn't like a L.A. cop and put the cuffs on so tight my hands would turn purple. "Does this mean we're going steady?" I asked.

"Now what are we going to do with him?" Manuel asked Sheila.

"Put him in the pit. We don't have time to mess with him right now. The shipment is coming in and Moralis will be here later."

Manuel waved the gun in the direction I was to walk, when I turned around outside, Sheila also had a silencer equipped pistol pointed at me. It wasn't as large as Manuel's, but any bullet hole in one's body is more than a little ouch.

Manuel poked me with his pistol. "Move it," he ordered.

I followed Sheila, with Manuel several steps behind me. We went to the horse barn and once inside, Manuel turned on the light. He unlocked the stall where I had found the guns. "Move," Sheila ordered, pushing me with her pistol.

"I had you all wrong," I told Sheila. "I figured you were only after the money. I had no idea you were in this deep."

"Deeper than you'll ever guess," Sheila said.

"It was all a crock, what you said about Sam. I wouldn't doubt you were the one who killed him."

"Roosevelt," Sheila said. "Your only problem is you think too much. If you would take everything at face value you might be able to figure more out."

Manuel moved several hay bales and uncovered a trap door and opened it. "There is a bed down there and a light switch."

I looked down. It was as dark as Jacob's tomb. "I thought I made reservations at a Hilton," I said.

It's hard going through a narrow door, no more than two feet by two feet, and down an almost vertical ladder, especially when the hole I was climbing into was dark and my hands were handcuffed behind my back. I made the first two steps and then slipped and fell about ten feet to the bottom of the hole. I hit like a rock thrown off of a bridge.

"That had to hurt," my Guardian Angel grimaced.

"Get up and head towards the ladder," Manuel ordered, but I thought there was a trace of concern in his voice.

"Now, to your left is the light switch."

I found the switch with my shoulder and pushed it on with my elbow. The room was concrete, about ten feet by ten feet, and there was a cot. On one wall was a steal door with the hinges set in the concrete. At one time there had been a handle on the door, but it had been removed. I know there is a tunnel on the other side of the door that goes to Lisa's house. Judging by the age of the two homes, I figure the bunker had been made in the fifties as a bomb shelter. In those days, America felt Russia would at any moment be raining atom bombs on us and everybody ran around digging holes in the ground and stocking them with enough food they thought they could out live 100,000 years of radiation. The trap door shut without Sheila or Manuel saying goodbye. Not good manners.

I heard the thud of hay bales being tossed over the door. I sat on the bed and knew they'd been expecting me. There was a blue blanket on the cot and a pillow with a pillowcase that matched the blanket - a lady's touch. There was also a pitcher of water with a cup. That was all well and good, but pouring water from a pitcher into a cup with my hands handcuffed behind my back would not be an easy task.

"At least you were right about the tunnel," my Guardian Angel said adding solemnly, "sadly, enlightenment normally only comes right before death."

I lay on the bed and shut my eyes. I had been so far off base in my calculations that I make the word wrong seem right. About the only thing I know is that Sheila and Manuel are expecting a shipment of heroin tonight and that after it comes in Moralis is coming over.

I have no doubt that after the shipment comes in, I will probably be taking a journey - a journey to never never land, but with no magic carpet to get me back. And, my Guardian Angel will soon be looking for another job.

"Remember what I said about Madonna," my Guardian Angel said a little too enthusiastically.

"You couldn't stand all the sex."

"I could try," he said with a grin like an old man watching a porno movie.

"Lisa, Lisa, I tried to send out with mental telepathy, call Agent Price. Lisa, call Agent Price. Lisa, call Agent Price."

There was no response.

"The mental telepathy line is busy," my Guardian Angel said.

Not one to ever really feel defeated, I managed to make my way up the ladder by leaning into the rings as I took each step. I climbed as high as I could and then pushed on the door with my shoulders by straightening my legs. Sampson might have been able to break through the trap door but not me.

"Your hair is not long enough," my Guardian Angel said, "and you have more than one Delilah around you."

I descended the ladder like I had the first time, by falling.

200

"You are not a good basketball," my Guardian Angel said.

I examined the metal door. The hinges were encased by the concrete. The door was at least two or three inches thick. If I was in an old medieval dungeon, I could probably scratch through it in about 45 years. When I was a child my father was stationed in England. One day he took the family to tour a castle and like most kids I wanted to see the dungeon. On the walls of the dungeon were scrape marks the condemned had made with their steel manacles as they counted the days to their deaths. I don't think I will have to count too far.

I sat on the bed. There was nothing I could do but wait.

"Simplicity in life is not always good," my Guardian Angel said.

I don't know how long I sat staring at the gray concrete walls. It could have been twenty minutes or it could have been two hours. My watch was behind my back and my neck isn't made of rubber.

However long it was, I got up and turned off the light and made my way back to the bed in total darkness. It was the second darkest place I have ever been in my life. The other one was on bunker duty in Nam during the monsoon. When it was night, I couldn't see my hands in front of my face. I would like to put my hand in front of my face and see if I could see it, but handcuffs have a way of putting hands out of commission.

I started replaying in my mind everything I thought was true about this case, and then I remembered Sheila's last words to me before I fell into the pit. "Roosevelt, you think too much. If you would just take everything at face value, you might be able to figure more out."

Face value, what is face value?

"Face value to you is being too full of yourself to listen to good advice," my Guardian Angel said.

"If you were more demonstrative and not a wise guy all the time I might listen to you more often," I replied.

"Roosevelt, I don't have to be nice," he said.

Suddenly I was filled with questions. Why didn't Manuel and Sheila kill me? Killing me now or later wouldn't make much difference. They could have shot me and tossed me in the river and some guy fishing for catfish in Missouri would have snagged me in about a week. Why did Manuel ask Sheila what to do with me? It was strange for a Latin man to ask a woman's advice on anything.

I don't know why, but I feel like bait. Fishermen say big bait catches big fish.

"If you think you are big bait your ego is really reaching," my Guardian Angel said.

"I can't give up yet," I said.

"For a man like you, getting killed with handcuffs on has to be embarrassing," my Guardian Angel said almost sadly. "It's not a manly thing, no Viking flair, no bravado."

I shook my head. I have no idea where some of the things my Guardian Angel says comes from.

I shut my eyes. If I was going to the big discount store in the sky I want to make peace with the world.

CHAPTER 17
SURPRISE - SURPRISE

The complete darkness I was in acted like a narcotic. My mind was filled with colored pictures of things I'd done throughout my life. I could see the blue rippling water of a small stream I fished as a boy in Washington State. I could see, in complete detail, the old lady who used to live by the stream and the apple tree she would let me climb to get one of the best apples at the top of the tree. I could see a beaver pond high in the mountains of Colorado filled with small, brightly colored, brook trout. I would put two flies on my line and catch them two at a time. I saw my grandmother standing on the front porch of her farmhouse and talking to the mailman. I saw myself dressed in green fatigues and standing on the deck of a ship as we slowly advanced on Vietnam, and I remembered how the ocean turned from a deep blue to a pale, dirty green. I ran the gauntlet of emotions - sad, happy, carefree, lonely, in love.

My life paraded through my mind like a movie.

"A bad movie that would only show at some small obscure theater on a back street in Baltimore," my Guardian Angel said sarcastically.

There is always a jerk in the crowd, that, with age, I have learned to ignore.

I was reliving my first rock concert when I heard the trapdoor open. A flashlight beam cut through the darkness. "Turn on the light and come on up here," Manuel ordered. "What are you, some kind of nut?"

I took it Manuel had never searched for his inner self.

I struggled to my feet, turned on the light, and had to let my eyes adjust to the sudden brightness. I slowly inched my way up the ladder. Manuel grabbed my shoulder and pulled me up the last several feet.

He didn't ask, "How have you been?" But pointed with his big shiny pistol for me to walk. Pistols have a way of cutting short the need for conversation.

When we got to the house, the door swung open and Sheila stepped back to let me pass.

"Did you get your load of heroin so all the little boys and girls in Chicago can throw up and roll in the gutter?" I asked Sheila.

"Keep your mouth shut," Manuel said.

"If I don't, will you kill me?"

"If you don't, I'll tape your mouth shut."

"Why did you bring me up here?" I asked Sheila, ignoring Manuel.

Sheila looked agitated and was strung as tight as a rock star before a concert that had forgotten to blow dry his hair. "A couple of people want to ask you some questions," Sheila answered me, like at the moment I was the least of her worries.

She looked nervously over at Manuel. Manuel seemed about as nervous as a boa constrictor.

"I think Lisa has forgotten about you," my Guardian Angel said. "She has had hours to call Agent Price."

"I told her to wait until mid-night," I told him.

"Who wants to see me?" I asked Sheila. "I bet it's not the Tooth Fairy."

Manuel laughed. Sheila gave him a look that would shut up a mother-in-law and didn't answer my question.

For the next fifteen minutes or so, there was no talking. Sheila paced back and forth across the living room, giving her impression of Churchill waiting for World War II to end. Manuel leaned up against the door jam between the living room and the kitchen. He had his, 'I'd like to shoot a white boy' pistol tucked in his belt, and looked like a Mexican border guard, who, for 10 bucks would let you bring anything you wanted into the country.

We all heard a car pull up to the front of the house. Sheila glanced at me and for a brief instant I thought I saw concern in her eyes.

Manuel looked at the door, looked at Sheila, and then looked at me. I looked at the door. My Guardian Angel looked at the door. It was a 'looking' happening.

"It's been a good run," my Guardian Angel said, "and I want you to know that I have done my best to protect you even though you are boring."

"Thanks," I said, about as thankful as a hungry man eating his pet chicken.

Sheila opened the door before the person outside had time to knock. She didn't say hello, she didn't say come on in, she didn't say anything as Detective Owens walked into the room with as much pomp as Prince Charles visiting a private all girls' college.

"Roosevelt," he said, grinning like a judge at a condemned murderer, "you've done it up good this time."

"I hate dirty cops," my Guardian Angel said sneering at Owens.

204

"I'm not surprised to see you," I said, like seeing Owens was the most boring thing that had happened to me in years. "I heard your voice over here one night."

"That was the night we loaded the truck. We thought we saw somebody lurking in the bushes."

"I guess I'm about as sneaky as a 747 taking off."

"I also take it, it was you the boys took some potshots at?" Owens said.

"I'm glad they were lousy shots," I replied.

"I've tried to kill you two times but I always missed," Owens said sadly.

Sheila gave Owens a darting glare and it looked like the gray cells in her brain were working overtime.

Owens, still grinning, hit me with a right cross so hard it slammed me back into the chair. I sat back up, blood running from a cut on my cheek. "You sticking your hippie nose into my business has caused me nothing but grief. You burned down the two Pussy Cats and because of you I had to kill Greasy Ed. Who knows what that idiot told you?"

"At least you know Lisa didn't kill Greasy Ed," my Guardian Angel said.

"Greasy Ed didn't tell me anything," I told Owens.

"His tough luck," Owens said coldly.

"Real tough luck," my Guardian Angel said.

I noticed Manuel do a double take when Owens mentioned Greasy Ed.

"That's why Greasy Ed looked so surprised," I said. "He thought you were his friend."

Owens grinned. "Did the stuff come in?" he asked Sheila, with an emphasis on, 'stuff'.

"Right on time," Sheila answered.

"I'll deal with you later," he told me.

"Watch this dogface," he ordered Manuel - the dogface being me.

"Yes, sir," Manuel answered as crisp as an Army private to a Captain.

I thought Owens was the only dogface.

"Show me," Owens told Sheila.

Sheila didn't take off her blouse but they both went out the front door. Manuel went into the kitchen and brought back a small dishtowel.

He wiped the blood off of my face but didn't say anything, although I could tell he wasn't happy about something.

"He doesn't like me because I slept with his ex-wife," I told Manuel.

"He doesn't like himself," Manuel replied. "He is a man consumed with hate and power."

It was a strange statement for a crook to say who sells guns and heroin.

"I figured you were tied up in all of this for a long time," I told Manuel. "But Sheila, I had her all wrong."

"Don't judge her, Roosevelt," Manuel said. "People do things for many reasons, not all of which are obvious."

"It's hard not to judge people when what they do harms people."

"You are a strange man," Manuel said. "You run around looking for trouble instead of being smart and looking for peace. We all would have been better off if you had never blown into town."

"You can say that again," I said.

"We all would have been better off if you had never blown into town," he said and smiled at me.

"Not funny," I said.

"I thought it was funny," my Guardian Angel grinned.

"Life needs a little humor now and then. Even when it is the darkest, one must remember, it can always get darker," Manuel said.

At the moment I didn't feel like my life was all sunshine. "I don't need wisdom when I'm about to die," I told Manuel.

Sheila and Owens came back into the house. Owens was grinning like looking at heroin was the happiest thing he does in his life. "The guy from Chicago will be here tomorrow night to pick up this load," Owens said to Manuel. "After that we're going to have to change our operation thanks to old Roosevelt here."

"It's about time anyway," Manuel said. "The Browne's will be back soon."

"The Browne's are dead," I said.

"Shut-up Roosevelt," Owens snapped, glaring at me.

Sheila and Manuel looked shocked.

"They found them in the trunk of a car in Mexico, shot and slightly overripe," I continued.

Owens moved quicker than I would have ever given him credit for. His leg was a blur as he kicked me in the chest and then punched me twice on the side of the head with a not too bad combination.

206

"Leave him alone," Sheila yelled, grabbing his arm.

Owens poised over me like a boxer who had his man down for the ten count. His face was beet red and he was gasping for breath he was so angry. He twisted away from Sheila but didn't say anything to her.

"We had to take them out," Owens told Sheila, after he had regained his breath.

"There was no need to kill them," Sheila said angrily.

"You just do your job, you work for me, remember?" Owens snapped.

I wondered what Sheila's job is?

Sheila looked at Manuel as if she was trying to tell him something. Manuel had a distant glare to his eyes.

"When is Moralis getting here?" Owens asked in an agitated voice.

"I'm not his mother," Sheila answered curtly.

Owens gave her a dirty look, but didn't say anything.

The room fell into a deep heavy silence.

"This den of thieves is having a little discord," my Guardian Angel said.

"Out of curiosity," I said, breaking the silence. "What are you going to do with me?"

"I'm going to kill you myself," Owens said, like killing me would take a lot of deliberation. "And to make it more pleasurable I'm going to choke you to death. A bullet would be too quick and painless."

"That's nice, you're all heart," I replied.

Sheila gave Manuel the, trying to communicate, look again.

I didn't figure anybody in the room except me was upset over my ultimate death. I did know that I would not go down as easily as Owens thought. Before I die, I would get in at least one good lick.

In Vietnam, the most afraid I had been was at night before I fell asleep. I didn't want to get killed while I was sleeping. It always scared me that I would die and not know it. I always wondered if you died and didn't know it, were you really dead. It's one of those mind twisters you really don't want to get into on anything heavier than coffee.

Another car pulled up outside. I hoped it was Lisa and Agent Price and a posse of sixteen agents riding in to save me.

"Dream on," my Guardian Angel said.

Manuel opened the door. Moralis and the man he had been with at Sam's funeral walked in. "So this is the guy who burned our bars?" Moralis said to Owens.

It was a strange way to say hello.

"What's the matter, you don't like naked women?" he asked me, and then laughed so hard it sounded like he was auditioning for track laughter that would run on a TV comedy – a show that wasn't really funny.

"I wish somebody would have burnt them sooner. The insurance paid more than they made," he said.

"You should pay me for the favor," I said.

Moralis nodded to the ape that came in the door with him. He was so big, he made Greasy Ed look like a midget. The ape without even a hello or a smile, backhanded me on the right side of my face and then on the left. It felt like I had been hit with two sledgehammers and let me know Moralis doesn't like my brand of humor.

My head sagged and I forced myself not to pass out. I felt a trickle of blood oozing out of my nose and the ringing in my ears was as loud as if I was standing in the middle of a hundred-member bell band playing Silent Night.

"Don't mess him up," Owens said casually. "I want him in good shape when I kill him."

This time Manuel didn't wipe my face off with a towel. But looked at me like a pig that he had raised to slaughter, and although he was sad about killing it, the bacon would be good.

"Now that the guests are all here, I guess you want me to sing and dance," I said.

"How much did you tell the Feds?" Owens demanded.

"I told them everything I know," I lied.

"Lovely Lisa is a snitch," my Guardian Angel said, "maybe I was wrong about her being an undercover cop.

"Did you tell them about me?" Owens asked.

"No, I didn't."

Owens smiled. "You wanted to wrap this up all by yourself. You wanted to catch whoever killed Sam just for your own stupid ego. Well, I hate to disappoint you Roosevelt, but nobody here killed Sam. Sam's death is all a mystery to us."

"I think he is telling the truth," my Guardian Angel said.

"I know he is," I replied.

My Guardian Angel gave me a questioning look.

"What I can't figure, Owens, is why you would even want to be involved? You're so close to retirement you could take a nap and wake up with your pension."

"My pension isn't big enough to feed a goldfish," Owens said. "You spend your life watching out for good old American Joe, you get shot at, spit on, run into every kind of scum ball there is in the world and for what? A watch, a badge mounted on an oak plaque, and about $1,000 a month. $1,000 in this world won't even pay the rent."

"A dirty cop is the worst kind of crook there is," I said disdainfully.

"You lousy bastard," Owens yelled at me and started raining blows on my head and shoulders like I was a drought that, he, the rain man was going to break.

I couldn't take it anymore and figured I might as well get my lick in while I could. I came straight up out of the chair and slammed the top of my head into Owens's chin. His teeth banged together like a 300-lb. man doing a belly flop at the pool. Owens grunted and fell back and I brought my knee up into his groin. As he sagged over, I kneed him once again in the face. Out of the corner of my eye I saw Moralis's bodyguard coming at me and I spun and kicked him in the ribs. He went down like Muhammad Ali in his prime had hit him with a left hook just below the heart. Owens started to move - I kicked him in the chest, trying to hit him in the throat. I was about to make a break for the door when a right cross from Moralis put me down for the count. Before I blacked out I wondered why Manuel hadn't gotten in on the fight.

When I came to I was in the chair, but now, besides my hands being cuffed behind my back, my ankles were tied with a piece of rope. Owens was laid out on the couch, groaning. Moralis's ape was sitting in a chair holding his ribs, with Moralis standing next to him.

Neither Sheila nor Manuel was helping either one of them. I could hardly breathe because of the blood trickling out of my nose.

"That was a brave thing to do," my Guardian Angel said to me. "I want you to know that whoever I go to in my next assignment I will always remember your last valiant act. Dumb but valiant."

Owens, in more pain than he had ever experienced in his life, in between grunts and grimaces, said. "I'll kill you for this. I'll cut your guts out and feed them to the birds."

"I don't like crooked cops, and I don't like cops that lie. You told me you would choke me to death," I said defiantly. I couldn't think of anything else to say and I tried to spit at him but my lips were so swollen I would have been last at a watermelon seed spitting contest.

"Where's the money?" Moralis demanded.

"What money?" I replied, like I didn't even know what a one-dollar bill looked like.

"Don't be smart Roosevelt," Moralis warned, "just tell us where the million is that Sam had."

"Don't tell them," my Guardian Angel said.

"Why not?" I asked.

"I don't know, but don't," he told me.

"Since I am about to die I'll listen to you."

"What money are they talking about? Do you have any idea?" I asked Sheila.

"What money, Moralis?" Sheila asked which caught me as odd as she knew 'what money.'

"Sam had a million over at his house that was ours. We know Roosevelt and Lisa found it. Now, where is it?"

"Lisa is a double snitch," my Guardian Angel said. "And maybe the little double snitch, undercover cop, ran away with the money."

"Where's Lisa?" I asked with concern. "You better have not done anything to her."

"Why?" Owens said hoarsely, sitting up on the sofa with about as much effort as a fat dog takes to roll over. "Do you think we would hurt your little lovebird?"

I tried to jump up, but forgot my feet were tied, and fell on my face trying to get to Owens. My head sounded like a walnut breaking when I hit the floor.

Manuel and Sheila picked me up and put me back in the chair.

"You're not a good acrobat," Moralis said.

His ape had recovered and he chuckled. If I'd had a banana I would toss him one.

"I'll ask you again," Moralis warned, "Where is the money?"

"I want to know that Lisa is ok, then I might tell you."

The ape took a knife out of his pocket and opened it. I could tell he spent hours of quality time sitting around sharpening it and that it was sharp enough to cut hair. He looked at me like it would give him great pleasure to turn me into long, thin strips of meat that a cannibal could make fajitas out of.

"If I let Hector cut your ears off, you won't worry about Lisa. Now tell us where the money is," Moralis demanded.

"If you kill me, you won't find the money," I said, trying to sound brave, although, to me, my voice sounded as brave as Robin threatening Batman.

Owens looked at me like I was the smartest guy in the class and he hated my guts.

Moralis glared at me and I thought he was going to come over and take his turn at me but he went outside. He was gone no more than 30 seconds. When he came back he wasn't being followed by the ever-trusting Lassie, but by Lisa, who had a snub nosed 38 clutched in her hand.

If I was a tire I would be a blowout.

"Oh boy, oh boy," my Guardian Angel said.

"Roosevelt, where did you put the money?" Lisa demanded.

"I don't think she loves you anymore," my Guardian Angel said, "and my undercover cop idea just flew out the window."

"Surprise, surprise," I said to Lisa.

Lisa ran at me like a house cat after a bird. After being hit by Hector and Owens and Moralis, her slap almost felt good.

"I see I didn't have to worry about you," I said. "Thanks for calling Price."

Lisa started to laugh. "You're so stupid Roosevelt. I don't know how you ever solved that kidnapping case that got you on TV. From what I've seen, you don't know if you're going forward or backward most of the time."

"He is a product of the 60's," my Guardian Angel said. "There is no difference between forward and backward."

"Yea, but I'm a rich forward or backward," I said to Lisa.

She slapped me again.

"Where did you put the money Roosevelt? You no good thief," Lisa said like she was Miss Goody Two Shoes.

"You know, at first I thought you had killed Sam," I told Lisa, ignoring her question. "But I know that you didn't. And then I thought you killed Greasy Ed. But good old crooked cop Owens over there already confessed to killing Greasy Ed. But in all truth I didn't think you were involved with these people."

Lisa looked like she wanted to say something, but she couldn't.

"Sheila, I had you pegged wrong all along. All I ever thought about you was when you were a young hippie and out to see the world, and what a disappointment it had all become. I thought you were greedy but I didn't think you would ever hang out with people like this."

Sheila couldn't look me in the eyes. It might be the fact my face looks like a boxer that had never won a fight.

"Enough of all this," Moralis said. "Tell us where the money is so Owens can kill you and we can all go home."

Owens, with the word 'kill' ringing in his ear, managed to sit up.

"You have to answer me one question?" I said.

"What is it?" Owens demanded.

"I suppose you people made all that money-selling heroin."

Moralis laughed, like heroin was a funny word. "Of course we made it selling heroin. What do you think? We made it selling Girl Scout cookies."

"Kill me," I said.

My Guardian Angel was down on his hands and knees praying, he was proud of me. I was going to die a good and honorable death. I have no doubt they will find the money, but I will not tell them where it is. I don't want any heroin karma on my soul. I am going to have one tough fight to get past St. Peter anyway.

Owens took his pistol out of the holster and before anyone knew what was happening, he pointed the pistol at my head. I jumped as far as one can with their legs tied together and their hands handcuffed behind their back, but it was too late. There was a loud bang, and everything, as if by magic, went into slow motion. I saw a small trace of smoke leave the barrel. I felt a dart of pain on the left side of my head. As I was falling to the floor I heard other gunshots, then - everything was dark, darker than death. I didn't hear my Guardian Angel tell me, "I'm sorry Roosevelt, but you knew your life had to end this way. I will never forget you."

CHAPTER 18
DUMB AS A ROCK - SMART AS A WHIP

The room came in and out of focus like everything was shrouded with pale silk - silk so fine the breeze from a butterfly's wings would make it move. The room was semi-gloss white and devoid of adornment. "I must be in heaven," I sighed, but then I smelled rubbing alcohol and realized with a jolt - I was not in heaven - I was in a hospital. I had a cheap whiskey headache and not enough energy to fall out of bed, let alone try to stand. I had no recollection of how I had gotten here or how long I'd been here. There was nobody else in the room and for some reason, somebody had turned on the TV, but the sound was off.

There was a window in the room but the window faced directly into a brick wall. All I could see was the wall and about a two inch layer of pigeon poop on the windowsill. At the moment, there were no pigeons to go with the poop.

I felt at peace. Maybe I had found my center. "Get off it, dream boy, your center is miles beyond your grasp," my Guardian Angel said.

"It's good to hear your voice," I said, as my peaceful feeling sailed out the window.

"It is good to hear yours, also," he said, but he did not sound too convincing.

"Why didn't you warn me I was about to get shot?" I asked my Guardian Angel, but not in anger, since I was not dead he had not completely failed.

"I was too late," he replied. "I think I am getting slower. These last few weeks have been hard on me what with looking at a half naked Lisa all the time."

I felt around my head. The complete left side of my head was covered with a bandage. Thankfully, my head had not been shaved - long hair is an ego thing for me.

"It's tougher to be cool now, it takes brains or a Gold Visa Card," my Guardian Angel said. "All it took in the 60's was long hair and beads and dirty feet."

"How did I get here?" I asked.

"I'm not telling you. You need another good surprise," he said.

"You have to tell me. I am your master," I demanded, slightly peeved. "And besides, I am about surprised out."

"You're funny," he said and stuck his tongue out at me.

Shutting my eyes I instantly went to sleep. I was too tired to argue with my Guardian Angel.

I don't know how long I slept, but when I woke up a nurse was peering at my face. She jumped back when I opened my eyes. "Oh, Mr. Roosevelt," she said, "you startled me. "You've been in a coma for six days."

"Six days," I mumbled.

Six days of having no recollection of passing time. It was the first time in my life I had experienced such a thing. What a burden time is.

"What's your name?" I asked the nurse, my words coming out in what seemed another person's voice.

"Leslie, Leslie Nichols."

"Leslie, you are the most beautiful lady I have ever seen in my life," I said.

She was really not that pretty but she was handsome and the smile she gave me was so happy it would have made Castro want to shave.

"What happened to me?" I asked Leslie.

"A bullet put a two-inch crease in the left side of your head. You were extremely lucky," she said.

"Who brought me here?" I asked, since my Guardian Angel was on an information strike.

"I don't know," Leslie said, and went around the room doing all the little things nurses do. I wondered if she was paid off by my Guardian Angel.

Leslie waved at me as she left.

The remote to the TV was on my bedside table and I turned off the TV. I looked at the pigeon poop. After thinking I was dead the pigeon poop is beautiful - but I was still puzzled as to how I got to the hospital, and adding to my confusion, I wondered where all the pigeons were?

Nurse Leslie, still smiling, brought me dinner. I had all the food groups, a vegetable, salad, beef, milk, a slice of wheat bread with margarine, a glass of water, a piece of cake, and decaffeinated coffee.

"People in the modern world have to be sick to eat right," my Guardian Angel said.

I ate everything and wished I could have seconds. I have never been a picky eater. I have always felt you eat because you have to.

When God invented us, he told one of his angels, "I'll mess with these guys, I'll make them spend half of their time eating and the other half killing each other over food and Me."

Think how simple life would be if we didn't have to eat?

"You could lie around all day and drink beer," my Guardian Angel said with a merry look.

I was enjoying my full stomach when a nurse came in that should have been a female drill sergeant. She also had a case of lockjaw. She filled a syringe, rubbed my arm with an alcohol swab, and with as much emotion as she paid her bills, gave me a shot.

I was asleep before she left the room. My last thought being, if I had a hundred gallons of this stuff I could make a fortune in Seattle.

My sleep was a kaleidoscope of dreams, all in living color and wrap around high fidelity sound. Detective Owens' face loomed before me. His hand came up holding a pistol that was as big as a bazooka, the pistol went off, but instead of a slug slamming into me, the air was filled with multi-colored streamers, that as they floated to the earth spelled out - Roosevelt, you be a fool.

Manuel was jacking up Matilda and stealing the tires.

Margaret was in a grassy meadow filled with yellow daffodils. She was sobbing.

Rick and Kathy were in a living room watching a TV show that played over and over again. The TV monster had sucked out their brain.

A million dollars was flying south for the winter. Each bill had wings and, as they sailed over lakes and ponds, hunters shot them out of the sky and stuffed them in their pockets, many shot over their limit.

Sam was sitting on a cloud with three other men, who I took to be angels, they were wondering what happened to Country Joe and The Fish.

Moralis and his bodyguard were playing jacks in hell.

My Guardian Angel was taking photographs of two women for the feature spread in a men's magazine.

Lisa, Sheila, and Manuel were sitting in a bar, drinking, and telling jokes about me.

Greasy Ed was flipping hamburgers that smelled delicious.

In my last dream I was in Matilda and trying to drive, but the harder I pushed on the gas pedal, the slower the car went. I was being chased by corn stalks holding M-16's at port arms that were hollering at me, "You can't get away from Iowa."

When I woke up in the morning, I felt as though I had not slept at all. Nurse Leslie was standing by the bed looking as fresh and starched as a cadet at the Air Force Academy. "You had better get out of bed and clean up. You're going to have some visitors."

The shower was wonderful. I shaved my neck and brushed my teeth - surprisingly, my face had only a few nicks on it from the love pats Owens and his cronies had bestowed on me.

Leslie had laid my clothes out for me. After I had put on my Levi's, boots, and shirt, I still felt tired and beat up but I could see the end of the rainbow.

"Don't even think about buying a pair of red shoes and taking singing lessons," my Guardian Angel said.

"There now, don't you feel better?" Nurse Leslie asked me, sounding like a mother who was leaving her child at kindergarten for the first time.

"Yes," I said. "I feel better now."

"Enjoy your friends," Leslie said happily, like her favorite thing in the world was to watch men put on their clothes.

"I think it would only be fair, since most people in a hospital are half-naked, that the nurses should have to be naked also," my Guardian Angel said.

"It's would be a good marketing ploy," I said.

I sat in a chair and wondered who would be coming to see me? The only person I could think of was Agent Price, but Leslie had said visitors. The only people Agent Price would have with him would be other agents to help him with my arrest for obstructing justice.

There was a knock on the door and completely out of character my heart sped up. I didn't feel like saying come in. So I said, "Ali outs in free."

The door swung open. Sheila, Lisa, and Manuel came into the room looking as happy and carefree as the Three Musketeers after they had been out all night killing the Cardinal's men.

My Guardian Angel laughed. I was so much in shock I didn't stand.

Both Lisa and Sheila were carrying purses. I figured they each had a pistol with a silencer on it and was going to make sure I was killed properly this time.

Sheila kissed me on my left cheek. Lisa kissed me on my right cheek. "The kiss of death," I muttered.

Luckily, Manuel didn't want to kiss me.

216

"Did you sell Matilda's tires?" I asked him.

"Volkswagen tires aren't worth the time to steal," he said, and winked at me.

"I take it you all have come to tell me you found the money," I said.

"Putting the money in the trunk of your car wasn't too imaginative," Lisa said, like she was disappointed in me.

"Imagination is for artists," my Guardian Angel said. "Roosevelt can't even finger-paint."

Lisa reached into her purse. I didn't have the energy to try and stop her. Sheila also reached into her purse. It was going to be dueling pistols to see who could shoot me first. But, their hands didn't emerge with pistols - both had a black leather folder that they flipped open and stuck in front of my face. I read quickly, Special Agent Sheila Wrench, and, Special Agent Lisa Wrench, on their picture I.D.'s.

My Guardian Angel started doing a jig and pointed his finger at me. "I was right. I was always right."

Manuel showed me his shiny badge and a picture I.D., it read - Special Agent Manuel Hernandez. "It was true, though, I did pick fruit when I was 13," Manuel said.

I felt as dumb as a rock.

"It's an amazing turn of events, isn't it?" my Guardian Angel said puffed up like a puffer fish after turning the tables on a shark.

My dumbness turned into aggravation. "You used me," I sputtered to their three smiling faces.

"We had to Roosevelt, you fell right into the middle of our investigation," Sheila said.

"What investigation?" I blurted, my mind racing like a cheap top bought from a vendor in Mexico.

Lisa touched my hand. "That's why we're all here, to explain everything to you. We figure we at least owe you that much."

"You almost got me killed," I shouted. "Look at my head."

"The bandage helps your looks," Manuel said.

"It doesn't cover his face enough," my Guardian Angel said.

I cooled down. They have to be the only reason I am alive, and believe me, I do enjoy being alive.

"Let me start from the beginning," Sheila said and sat on the bed.

I figured the story was going to take a long time if she had to sit.

"Years ago, after Sam had left the commune in New Mexico, he came back here," Sheila started.

"Tell me something I don't know," I cut in. I have always been a - let's get to the point - type of guy.

"Shut up Roosevelt," Sheila ordered - her special agent personality coming through. "I don't have to tell you anything if I don't want to."

"Go on," I said. "Sorry."

I've learned that telling a woman I'm sorry, even when I'm not, is always a wise thing to do.

"As I was saying," Sheila went on. "When Sam came back to Iowa he was completely disillusioned. Nothing the hippies had stood for was happening. Pot wasn't the road to the soul. Acid only made people jump out of windows and sit around on the ground and eat dirt. Timothy Leary became a politician and all the rock and roll stars bought 10 million dollar homes and shares in oil stocks. Dope suddenly became a big business and instead of a bunch of freaks running off to Mexico to bring back enough smoke for their friends, tough guys with guns started controlling the pot scene. It was then Sam and I met. I was just like him, angry, fed up, disillusioned. Soon after we were married we were approached by the F.B.I. to become undercover agents. My Uncle was in the F.B.I. and he had set it up. Sam and I decided to make a career move and we became agents."

I started to speak. "No, Roosevelt, we didn't bust long hairs for a few joints," Sheila said.

She had read my mind. I felt relieved.

"You were telling me the truth about going to Frisco, weren't you?" I asked Sheila.

Sheila smiled at me, an almost sad smile. "Yes I was."

I smiled back. Lost dreams are lost dreams. They never come back.

"I was also telling you the truth about Sam getting involved with guys in New Mexico who were bringing small amounts of pot into the country."

"I suppose that's good," I said.

"After our training, Sam and I worked on cases all over the country. It was perfect. A man and a woman, and later with kids, we got in with big time dope dealers from here to New York. And then by accident, three years ago, one of the people we had busted knew the original people Sam had worked with in New Mexico. They were now smuggling heroin into the country and guns into Mexico. The department thought it was worth a try for Sam to approach them and see if he could get back in. Sam made a trip to Nogales and made it look like an accident that he ran into Moralis. Moralis has a home in Nogales and his business hub is out of there. Moralis took him in with open arms - like a long lost brother. Sam told him he could supply stash houses and he had a man in Chicago that could distribute."

"Moralis took the bait, the hook, and the sinker," I said.

"He was so happy, he wanted Sam to become one of his partners," Sheila went on, "and, he even centered his operation out of Des Moines. A special task force consisting of Sam, Lisa, Manuel, and me, was put together for this case. We were told to keep Agent Price informed of our activities. The Feds paid the rent on the house Lisa and Sam lived in and Sam got Manuel in with Moralis. Sam also talked Moralis into renting the Browne's house to work out of. The Browne's knew exactly what was going on, he is a retired C.I.A. agent. Moralis told them he would give them $20,000 for two months, all they had to do was take a vacation. The Browne's told Moralis where they could be contacted in Mexico if anything went wrong."

"Wrong enough they got killed," I said sarcastically.

"They are not dead," Lisa stated.

"But, but...." I stammered, taken completely off guard.

"I know," Lisa went on. "Your Border Patrol friend said they had been found dead. It was all done by computer. Every law enforcement agency in the country thought they were dead. We couldn't afford for anybody to know the truth."

"But Owens said he had them killed," I said, feeling like a bird with no wings.

"Owens always made his calls from the same pay phone. It wasn't far from his house and he was too lazy to drive to another one. We bugged the phone. When he contacted a man to arrange the hit on the Browne's all we did was have the Mexican authorities grab him and then we put out the death notification on the computer. Owens couldn't have had them killed anyway. The Browne's made it look like they went to Mexico. They really went to Hawaii. They will be back in a few days."

"Bugging pay phones is illegal," I said.

"Pay phone, did somebody say pay phone?" Manuel said trying to look like an alter boy who coveted the Mother Superior.

"We could have never used the tapes in court is all," Sheila said, looking at me like she was finally realizing how stupid I really am.

"Now you know what I have to put up with," my Guardian Angel said.

"Why did Owens want the Browne's dead?" I asked.

"The only reason we can think of is he didn't want to pay them. More money for him," Manuel replied.

Sheila continued. "What we've been doing for the past two years is working in conjunction with the Mexican authorities and building a case on Moralis and everybody around him. We were about to wrap it all up when Sam was killed and you happened to bless us with your smiling old hippie detective face."

"Roosevelt has the knack of showing up when he isn't wanted," my Guardian Angel said.

"We have the growers, the refiners, the storage people. We have the big boy in Mexico and most of his organization. We have the smugglers, and the drivers, and the outlets in cities from here to the East Coast," Lisa said.

"But what about the fake kidnapping?" I asked.

Sheila and Lisa looked at me like little kids who had been caught stealing cookies. "I thought it was a dumb idea," Manuel said. "But I'm not the boss."

"Who is?" I asked.

Lisa smiled.

"A few days before Sam was killed he hid a million at the house," Sheila said, "but we didn't know where he put it. Lisa had been gone and he didn't tell anyone else. It was money he was stashing for Moralis and Owens. When he was killed, and you were there, we knew you would want to solve his murder so we came up with the idea of the kidnapping to keep you occupied. The only thing that screwed it up was you figured it all out. We never dreamed you would be so lucky," Lisa said. "How can someone solve a kidnapping that is not a kidnapping?"

"With Roosevelt it is always luck," my Guardian Angel said.

"It would have been a lot easier if you would have told me what was going on," I said.

"We know that now," Lisa replied. "But we decided it was better not to tell you. We couldn't afford a leak after all the years of work and we didn't know if we could trust you. Then, after the money was found, and we wanted you gone, you wouldn't leave."

"You can't blame anybody except yourself," my Guardian Angel said. "You sure can't blame me. I told you to hot foot out of here from the start. And, old wise one, if you remember, I told you to think about the fact that Sheila and Lisa were always in communication."

"Why did Sam tell me he was in trouble and had messed his life up and ask me to come over to the house?" I asked.

"You were always his hero. Plus, he was getting tired of what he was doing. When this case was over he was going to get out and try to live a normal life," Lisa said.

"He also told me he would introduce me to the kids," I said.

"Under all the pressure he was under he probably forgot they were at camp," Lisa said.

"When Sam got shot for an instant he looked relieved," I said, "as if he wanted to die."

"Death is often a relief," My Guardian Angel said, which he should know since he has been dead for almost 700 years.

"Sam had been depressed. He was having a lot of trouble with Margaret and I think he was beginning to wonder if our marriage had been a mistake," Lisa said, in a voice I knew it saddened her deeply.

"Right after Sam was killed I took a card out of his pocket with C'est La Vie Mother Goose written on it," I said.

"I gave him that card right after our divorce," Sheila said. "Why he had it in his pocket I have no idea."

"He also had a key in his pocket and I discovered the key fit the lock to the tennis court at Sam's and the tennis court at the Browne's."

"Sam always locked the tennis court. He and the Browne's played tennis at both courts and they each had keys to both of them," Lisa said.

"Yes, but, why lock a tennis court?"

"Kids would get in and use the volley machine and not pick up the balls," Lisa said.

"Too simple," my Guardian Angel said.

"Lisa, it always bothered me that you drive Sam's Lincoln," I said.

"He loved that car and it makes me feel close to him," she replied, giving me a sad little pixie smile.

"The way I've investigated this case it is no wonder, I couldn't even get shot good," I said.

Then I gave Sheila a dirty look. "You didn't have to hit me on the head so hard the night you ransacked the house."

"It was just a love pat," she grinned, adding. "You didn't have to hit me so hard, either."

"I'm sorry," I said, which I truly was.

"Apology accepted."

"Trashing the house while I was sitting by the river was not a bad idea," I said. "It confused me enough to keep me off track for a while longer."

"Lisa and I did it, there was nobody else," Sheila said.

"And the box with the kid's things in it wasn't bad either."

"I thought it was original," Lisa said.

"Sheila, you typed the kidnap notes on a computer that used to be in Margaret's room at Sam's, didn't you?"

"Yes I did."

"Good deduction skills, Roosevelt," my Guardian Angel said.

"I know you didn't shoot at me when I left your house after our soup dinner," I told Sheila. "I knew it wasn't you from the beginning. As I got into Matilda you turned the porch light off. There was no way you could have gone out the back door, run up the street, and shot at me."

"Why did you accuse me and then go along with my story?" Sheila asked.

"Looking for clues for Sam's murder," I said.

"It must have been one of the two times Owens tried to kill you," my Guardian Angel said.

"No kidding, brainchild," I replied.

"How did Owens get involved with Moralis?" I asked Manuel.

"Owens at one time was a narcotic's officer in El Paso, when he took a job in Des Moines he investigated Moralis, something made Owens want to go crooked and he offered Moralis protection for a piece of the action. In time they became partners."

"Owens will never see the outside world again. The tapes from his house, along with all the other tapes we have of him, will put him away for so long he'll forget what the sun looks like," Lisa said with pride in her voice.

"We also bugged Moralis' house and his car," Manuel said.

"There is also the 15 pounds of heroin that came in the other night," Sheila said.

I whistled.

"How is Moralis?" I asked.

"When Owens shot you, Sheila shot Owens in the arm. Moralis and his bodyguard drew their guns and Manuel and I sent them on an express train to hell. They won't have to hire a lawyer," Lisa answered.

Manuel and Lisa looked about as disturbed at killing the two men as if they had stepped on two cockroaches.

"Thanks, Sheila, for saving me," I said.

She smiled at me, but I had a feeling she had mixed thoughts over saving me. I couldn't blame her.

"I take it the M-16's I discovered in the corrals were supplied by the Feds," I said.

"Yes they were," Manuel said, "and none of them ever made it to Mexico."

"How about the heroin that has been smuggled in for the past two years?" I asked.

"Most of it we intercepted, but some of it we had to let through to get as many convictions as we could," Sheila said. "It's not good, but it's part of the game. No matter what we do there will always be heroin."

"Sadly there are many lost souls in this world," my Guardian Angel said.

"I don't understand how you and Lisa get along so well?" I said to Sheila.

Sheila didn't look disturbed. "Sam and I were over before Lisa, our relationship had been stale for years. Lisa and Sam started dating after the divorce. We all got along. I was glad to see them both happy and it in no way jeopardized the case. The kids accepted what happened as well as they could and stayed at both houses. I had already been entrenched in Moralis' topless bars, and the Outer Limits," Sheila said, not looking ashamed.

"When Sam married me," Lisa said. "It was easy for him to introduce me to Moralis."

"I should have known all along what was really going on, the signs were all there. There were too many things that happened that both of your reactions were wrong," I said.

"We were telling you so many lies it was getting to the point we were forgetting what we had told you," Sheila said.

"Well, I know one thing," I said with conviction. "There's a tunnel that runs between those two houses."

"Bingo, you win two cigars," Manuel said. "The tunnel goes from the hole we put you in to the barbecue pit at Lisa's."

"We never used it for anything," Manuel said.

"Both of those houses were built at the same time and they had a connecting bomb shelter built," Lisa said. "When the Agency rented the house to use for our sting they built a barbecue pit to cover up the entrance to the tunnel. They didn't want any visitors they didn't know about."

"The night I was listening behind your window some guy snuck up behind me and caught me by surprise," I said to Manuel.

"I missed you on purpose. Good thing you're a good swimmer," Manuel said. "And they were lousy shots. If they would have caught you, I would have had to let them kill you. But rest assured they would all have gotten time for your murder."

My karma is much better than I thought, but somebody doing time after they had killed me is not my idea of payback.

"The worse thing about this case is we've never been able to find out who killed Sam," Lisa said sadly. "If it would have been ordered by Moralis we would have found out through our wire taps and recording devices. The same thing with Owens."

"Being an agent is why you take death so well," I said to Lisa.

"In this line of work you have to. We all know the rules. Sam knew them as well as anybody else. Plus, I couldn't let myself get too emotional right when we were about to close the case."

Sheila hung her head.

"You two don't have a big insurance policy left to you from Sam, do you?" I asked Lisa and Sheila.

They both shook their heads. "That was all part of the cover to keep you confused," Lisa said. "Whenever I told you I was going to see an attorney I was really going over to see Manuel and keep him posted on what you were doing, or going to see Agent Price."

"The kids will get his retirement, when people are killed in the line of duty their kids get taken care of," Sheila said.

"Why didn't the kids go to the funeral?" I asked. "It has always troubled me."

"They didn't want to. They wanted to remember their father as being alive," Sheila said.

I couldn't blame them, our modern funerals have always seemed strange to me. I would rather my last memory of a person be one of them alive, not laid out in a box like a wax dummy. The phrase spoken by people looking in a casket, "Oh, he looks so natural," has always bothered me. Do they really mean that while the person was alive he looked like he was dead?

"Greasy Ed really didn't know what was going on, did he?" I asked.

"Owens and Moralis used him to pass information, but he was not a big player," Lisa said.

"Why did Owens kill him then?" I asked.

"We think Owens thought Greasy Ed had told you things after you beat him up," Sheila said.

"The restaurant was in your name, Lisa, because it was set up by the Feds for Moralis to clean small amounts of money," I said.

"Mostly Moralis used it for a meeting place. It had more microphones in it than the American Embassy in Moscow. We did sell it to the two black men, though."

"Good, they needed a break," I said.

"They said to tell you hello and if you need a job to come on by," Lisa said with a grin.

"A career change in mid-life is scary," my Guardian Angel said.

"What's going to happen now?" I asked to any of the three that wished to answer.

"You won't have to go to court and testify," Lisa said. "We have enough on Owens without you and I've been transferred to another case in Florida."

"I'm going back to a desk job in L.A.," Manuel said.

"I'm getting out," Sheila said. "Sam and I bought my house years ago, and throughout all the turmoil, I have managed to keep it. I'm going to run my store and watch my kids grow into adults."

"I have a question," Manuel said. "How have you ever managed to solve a case, Roosevelt?"

"I solved the fake kidnapping. Does solving something that did not happen count?"

They all shook their heads in disbelief.

"I think it should," my Guardian Angel said. "You showed great intuitive power, which surprised me probably more than it did you."

"Does this mean I have to give back the money you gave me?" I asked Lisa. "It has to be government money."

"It's yours," Lisa said. "Do us a favor and don't claim it."

"It never crossed my mind," I answered truthfully.

"The doctor said you would be discharged tomorrow," Sheila informed me. "You really were lucky, you know?"

"The sooner the better," I replied. "It's time for me to get out of Iowa."

Manuel shook my hand. "Sorry I wasn't a heroin dealer," he said to me.

"Enjoy your desk," I told him. "And sorry I kicked you behind your house."

"I'll bring the car to the front door," Manuel said to Sheila and Lisa and left the room.

Lisa kissed me on the cheek. "I don't see anyway I can forget you. You are the only man in my life I have met who has morals. I think under different circumstances I could have fallen in love with you."

"My luck," I said. "If I ever see you again, I hope people aren't shooting at me and I want you to know I will always consider you a friend"

Lisa winked at me as she shut the door.

"When I get out of here I'll come by," I told Sheila.

She patted me on the arm and started to leave. Sheila was carrying a heavy load, one I hoped to make lighter. By the door, she turned. "Agent Price has your car. When you're discharged, take a cab over and see him. The Agency will reimburse you for the cab."

I waved at her. A small smile crossed her lips. I could see her at 18, sitting in a park in Frisco and thumping on a set of bongos. Innocence is fleeting in this world of ours.

I gazed out the window into the brick wall. What was I supposed to do now? The murderer was still free. At times I may be dumb as a rock, but there are also times I'm as smart as a whip. This time I wished I had remained dumb.

"You know who killed Sam, don't you?" my Guardian Angel said.

"Yes, I do," I said with a heavy heart.

"Tell me, please? I can't figure it out."

"No," I replied.

226

CHAPTER 19
A TANK FULL OF GAS

When I was released from the hospital the bandage had been removed from my head. The wound had healed nicely. The doctor told me to try and avoid bullets. I didn't bother to tell him I know I have a date with another bullet. Bullets and I are predestined.

"There are many careers that bullets are not part of the picture," my Guardian Angel said. "Life is all decisions."

He sounded like an underpaid therapist.

My bill had been paid. I didn't bother to ask by who.

The hot muggy air felt good after the days under fluorescent light.

The cab driver wasn't in a jolly mood and was in less of one when I told him to take me to the Federal Building. There is something about mainstream America that both hates and loves their police. I've always said I don't like police, but what would we do without them? When somebody rapes someone, or there is a robbery, or a murder, you don't call your local plumber. There are a lot of not nice people in this world. Without police the not nice would beat the spaghetti out of the nice people. It's sad, but it's true. I should really say I don't like some laws that the police are made to enforce.

Entering Agent Price's office his smile was so large there was doubt he would get smile lines before he was 40.

"Glad to see you up and about, Roosevelt," he said, shaking my hand so hard I felt like an old time water pump.

Four agents were standing around the water fountain. They must fill it with gin. "I'm sorry about what happened to you," Price said, "but I told you to get out of town."

"I should have listened," I lied.

Price made a phone call. "Bring that black Volkswagen to the front."

Matilda would be happy to see me.

"We found your $5000 in the car," Price said. "We put it back where you hid it."

I was going to tell him they had no right to search my vehicle, but decided against it.

"We also got your belongings from Lisa's. Sheila has them, she said you were going to come by before you left town."

Price walked with me to the street. Matilda looked so good I wanted to kiss her. The bullet holes had been fixed and she had a new black paint job.

"We couldn't do anything about that ugly headliner with the flowers on it," Price said.

"I painted the headliner in 1967 and thought, at the time, it was a work of art," I said. "I painted the flowers as a symbol of peace and hoped peace would take over the world. Now, all that is left of the dream of peace are the flowers on the headliner."

"It's truly too bad," my Guardian Angel said.

"Maybe one day the world will have peace," Agent Price said.

"Thanks for taking care of Matilda," I told Price.

"Roosevelt, do me a favor and don't ever come back to Iowa."

I didn't answer him. Iowa is full of good people and I was now used to the humidity.

Matilda, as usual, started with one turn of the key.

"It's too bad you didn't meet the love of your life while you were here," my Guardian Angel said.

"The ladies here only wanted me for my body," I said with a wry grin.

The closer I got to Sheila's, the more I wanted to turn around. The fact she has my suitcase and pistol wasn't why I was going to her house, nor was it out of a sense of justice.

Sheila's neighbor was once again mowing his yard and he waved. Sheila opened the door before I could knock. There were no dogs and I didn't ask where they were.

"Maybe they are underneath a car tire," my Guardian Angel said.

"Price called and told me you were on your way," Sheila said, looking worried.

Sheila was wearing a bright blue summer dress, but there were dark circles under her eyes. I followed her to the kitchen. She poured two glasses of iced tea without asking if I wanted one and we sat at the table.

"Are the kids here?" I asked, feeling like the Grinch that stole Christmas.

"Margaret took them swimming. She is not a bad kid, Roosevelt."

"I know," I said.

"Oh Roosevelt," Sheila lamented. "Life is a big mind game. Who knows up from down?"

228

"Not me," I said.

"I don't either," my Guardian Angel said.

Sheila sipped on her tea, set her glass down and took a deep breath. "You know I killed Sam, don't you?"

I held Sheila's hand tenderly and squeezed it reassuringly.

"I know who killed Sam, Sheila," I said. "And I know it wasn't you."

Sheila's eyes filled with fear. "It was me Roosevelt," she pleaded.

"You don't have to lie," I said.

Sheila pulled her hand out of mine and held back a sob. "What are you going to do about Margaret?" she asked in a halting voice.

"I came by to get my things. I'm on my way to Colorado. When I lived in New Mexico, I used to go to southern Colorado, near a town called Platoro. It's beautiful country. No ski resorts nearby to ruin anything, no big motels, only a few dirt roads and trails that go back into the high mountains. I'm going trout fishing, look at the wildflowers, and spend my nights trying to count the stars."

"You know why Margaret.......?" I cut Sheila off.

"It doesn't matter," I said softly. "You know she loves you, she confided in you."

Sheila started to cry. "You're ok, Roosevelt."

"Have you ever been trout fishing?" I asked her.

"No, I never have," Sheila said, wiping her eyes with the back of her hand.

"After a few weeks of no people with only the sounds of nature I feel rejuvenated. I'm ready to go out and battle life once again."

"I'd like to go with you," Sheila said.

We both laughed lightly, knowing likes and reality are two different things, and life is all timing.

"I have to get going," I said, feeling sad.

I got up and Sheila followed me. The TV was gone. "TV break?" I asked.

"I gave it away," she said. "The kids are going to learn how to think."

She got my things.

Standing by the door, we looked at each other as if it was 40 years earlier. She would have had long hair and been wearing a peace sign. I would have had a brain full of philosophy intermingled with infantry boots. We hugged each other, said nothing, and I headed to Matilda as she closed the door.

The man across the street finished mowing his yard. He waved and I waved back. A small portion of me envied his life. I didn't look back as I drove away.

"Don't talk to me until I cross into Nebraska," I told my Guardian Angel.

Matilda purred down I-80. The wind blew through my hair. The truckers blasted by me like I was driving in reverse. Occasionally people gazed at Matilda as they sped by and smiled.

It was late afternoon when I crossed the state line into Nebraska and pulled into a rest area.

"I want to know how you knew Margaret shot her father?" my Guardian Angel asked me as soon as I shut off Matilda.

"It doesn't matter," I said.

"Please," he begged.

I hesitated for a few moments before deciding to tell him. "The clues were all there."

"What clues?"

"The fact she was on the rifle team. The fact she thought her father abandoned her. The look on Sheila's face whenever the topic came up. Her remoteness. And if Owens didn't shoot him who else would have?

"Lisa or Sheila?"

I shook my head.

"She murdered her father. How can you let her go?" my Guardian Angel asked in astonishment.

"I am not God or the police."

"Where would she have gotten the 243?"

"It was Sam's. There were photographs of him deer hunting in his den, in several of them he was holding a rifle, but there was no rifle in the room. I would bet everything his rifle was a 243. I bet Margaret snuck it out of the house."

"Lisa would have missed the gun."

"Margaret had been at the house with Lisa when Sam and I drove up. Lisa, although wearing a bathing suit when she ran out to where Sam had been shot had been in the house. Remember she didn't have any lotion on and there was not one time when she went to the pool that she didn't have lotion. She couldn't turn in Margaret."

"It had to be tough on both Sheila and Lisa."

"They both were in more pain than they put on."

"Where do you think Margaret was when she shot Sam?"

"She stood on a chair and shot Sam from the swimming pool through one of the ventilation vents."

"How did Margaret get away?"

"She swam, ditching the rifle in the river. Remember she was going to go to a swimming camp, she has to be a good swimmer. She wouldn't have had to swim far before she could get out of the river, go to a store and call Sheila or a friend and get a ride home - it doesn't really matter. She got away."

"Good, Roosevelt, very good," my Guardian Angel said.

"Margaret isn't a bad kid. She is sad and lonely but she is not evil. She shot Sam on impulse, not realizing at the time what a terrible thing she was doing. She does now. Hopefully she will turn her life around. I've thought about it a long time, it's been a tough decision, I could be wrong by not turning her in, but, she has a loving mother and I really don't want to hurt Sheila."

"It will be a hard thing for Margaret to live with throughout her life," my Guardian Angel said.

"That could be the worst punishment of all," I replied.

"Roosevelt, you aren't always a jerk," my Guardian Angel said.

"One day you won't be stuck with me," I said.

My Guardian Angel put his hand on my shoulder. He is not a very touchy angel and it surprised me. "No, I think you and I are stuck with each other, but I can always dream. What is life without dreams?" he smiled.

"In your case it is, what is death without dreams," I smiled back.

I started Matilda.

"Somewhere on this road off life you'll find yourself and a person to love," my Guardian Angel said.

"There are no guarantees," I said.

"Keep rolling the dice, Roosevelt," he said.

Driving away from the rest area my Guardian Angel and I were humming an old Beatles song - something about yellow submarines. I felt good. I was alive. The bad guys had lost. I was going trout fishing in Colorado. This story has a happy ending. Many don't. Good had come out of a bucket full of lies.

THE END

OTHER BOB ROOSEVELT MYSTERIES

BOOK TWO - TROUT FISHING FOR BODIES
BOOK THREE - DOUBLE BOGEY MURDER
BOOK FOUR – FROGS DON'T CROAK IN THE WINTER
COMING SOON – BEACH BUM TANGO

You can see more of Robert K. Swisher's novels at
http://www.swisherbooks.com/

CPSIA information can be obtained
at www.ICGtesting.com
Printed in the USA
LVHW020842300620
659359LV00002B/209